Also by Jerry Mevissen

Nimrod Chronicles
Broken Hart

GOOD SHEPHERD

GOOD SHEPHERD

Short Stories

by Jerry Mevissen

JACKPINE WRITERS' BLOC

Published by the Jackpine Writers' Bloc, Inc.
© Copyright 2014 Jerry Mevissen
All Rights Reserved
Nimrod MN, 56477

This is a work of fiction. Any resemblance to actual persons,
living or dead, events or locales is entirely coincidental.
Some of the works in this book have been previously published in the following:
"The Talking Stick, Volumes 14 and 20."

Edited by Deb Schlueter and Sharon Harris
Layout and cover design by Tarah L. Wolff
This book was set in *DejaVu Serif,* a typeface printed in size 10.8

For Megan, Michael, Peter, Rachel and Sarah

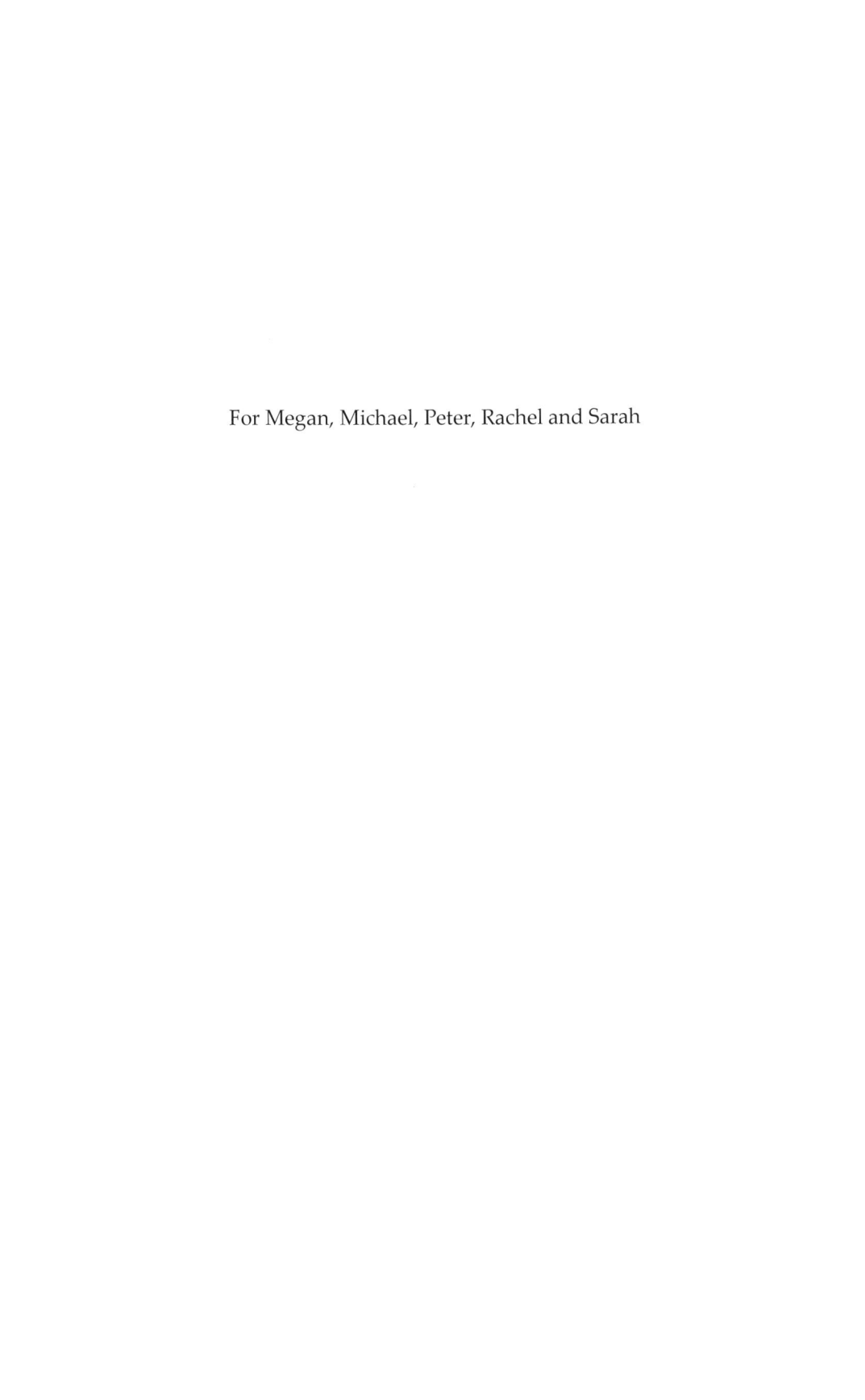

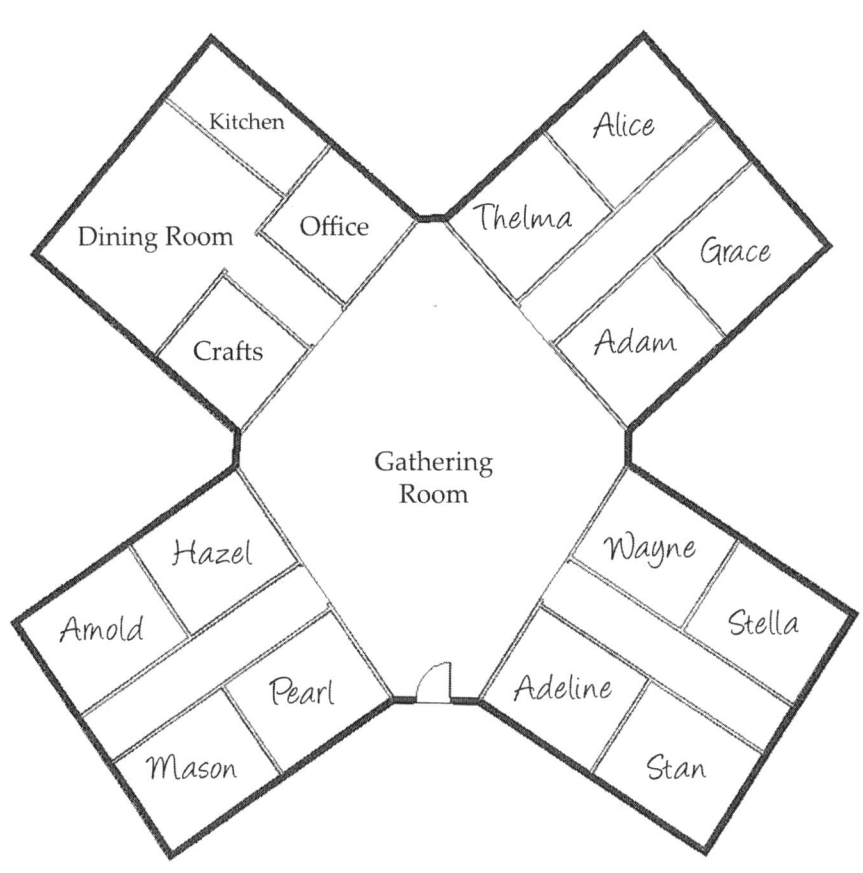

Good Shepherd
Assisted Living Center

- Kitchen
- Dining Room
- Office
- Crafts
- Thelma
- Alice
- Grace
- Adam
- Gathering Room
- Hazel
- Arnold
- Pearl
- Mason
- Wayne
- Stella
- Adeline
- Stan

Contents

Wildcat ∞ 1

Men ∞ 23

Widow Maker ∞ 47

Johnny ∞ 61

Familiar Quotations ∞ 81

Garden of Eden ∞ 99

May Day ∞ 125

Cameo ∞ 141

Sisters ∞ 169

Satyr ∞ 185

Hug ∞ 207

Sweet Spot ∞ 227

Pearl Witte

Welcome to Good Shepherd Assisted Living in Browns Prairie, Minnesota. We're hosting a reception on October 24, and you're invited. You'll have an opportunity to view our charming home: twelve apartments, Gathering Room, kitchen & dining, and crafts room.

You'll meet our staff: Director Mrs. Fitzgerald, Nurse Betty Brockett, visiting physician Dr. Harold Provence, and aide Mary.

Best of all, you'll meet my friends and neighbors and their families. Please join us for dinner and conversation. Take the opportunity to get acquainted. As a friend said, "Listening to your stories is like looking in a mirror."

We hope to see you on October 24.

Pearl

Good Shepherd

Wildcat

Saturday morning in November, and a harsh rain pelted against the window. Cliff Benson stood in the kitchen, quiet except for the hum of the refrigerator. The room was dark and chilly. He could turn on the lights or the radio, or he could brew a pot of coffee. But he stood there, braced against the cupboard, as if the kitchen were his tomb.

Earlier this morning, he felt uncertain, suspicious. He knew she feigned sleep when he lay in bed tracing finger designs on her back. Later, standing in the doorway before he left the bedroom, he wondered what excuse she might invent to leave and use the morning free of him.

The upstairs plumbing rattled, and he heard the rumble of the shower. Mary Jane was out of bed and from the sound of it, preparing to leave for the day. Her son Andy would sleep through the rumble, would likely sleep all morning.

Cliff switched the light on, brewed a pot of coffee, and set two mugs on the table. He checked the calendar where Mary Jane noted her schedule commitments. Today was blank. Had she mentioned leaving? He didn't recall. He turned on the radio to hear the weatherman forecast showers, turning to sleet, then snow.

Rain smearing the window made him shiver. Today he had planned a day of home work, mulching leaves one final time before snow fell. He planned to linger over coffee with Mary Jane, keeping one conjugal eye on her to quell his suspicions. Her new diversion, oil painting, had generated a new set of friends, artists he didn't know or trust. He wanted to share her enthusiasm and to understand it. To listen to her talk about finding her artistic niche—texture. He wanted to state with confidence, "I can see what you're going for, what you're achieving."

Instead, when she presented a painting to him, he had asked with a child's innocence, "What is it?"

"It's a painting, darling," she snapped. "Must it be something more than a painting?"

"I was looking for a subject."

"If there is a subject, it's texture. See how the steel glimmers beside the dull slate? And how the gray wool scarf softens the entire piece?"

End of questioning.

The rumble of the upstairs shower stopped, and Mary Jane appeared on the staircase wrapped in a white terrycloth robe, her wet hair capped in a white towel. Cliff walked to the entry hall mirror and flattened a few gray strands of hair. He rubbed his chin and felt Saturday morning stubble. He inhaled and sucked in his gut; the gray sweatshirt and pants did little to conceal his belly. *You are not an artist's husband*, he whispered to his image.

Cliff returned to the kitchen and poured coffee. Mary Jane padded down the stairs singing, "Oh, what a beautiful morning." She stood in the kitchen doorway buffing her nails. "Good morning, darling." She loosened the towel, tilted her head back, and shook red ringlets. Her skin was a soft, transparent pink that smelled of scented soap and seemed to say *look, but don't touch*.

Cliff approached her, his arms extended.

"Not this morning, darling. I'm running late." She reached for her coffee. "I'll drink this while I do my hair."

"You have an appointment today? There's nothing on the calendar."

"Don't you remember my telling you about the Gallery Crawl this weekend? Ten galleries today and a workshop tomorrow."

"I thought you and I and Andy would do something together. Have lunch, maybe. See a matinee. Stop to see Mother at Good Shepherd."

She tousled her hair with the towel.

"What time will you be home?" he asked. He took her arm, pressing it until she turned to him. She lifted her eyes in a grimace and pulled away.

"I don't know, darling," she said, walking to the stairway.

"Shall we wait dinner?"

"I said I don't know. We have ten galleries to visit. The last one is hosting a reception. Appetizers, I suspect. You and Andy go ahead," she said, heading up the stairs. "I know you want me to be successful, and I need the exposure." She tilted her head and smiled. "Now be a sweetheart and carry my painting valise to the car."

Cliff closed his eyes and inhaled the air where she had stood.

When Mary Jane waved her fingers goodbye, Cliff tapped his shirt pocket for a cigarette, forgetting he had dumped the habit when Andy arrived. He finished his coffee and wrote a note. "Off to see Grandma for a couple hours. Your favorite raisin bagel is in the toaster. I'll probably be back before you rise. What do you want to do this weekend?"

Cliff backed his '87 Mazda out of the garage, mindful of Andy's bicycle which he had flattened the week before, and the garbage cans at the curb which he had sent careening into the street. He struggled in the fogged light of morning with the dread of seeing his mother's fading condition. And further, he was nagged by a gut feeling of some task undone—the Mr. Coffee left on, the front door unlocked, the telephone bill, due today, on the table. The stuff Mary Jane noted and recalled at inconvenient intervals, like an employee evaluation to justify the denial of promotion.

His uncertainty, his suspicions of Mary Jane dogged him. She had gushed over the talent and sophistication of her art instructor, had dropped barefaced hints of an affair. She flaunted the clues—new diet and exercise regimen, a shift to brighter colors in her wardrobe, reasons to stay late at the studio. Wasn't anything new?

And the alcohol. Or was it drugs? Or both? Cliff suspected a problem when she stowed the gin bottle in a seldom-used cupboard above the refrigerator.

"You're no fun anymore, darling," she said one night after returning late from a gallery opening. Her focus shifted, her eyes searched for safe landing. "I'm not letting my life slip by waiting for you."

"You and Andy have dinner without me," Cliff heard several days a week. Mary Jane would select from her litany of excuses. "I'm working late at the studio." Or, "I'm going to work out at the gym." Or, "I've shopping to do." If this were a solo act or she had an accomplice, Cliff didn't know. What he did know was that Andy's care had defaulted to him.

If only I could ask for time with you, Cliff thought. *Time to prove I'm more than a caretaker for your son. More than a financier who bankrolls your endless diversions. Time to prove I'm lovable and . . . And to prove I love you. If only I could ask for that.*

Mother. She had been at Good Shepherd for two years, had settled in, made it her home as best she could. The staff found her grumpy and hard to please. Especially the males, her yelling at the night shift aide, "Get your hands off me!" and the male residents, "Go sit at another table."

"Hazel can be so feisty," Director Mrs. Fitzgerald said. "Defiant, sometimes. She has difficulty accepting a compliment. Small talk even."

No surprise for Cliff, who had never heard his mother complimented in fifty years of marriage, and who regarded small talk as a waste of time. He recalled his father's penchant for criticism and his grandfather's dictum when Hazel was a young woman. After a second glass of wine at his grandfather's funeral, Hazel quoted him as saying, "Better find yerself a husband, and soon. You'll never amount to nothin'. As if bearing nine children, stretching a meager milk check through the lean years, and losing a soldier son were nothing."

Cliff tapped on her door at Good Shepherd and opened it. Hazel lifted her gaze from the television. "I didn't expect you." She looked past him to confirm he was alone and returned to the screen.

"I got rained out," he said. "What're you watching, Mother?"

Hazel, in a cotton housedress dating back to her farm days, sat upright, gripping the remote, and fixed her stare at the screen. Her gray hair was parted on the side and chopped at a short length. Bits of flint peeked through her tight eyelids. Her lips were thin and bloodless, eroded by a lifetime of biting. "Nothing," she said.

Cliff glanced around the room, at the spare furniture and furnishings, stuff also reclaimed from the farm. On a table in front of the window stood a portrait of his brother Danny in Army uniform beside an encased three-cornered flag.

The rain continued and formed droplets on the window that blurred the lawn and garden. Linden leaves spiraled down and clung to water-logged benches with *In loving memory of* plaques. Cliff walked to the window and placed his hand on the flag. Red sumac at the garden's edge wore the bold hue of dried blood. A squirrel crawled from a branch to a bird feeder chain, grasped it with his back feet, and inched down to sunflower seeds. "Look at that fellow, Mother."

The television audience erupted in hysteria and then applauded.

"They love you," Cliff said to the squirrel. "Go for it."

Hazel clicked the television off. She rose and grabbed her walker. "Time for treats," she muttered.

Despite the gray November, the Gathering Room was merry as May. A bold floral print wallpaper—pink and rose hollyhocks, yellow and orange tulips, heavenly blue morning glories glared behind a wainscot of white picket fence. Parakeets twittered in a cage amid intertwined ficus trees. Tropical fish with bulging bellies and vacuous eyes swam in never ending circles, hesitating at the glass wall as if to ask, *What am I doing here?* It was a kindergarten room, a nursery.

A nurse's aide with HI, MY NAME IS MARY tagged on her smock poured nectar in plastic, weighted cups. She could have been a nursing student in the local community college, an immigrant. Maybe Filipino, or East Indian. Hazel steered her walker around Mary's extended arm and poured her own cup and handed it to Cliff. "I don't trust some of these people," she said, not in a whisper. She walked a few steps, then stopped to catch her breath, refusing Cliff's offer of a steady arm.

They sat by the fireplace, spared of conversation. "Would you like to go for a ride, Mother?" Cliff asked after a long silence. He glanced at his watch and twirled the cup in his hands. Hazel stared at a robed resident wearing a white crash helmet. She pointed.

"Maxwell. Not long for this world." His long neck bent like a heron's, his ropy arms were mottled and bruised. He maneuvered his wheelchair toward them, his twiggy legs lost in white surgical stockings and his feet sporting multi-colored harlequin slippers. "Probably a terrorist," she said.

Cliff saw his slight carriage, small gold rimmed glasses, and serene Gandhi-like deportment. "Probably a prophet." He chugged his nectar. "Let's get out of here."

A peppy lady in a pink velour jogging suit and pink tennis shoes shuffled toward them. "Got a date, Hazel?"

Hazel rose and headed to the door. "Bucket mouth," she said.

The lady grabbed Cliff's arm. "I'm Pearl," she said. "Hazel's neighbor down the hall. And the arts and crafts coordinator. Check it out." She pointed to a bulletin board with cutout leaves of autumn-colored construction paper. "It's like I'm still teaching fourth grade."

"Pleased to meet you, Mrs. . . ." Cliff said.

Hazel waited at the door.

"*Miz*, if you please. Never been married and never will. Unless I find Mr. Wonderful. The Good Shepherd-ers are all the family I need. And we're one, big, happy flock, aren't we, Hazel? You know, we're valuable in our old age." She brimmed at the prospect of telling her current joke to a newcomer. "We have silver in our hair, gold in our teeth, titanium in our knees, and plenty of gas in our stomach." She cackled until she coughed.

They drove to the strip mall, a collection of discount and dollar stores, a municipal building, and a café within walking distance of Good Shepherd. Cliff often stopped at Muni Liquor in the mall to buy beer for his mother. The six-pack cases were empty when he checked her refrigerator, although she claimed to drink only one or two. "The cleaning lady has itchy fingers," she said.

He grabbed two six-packs of beer marked SALE from an end cap display and placed them on the checkout counter. The cashier was new to him, a tall woman with tanned muscular arms. Her short, sleeveless T-shirt revealed a bronze midriff above snug blue jeans. Her hair was short, a metallic auburn. No makeup. A tattoo of barbed wire encircled her wrist.

"Trying to impress someone?" she said with a playful tease.

"It's for my mother at Good Shepherd. She says she doesn't drink, but it's gone in a week." He wrote a check and handed it to her.

"Some mothers get roses. Others get beer on sale."

Her cheekiness, her bold familiarity staggered Cliff for a moment. "Good girls get diamond bracelets." He pointed. "Bad girls get barbed wire."

She chuckled and reached to touch his arm. Cliff grabbed the six-packs and headed for the door. She glanced at the check. "Goodbye, Mr. Benson," she called. "Mr. Clifford Benson." Through the window, she watched him open the car door, saw his mother look at him, then turn to look at her. She waved.

Cliff dialed his home number in Hazel's apartment, then hung up before the phone rang, remembering Andy might still be sleeping and Mary Jane was gallery hopping. If she were home, she'd be irritated for his acting like a doting parent checking on her.

"What's Mary Jane doing? I haven't seen her for months," Hazel asked. "Still doing her artsy-fartsy thing?"

Cliff hesitated. "She has a gallery tour this weekend. A workshop tomorrow. She's dedicated to her painting. She gives it her all."

Hazel gave him the maternal *don't lie to me* look. "Sounds like there might be trouble in paradise."

"Things are fine. Busy, that's all." He turned away and patted his shirt pocket. "I'd better get going. I told Andy I'd help him with a school project."

"Whose kid is he?" Hazel asked. She shrugged her shoulders and reached for the remote.

It was noon when Cliff left Good Shepherd for home. Rain to sleet fell hard and hammered the Mazda's roof. Past the strip mall, he saw a figure walking, a woman in jeans, a child's pink umbrella shielding her head. She walked straight ahead, waving a hitchhiking thumb without looking back. When Cliff slowed to keep from splashing her, he saw her hair—short, metallic auburn.

She turned toward the car, a smile of confidence and gratitude, and reached for the handle. He hit the brakes. "This is sweet of you," she said, sliding into the Mazda. "My truck's in for a brake job. I thought it would be done by now." She hadn't looked at him, hadn't met his gaze. She fussed with the umbrella. "Any chance you'd be going by Rancho Costello?"

He shifted the Mazda into gear and pulled into the lane of traffic. "Sure," he said. "Sold any more bargain beer?"

She glanced at him, then smiled. "Mr. Six-Pack! Good to see you again. How did Mother like her gift?"

Cliff shrugged. "Rancho Costello. You have horses?"

"I have a couple dogs."

Cliff was silent. He hadn't asked her if she wanted a ride. Just slowed down. Now she was in his car. He could smell her perfume, a musky aroma that hung in the air and tickled his nostrils. Best to drive safely. How would he explain this to Mary Jane?

"My name is Cheyenne," she said as if she sensed his apprehension. "Cheyenne, as in Wyoming because that's where I was conceived. My dad was a rancher before he was a wildcatter. Now he's a safety engineer at an oil drilling site. I work for the same company and pull samples on an oil rig. I'm burning up a couple weeks of vacation to patch up a domestic mess. And I'm burning up a few hours at the Muni to pay for a brake job."

"Happily married?" Cliff asked, and wondered why he asked.

"You got one out of two," she said.

They took the cutoff to Rancho Costello, quiet except for rain drumming and windshield wipers beating a bass line. The development was an area of treeless, small acreage lots, modest rectangular prefab houses in an erratic panoply of pastel colors—lemon yellow, robin's egg blue, lime green. Beside the houses, outsized pole barns and sheds, split rail fences extending to the road. Horses stood in lean-tos, their heads bowed in an "End of the Trail" pose. Dogs approached them on gravel driveways, barked, then retreated.

"How's your mother at Good Shepherd?" Cheyenne asked.

"Fine. How'd you know?"

"You told me. My aunt lived there."

"Will you be here next weekend?" Cliff changed the subject.

"I head back to Montana next Sunday. If my patience holds out."

At home, Cliff and Andy settled in front of the computer and googled raptors. Birds of prey: eagles, ospreys, kites, hawks, buzzards, vultures, owls.

"Interesting birds," Cliff said, as Andy took notes. Andy settled on eagles for his project, fascinated by their return from near extinction, their nesting habitat near his home, their national symbolism.

"I've never seen an eagle," he said.

"I know where we can view them. They hang around until the lakes and rivers freeze. We can go tomorrow." Cliff paused. "Unless your mother has plans for you."

Andy shot him a quizzical glance. Cliff saw the boy's skepticism, as if he realized the irony, the lie in Cliff's comment. The "little boy" expression, the grieved conclusion, the cynical acceptance that said, *Sure, she has plans for me.*

Andy stood, headed for the door, then turned around. His cherubic face resembled his mother's—red hair, fair skin sprinkled with freckles. "I told her about my report on raptors, but I'm not sure she heard me. Funny, because she used to talk about eagles that nested at the farm. I thought she'd be interested in this."

"She has a lot on her mind. Her classes, her studio time . . ."

"It was the same thing with Dad. His job, Rotary Club, fishing trips."

"Don't be hard on them."

When Mary Jane returned from the Gallery Crawl at eight, Cliff and Andy were watching television and finishing a boxed pizza. She busied herself in the kitchen, checked the answering machine, and poured a glass of wine.

"How was your day?" Cliff asked.

"Hectic," she said. "Hectic, but fun, exciting. And I have news, darling. The curator at Galactic Gallery liked two of my paintings. He wants to display them. Of course, they have to be framed first. But he'll do that."

"What will that cost?"

She snapped her hand open in a matter-of-fact gesture. "It'll cost whatever it costs, darling. Must you be an accountant twenty-four hours a day?" She filled the wine glass. "I'm tired, and I have a busy day tomorrow. Good night, you two." She walked upstairs with the glass and closed the bedroom door behind her.

"Guess I'll turn in too," Andy said. "Goodnight, Dad."

Cliff turned the television off and scanned the paper. He flunked the sudoku, then started a crossword puzzle. He thought of calling Mother. But why? The memory of the auburn-haired clerk appeared. Cheyenne. This time, she stood along the highway, her hand resting on jutted hip, her thumb extended, her grin bawdy. Cliff twisted his wedding ring with his thumb, a habit he practiced while driving. Had she noticed?

He surveyed the living room and decided to sleep an hour or two on the couch. He rose to use the bathroom, another challenge for Mary Jane. Early in their marriage, she had taped THREE

RULES to the bathroom door, which Cliff called his emasculation proclamation.
1. SCRUB THE SKID MARKS OUT OF THE BOWL
2. PUT THE TOILET SEAT DOWN
3. SIT DOWN WHEN YOU PISS. I'M TIRED OF WIPING WET TILES

On Sunday, Cliff and Andy drove to the Raptor Center, quiet except for rain, the monotonous clack of windshield wipers, the hiss of tires on wet pavement. The incessant drizzle kept the binoculared birders away, kept the Center's parking lot empty except for the naturalist's car.

In the Interpretive Center, they listened to audio tracks that informed backlit photographs. They watched a video where parent eagles taught a young eaglet to fly. Watched them nudge it from the nest, the young bird fumbling and tumbling, flopping its stubby wings, nose diving. Andy gasped and held Cliff's arm, held it until the parent eagle swooped beneath the eaglet, catching it on its back. The eagle soared upward and canted, dislodging its rider, repeating the process until the eaglet flew, clumsily at first, but independent. Andy smiled. "Let's watch it again."

Later, at the dinner table, Andy said, "We're studying drugs in health class. Meth, opium, *marijuana*. Did you know marijuana is Spanish for *Mary Jane*? That's a shocker, huh, Mom?"

Mary Jane choked on a bite of food and reached for her wine glass. Her fingers trembled as she lifted the glass and let the wine slide between her lips. She closed her eyes and held the glass in front of her, blocking Andy's stare.

Cliff shifted his gaze from mother to son, son to mother. Son, red-faced because he had exposed some embarrassment; mother, in her fluster, confessing guilt. She rose, picked up her plate, and retreated to the kitchen. Cliff heard ice cubes dropping in a glass.

Monday morning, Cliff huddled in his cubicle, grateful for the predictability of his job, the structured approach to accounting, the impregnable logic of mathematics. Tension dogged him all week: Mary Jane. Mother. The Muni clerk. Rain continued, like the annoying drip of a leaky faucet.

By Saturday, the trees were bare, their stark arms vulnerable and supplicating. If November were a color, it would be gray. Rain-soaked leaves settled in a drab carpet, defying the gust of a northern bluster. The bird feeder in the back yard was quiet, unattended. No wonder, since it was empty. Cliff padded around the house, mindful of his sleeping wife, although he heard a closet door's whisper, a dresser drawer's glide. He poured coffee and left for Good Shepherd.

The town had a weekend quiet to it. On Main Street, not a moving vehicle in sight, not a parked car. The street was wide and vacant, like the set of an old western movie. At the strip mall, he saw a Dodge pickup with Montana license plates.

Cheyenne recognized him when he approached the checkout counter with the on-sale six-packs. "Good morning, Mr. Benson."

Cliff stopped. "Good morning."

"If you don't mind an innocent suggestion, I think your mother would prefer blackberry brandy over beer."

"I beg your pardon?"

"I had a delivery run to Good Shepherd yesterday after work, and I met your mother. Nice lady. Lonesome though. Does she have sisters? Daughters?"

"Wait a minute. You met my mother? And she talked about being lonely? And she told you she preferred blackberry brandy?"

"The loneliness is my intuition. The blackberry brandy is my suggestion. She has trouble sleeping."

Cliff opened his mouth and waited for words. Cheyenne reached for a half-pint of brandy and waved it in front of him. He nodded *Yes*, and patted his shirt pocket for a cigarette.

"What took you so long?" Hazel sat on the edge of her chair, leaning forward on her walker, her brown wool coat slung over her arm.

"I didn't know you were expecting me," Cliff said. "Didn't know I was coming myself until I left the house this morning."

"I'd like to drive out to the farm," she said, dismissing the small talk with a flick of her hand. "What's in the bag?"

"The usual," Cliff said. "And a small brandy for your insomnia." He waited to hear about the diagnosis, irrespective of whose it was.

"So you talked to Cheyenne, huh? Good woman. There ought to be more like her." Hazel handed her coat to Cliff and turned. "I haven't been to the farm for months. I got word to them that I'd be out to pick up the rent."

The farm was the Benson family farm, bereft of Bensons since Gus died ten plus years ago. Neither Cliff nor his brothers or sisters were inclined to return after tasting the freedom of an eight-to-five job and life a couple rungs higher on the ladders of commerce and culture.

It was a short drive out of town, a drive Cliff had ridden, walked, biked, and hitchhiked thousands of times to and from school. The road was paved now, and once-proud dairy farms outside of town had been fractionalized into hobby farms. The red barns, white roofs, and blue Harvestore silos stood tall and vacant, decommissioned symbols of another era, like a VFW color guard at a Fourth of July parade.

Hazel disregarded the scenery and reached for a pack of cigarettes in her purse. "I had to get out today," she said. "Had to get away." She squeezed a cigarette out with a snap and pushed in the cigarette lighter.

Cliff cracked the window. "What's today?"

Hazel looked away and lit her cigarette. "November third. That's the day I got the telegram from the Department of Army about Danny." She inhaled and held the smoke in her throat.

"That's right," Cliff said. "When was that?"

"Yesterday."

"It seems like a lifetime ago. I was just a boy then."

"So was he." She sat quiet, inhaling and exhaling exaggerated puffs.

"You ought to quit smoking, Mother," Cliff said.

Hazel ignored him. She couldn't smoke at Good Shepherd, and that restriction had kept her on the farm, alone for eight years despite the urging of her children. Gus, of course, didn't cotton to her smoking, not because of the health hazard. *It's a stupid waste of money.* Once Gus was tucked out of sight beyond reproach, Hazel assumed the habit full tilt. A cigarette and beer before bed, another, then another until the night she had fallen asleep on the couch with a lighted cigarette, burning an accusing design on the pillow and scorching the drapes.

It was then she agreed to move to Good Shepherd. "It was my decision," she said. "I'm the one who decided to move."

"Tell me about your insomnia, Mother," Cliff said as they drove.

Hazel glanced and inhaled a deep breath. "She walked up to me in the Gathering Room and asked if I was Mrs. Benson. She said you drove her home last Saturday in the rain. I was leery of her at first. That tattoo on her wrist is disgusting. She talked about her job in Montana." Her voice mellowed after a pause, as if describing a pleasant memory. "I told her about the traffic noise outside. How they keep the room temperature so high. How Mr. Baxter next door flushes his toilet all hours of the night. She thought a shot of brandy at bedtime might help."

They drove beneath an expansive leaden gray sky, broken by rifts of inky clouds and graced with blackbirds flying random solo patterns. The rain had stopped, providing a brief reprieve. The pasture fence along the home place was taut, the posts straight and evenly spaced. The driveway was graded, the yard mowed, the shrubs below the eaves bundled in burlap. Cliff tapped the horn and helped Hazel from the car to her walker. She steadied herself on the cinder walk, took a few steps, and rested.

An Amish woman, Lydia, opened the door, silhouetted against the warm light of a kerosene lamp on the kitchen table. She wore a dark dress down to her ankles, behind a white apron pulled tight at the waist. A girl peeked from behind her skirt, dressed the same and holding a cloth doll by the arm. "Come in, Mrs. Benson." Lydia touched Hazel's arm as she climbed the step and walked across the open porch, past the glider swing that hung from the ceiling. Lydia's skin was a pale rose, her hair smoothed beneath a hanging veil bonnet.

The kitchen was sparse. Wood floors, painted cabinets, a bare Shaker table and chairs, a dominating Monarch stove stationed like a throne on the center wall, the kitchen's paucity defeated by the warmth of a wood fire and the aroma of cinnamon, nutmeg, ginger. *Pumpkin pie?* Cliff wondered.

"Please," Lydia said. "Let me take your coats. Sit down. Coffee?" She reached for an enameled blue percolator.

LeRoy, husband and father, entered the kitchen. He carried a toddler boy in his arms, cheeks like ripe peaches, Dutch boy haircut, denim pants and lavender shirt, a clone of his father. The man gave a deferential nod to Mrs. Benson and extended his hand to Cliff. "Welcome home," he said.

"We've had a busy fall," Lydia said, not waiting to be asked. "The harvest, of course. Third crop of hay to bale, four new calves, the machine shed re-roofed to keep the buggy dry. LeRoy's been a busy man."

LeRoy sucked an unlit pipe. His eyes kindled, his complexion blushed to a dark rose. A smile breached his trimmed beard. "Lydia's been the busy one," he said. "Canned dozens of quarts of carrots and beans and corn. Refinished the kitchen floor." He pointed to the gleaming pine planks below them. "Sewed curtains for the living room."

It was Lydia's turn to blush. She touched her husband's shoulder, the toddler pushing her hand away.

LeRoy and Cliff toured the farmstead: the whitewashed barn walls, the limed concrete aisle between the stanchioned dairy cows, the aroma of corn silage that transplanted Cliff to his youth. The haymow, stacked with verdant bales of alfalfa and upland hay; the corn field, plowed and ready for spring planting; the garden, barren except for a row of horseradish and rhubarb, their parched leaves in winter repose.

They returned to the house as Lydia was serving pie. "We're mindful of what we do here," Lydia said. "It's still your place, but we hope to own it some day. Soon. We have plans, don't we, LeRoy?" She glanced at him with a generous smile.

He nodded and beamed. "More bedrooms. More babies." He tickled the chin of the toddler, who sat in a highchair eating pumpkin pie with his fingers.

"I'm glad we made the trip," Cliff said on the way back to Good Shepherd. "Did you see how they pull together?"

"As it should be," Hazel snorted. "Hitched to the same wagon. Not like you and Mary Jane, pulling in different directions. What went wrong with you two?"

Cliff patted an empty shirt pocket for cigarettes. "Nothing," he said. "Everything."

"Then why don't you leave? Why did you get married in the first place?"

Cliff was silent. "I felt sorry for the boy. I had to take her in."

Hazel grunted. "She could have roosted in a tree."

Rain turned to snow when Cliff left Good Shepherd, soggy flakes like white polka dots against black trees. It was two o'clock, later than the time he had left last week. He drove past the Muni, wondering if he'd see the Montana-licensed pickup. It was gone. He slowed and drove into the mall parking lot. Nothing. He sat there, the engine idling, the windshield wipers pushing clumps of snow. A truck pulled up beside him, and the driver rolled down the window. "Looking for someone?"

Cliff stalled.

"Coffee?" Cheyenne lifted an imaginary cup to her lips. "I have to get back to Rancho Costello and let the dogs out. Follow me."

"Eager to return to the oil patch?" Cliff asked as they walked into the kitchen. The dogs, two black labs, scrambled and ran for the door. "How is life for a woman in a man's world? Figured out how to deal with those roughnecks?"

Cheyenne raised her hands in a karate pose. "They don't mess with a black belt."

Cliff noted the Wellington boots by the door, the canvas chore jacket hanging on a peg, the barren space in the yard where a semi-trailer had been parked. "Where's the old man?"

"Off on a three-day run to Detroit. Don't worry," she said. "When he's gone, he's gone." She poured reheated coffee.

"Mother said you had a good talk. Even said she liked you." He chuckled. "She hasn't liked anybody since Lucille Ball."

"I'm glad I was there for her. Early November is not her best time. She talked about your brother Danny. She misses him."

"I got a hint of that in the car."

"Her first son. Wounded on the other side of the planet. Devastating. Then the telegram."

"Danny was her favorite. She made no bones about that."

Cliff stirred his coffee and watched the dogs scramble in the yard. "And you? Did you get your domestic mess cleaned up?"

"As much as could be expected."

"Too early to celebrate?"

"No," she said. "Order the cake or the keg. If we wait for all the dust to settle, the party will never begin. And you. Making any progress with Mary Jane? Isn't that her name?"

Cliff didn't answer.

"What went wrong with you two?"

"Nothing. Everything." A sense of *déjà vu* floated over him. Women ganging up on him.

She touched his jacket sleeve, sliding the fabric between her fingers like a tailor assessing a fine wool. "Let me offer some friendly advice," Cheyenne said. She squared her shoulders forward in a counselor pose. "I know something about men. I've been married a few times, been in and out of relationships a few more. They were all jerks. All losers. But," she angled her jaw in a serious smile, "there are times when a woman has to fight for what she wants. When her man lays down and plays dead, where's the challenge?" She stared at Cliff, her hand resting on his sleeve.

He glanced out the window at large snowflakes floating to earth. "I have my wants. I have my needs. She knows that."

"Could you have this frank a conversation with your wife? Tell her your wants and needs in simple four letter words?" Cheyenne asked. "The answer is no. I see couples like you and Mary Jane driving to town or shopping at the Muni. Married forever. How do I know? They're not talking."

Cliff waited. He stared through the window, stared at the dogs outside racing in the snow, crouching, tugging at a chunk of rawhide.

"My dad was a wildcatter, and everybody loved him," Cheyenne said. "Neighbors, friends, the company he worked for. Well, almost everybody. Mother left as soon as I could make my own bed. Back to Minnesota. Dad loved the thrill of the chase, the challenge of the unknown. He was bored by predictability. Happiness for him was waking up the next morning. Success was getting his paycheck on Friday."

Cheyenne stood and poured refills. "I don't need much," she continued. "An occasional friend, a full-body hug now and then. And I'm not complaining. I went to a class reunion a few years back and couldn't wait to leave. I wouldn't trade places with any of them.

"Guess you could call me a caretaker, and that's a part of me I can't deny. My current husband? Not worth the effort. But one way or another, he'll be a better man when I leave him." She laughed. "I see my marriages as Junior Achievement projects—high energy, low expectation."

She sipped her coffee. "And as for you . . ."

Cliff felt the sting of female chastisement, like his wife saying "We have to talk."

"Who do you think benefits from your procrastination?" Cheyenne asked. "I know a little bit of the grief therapy gobbledygook, and you're in denial. How do I know? Don't ask. It's woman's intuition. You tried some wildcat exploration yourself, and it didn't work. Do you know how many more untapped oil fields there are on the planet?" She glared at Cliff. "And her son . . ."

"Andy," Cliff said.

"What does Andy think? That this is the way a marriage works?" Cliff returned to the window, toward a world being recreated in undeserved white purity.

"Go for it, man." Cheyenne touched his sleeve again, stretched her hand around his wrist, and pulled his arm toward her. She smiled. "Follow me."

Later, Cliff stood at the kitchen table, faked a sip from an empty cup. "I'd better get going. I promised Andy I'd be home."

Cheyenne entered the kitchen behind him, brushing her hair. "Your missus doesn't know what she's missin'."

Cliff looked for his jacket.

"I know how men are wired," Cheyenne said. "Right now, you're swimming in guilt, rushing for the door. But an hour from now, you'll wish you would have stuck around for seconds."

Cliff checked his pockets for keys and wallet.

"Before you leave, let me tell you the moral of the story. Not every husband and wife are compatible. You and Mary Jane aren't. Fang and I aren't. You and I wouldn't be. But take it from me, a loveless marriage is worse than no marriage at all."

Cliff looked at his watch and walked to the door for his shoes.

"But I noticed a spark of life in there." She pointed to the bedroom. "For a brief moment, you took charge, and you enjoyed yourself. You're capable of that. Not with me, long term. Not with Mary Jane. But someone. Someone for you. Someone for Andy."

Andy. Cliff recalled his awkward surprise at the dinner table, felt him clinging to his arm at the Raptor Center, sensed his fascination, his innocent jealousy, as he watched the protective antics of the parent eagles. His pleading eyes, tragic and hopeful.

Cheyenne continued. "Do you know my co-worker at the Muni? Ellie? Great lady. Cute. Funny. Hard working. Her husband walked out on her a couple years ago. Left her with a teenage daughter. Okay if I tell her about you?"

"I'm married," Cliff fired back.

"Oh, are you? I wouldn't have known."

Cliff slipped into his shoes and kept his back to her.

"Well, can I tell her about you?"

He hesitated, then patted his shirt pocket. "Ellie? Eloise Jenkins? Yeah," he said. "Yeah, I guess so."

On the drive home, Cliff toyed with stopping at Good Shepherd. Maybe tell Mother everything. Talk about his problem, hoping to clarify it, solve it. He had nowhere else to unload, no one else to unload before. Mother would pretend not to hear his story, wouldn't turn the television volume down while he disgorged every agonizing detail. At the end, she'd offer some perfunctory comment like, "Who's surprised?"

He stopped at the intersection where a left turn would take him home, a right turn to Good Shepherd.

Snow glided down the windshield and settled on the hood. It heaped on garbage can lids and mailboxes by the road. It whitened the rail fence that followed the highway toward the Muni and Good Shepherd, whitened everything, tempering the landscape, rendering it soothing, benevolent.

MEN

Bonnie Witte trudges six blocks to her job at the C-Store, her face snuggled in a scarf, her shoulders bracing into raw December headwind. Her steps are weighted, sluggish, as if winter may defeat her and force her back to the warm comfort of her room. Snow on the sidewalk is slush, and in the street, a murky grime. She stops at the curb and waits while a crawling city bus passes, spewing acrid diesel fumes in its wake. She plods past student housing, administration, the chemistry building, the gate to the campus mall, all abandoned on Christmas morning. The chapel carillon breaks the silence.

> *God rest ye merry gentlemen,*
> *Let nothing you dismay.*
> *Remember Christ our Savior*
> *Was born on Christmas day.*

Last night's horror weighs on her. And what's the lesson learned, the redeeming social value? None. She is used goods, humiliated, devastated beyond redemption. What's next? Next semester? Next year? Next rest of her life? A passing motorist honks in scorn. Student pedestrians laugh and jeer. She compares her trek to the walk on Calvary. She's not religious, but the thought of shared pain relieves her. Or is she being dramatic?

The C-Store is at the end of the block. She checks her watch—five before eleven. She opted to delay her return home during the semester break to compete in a swim meet and to work Christmas Eve and Christmas Day. Her father approves of her frugality in the unspoken manner of a practical man, an auto mechanic. Her mother rationalizes about how much more relaxed the holiday is "after all the Christmas hullabaloo is over."

To save us all from Satan's power
When we were gone astray.

Bonnie detours to an alley to avoid the annoying carol. The irony angers her. Merry Gentlemen? What gentlemen? There are none. Not her father, not her previous boyfriends, certainly not Scott Griffiss, her Comp & Lit professor. No gentleman would have degraded her the way Scott had.

In the C-Store, she punches the time clock and heads for the front counter, ignoring the clerk she relieves. She dons the mandatory reindeer antler headdress and scowls, as if daring a customer to stop. A car drives to the gas pump and inserts a credit card. Good.

Then another car parks outside the store entry. A single passenger sits inside, a man. "Oh, God," Bonnie says, "not him." Bitter bile gags her. Or is it blood from biting her lip? "Not him," Bonnie growls, "not him."

O tidings of comfort and joy, comfort and joy.
O tidings of comfort and joy.

Bonnie neared the end of the first semester of her second year at North State. Her Comp & Lit class was a two-year sequence taught by Mr. Scott Griffiss, a youngish professor given to affected speech and dramatic gestures. He dropped hints to his students of pursuing his PhD and being named Chair of the English Department. Tall and heavy-framed with a shock of sandy hair cantilevered from his forehead, he preferred to lecture using an overhead projector rather than a white board. Students speculated that using the board required him to turn his back to the class and expose an emerging bald spot.

Earlier in the semester, Mr. Griffiss had assigned his class to write their first paper on a character in Twentieth Century American Literature. Someone they would like to know. He lingered on the word *know*, as if giving it multiple interpretations: to perceive, to experience, to *know*, as in the biblical sense. The class, mostly young women, gave him a confused or embarrassed stare. He opened his arms, as if to offer help.

"Would you select a radical activist like Tom Joad in *Grapes of Wrath*? Or an idealist like Atticus Finch in *To Kill a Mockingbird*? Or a soldier of fortune like Jake Barnes in *The Sun Also Rises*? How about an adulterous socialite like *The Great Gatsby*?"

Bonnie was uncertain. She made an appointment to meet him in his office after class. "None of those characters appeals to me," she said. "I prefer someone more contemporary, less driven, more accessible." She flushed at the word *accessible* and fidgeted with her notebook.

He gave her a quiet, tolerant smile, sat back in his chair, and sucked his pen. Dribbles of sweat rolled down her side. He stood and placed a hand on her shoulder, as if evaluating a prospect. "Meet me for coffee at the Union and we'll discuss it. Wednesday afternoon at three. No, Tuesday afternoon," he corrected himself. "I play racquetball on Wednesday."

On Tuesday, Bonnie waited at the Union coffee shop. Rather than the jacket she wore to class, she wore a dress coat opened to expose a bright fuchsia sweater. She removed her glasses, then replaced them when passing students blurred to unrecognizable forms. With her notebook open and keeping one eye on the door, she glanced at the list of characters she'd like to know—Harry in *The Snows of Kilimanjaro*, but everyone would choose him. Cal in *East of Eden* was an obvious choice, but it may have been her infatuation with James Dean in the movie. She pushed hair out of her eyes and pretended to write. Her hands were shaking when she checked her watch. At three-thirty she left.

He didn't apologize when she saw him in class, and out of disgust for his absent-mindedness or ill manners, she submitted her paper "My Life With Tarzan."

In early December, Mr. Griffiss assigned his class their second paper, a biography of a living person, due before Christmas break. "Someone you know well enough to interview," he suggested. "Family members are the easiest. Think of someone unconventional, rebellious, an outcast, perhaps."

Aunt Pearl. Bonnie pounced on the inspiration. Aunt Pearl, Dad's sister in the Good Shepherd Assisted Living Home about a half-hour's drive away. Pearl and her dad Carl were siblings in a family of children named for precious and semi-precious stones—girls Crystal, Opal, Pearl, and Sapphire, and boys Garnet and Carl. The father objected to Coral.

Yes, Aunt Pearl. The mention of her name still brought a round of tsk-tsks and raised eyebrows at family gatherings. The legend Bonnie heard was that Pearl had had an affair with the priest-superintendent of the parochial elementary school where she taught. Their relationship was exposed, and she was banished, of course. She taught the balance of her career in Wisconsin public schools and now returned to spend her retirement years at Good Shepherd.

Yes, Aunt Pearl. Bonnie had met her at family reunions and received a Christmas card from her earlier in the week.

Bonnie called and thanked her for the card. They wiled away a few minutes in small talk before she announced her intentions and asked Aunt Pearl for permission to interview her for a term paper. "Aunt Pearl, could we meet at Good Shepherd on Monday evening, the sixth?"

"I'd welcome visitors from the Ku Klux Klan. But please, just call me Pearl."

Wreaths with billowing red bows festooned the front doors of Good Shepherd. Christmas-y snowflakes tumbled in front of paned windows and settled on entry planters stuffed with evergreens and plastic poinsettias. In the entry, Bonnie pushed the button under Pearl's mailbox.

A bouncy woman in a pink velour jogging suit opened the door. "Bonnie," she said. Pearl reached for Bonnie's arm and motioned her in. Bonnie recognized her—the busty frame and beehive hairdo that shone like spun sugar. Large rose-tinted glasses illuminated her forehead and cheeks with a healthy, happy glow.

"Come in. Come in. Let's sit here in the Gathering Room," Pearl said. "My apartment's a mess." They sat before the fireplace, its gas log casting contrived warmth and ambiance. *Family Circle* magazines fanned across the coffee table. Beside them, two residents sat at a card table assembling a jigsaw puzzle in concentrated silence. A robed resident in a Santa Claus hat sat at the upright piano offering an anguished one-finger rendition of "Silent Night." The room was warm, instantly warm, and smelled of agedness.

"You're looking well," Pearl said. "You have your mother's carriage. Shoulders back, girl."

Bonnie straightened and pushed hair out of her eyes. She forced a smile, then relaxed, shoulders sloping, round face flushed, head cocked and drooping.

"Tell me about yourself," Pearl said. "I can't believe you're in college already. And you're writing a paper? How's your father? I can't remember when I last saw you."

MEN

Bonnie smiled and held her aunt's hands. "Aunt Pearl. Pearl. I saw you at the family reunion."

"Well, that was years ago. This is our special occasion." Pearl stood. "Let's go to my apartment and celebrate, if you can find your way through the clutter. Could I interest you in a glass of wine? Or are students still teetotalers?" She tittered.

They walked past the pianist. "Play it again, Sam," Pearl said.

"The name's not Sam. It's Maxwell."

"Play it again, Maxwell."

When they walked the hall to Pearl's apartment, she pulled a key from her pocket. "Got to lock the doors," she said. "The man in the next wing is a sex maniac." She poked Bonnie. "I wish."

Furniture lined the apartment walls—flowered sofa, recliner, drop-leaf table and chairs, twin curio cabinets, a television turned on but muted, bookshelves labeled by genre: fiction, poetry, biography, reference. And everywhere, angels—figurines, a sofa throw, lamps, vases, plates, framed artwork, a small Christmas tree with angel ornaments. Bonnie surveyed the scene. "Must be tough to make it to the bathroom without being touched by an angel."

Pearl smiled. "It's Christmas. I know you came to interview me, but you must tell me a Christmas story first. Then I'll tell you mine." She poured two glasses of wine. "This will get you going."

Bonnie lifted her glass in a toast. "I could tell you my entire life story in two minutes." She gazed at the tree. "Would you like the sugar-coated sitting-on-Santa's-lap story or the traumatic coming-of-age-disappointment story? I have both." She sipped her wine.

"Your choice," Pearl said.

"Maybe a quick bit of Christmas humor first. I was in second grade and couldn't sing a note. Instead of putting me in the choir, Mrs. Delaney selected me to be the Blessed Virgin. I cradled a baby doll in swaddling clothes while the choir sang 'Silent Night.'" She closed her eyes, remembering, then shook her head with an embarrassed chuckle. "Hawley Shafer also couldn't sing a note, so he was Joseph. The guy was a ham, kept stomping the stage with his shepherd's crook, tickling the doll's chin, putting his hand on my shoulder and pulling me toward him. I knew the kids would razz me for the rest of the year. 'Bonnie and Hawley and their little rubber dolly.' I elbowed him in the you-know-where."

Pearl laughed. "Bonnie, that's terrible. What did your mother and dad say?"

"Dad wasn't there. Mother didn't comment." Bonnie sipped her wine. "How long before this kicks in? I may need a boost to tell you the rest of that year's story."

"Drink up."

"That was the Christmas I prayed for a doll, the popular doll that smiled and cried in television ads, the doll my friends wanted and asked of Santa. A soft, baby doll that I could feed and dress and love. I stayed in bed until seven o'clock that morning, our Christmas routine. I remember it was five to seven, and I smelled bacon and heard a carol from the record player. I counted backward from 300, then tumbled out of bed and dashed into the living room."

Bonnie twirled the wine in her glass.

"I sense disappointment in the works," Pearl said.

"The drapes were drawn, and the tree lights sparkled. Mother stood in the kitchen doorway, spatula in hand, wearing a red chenille bathrobe. Dad wasn't there. I found my package under the tree and was surprised at its size. Too flat for a doll. I ripped the bow and wrapping paper, held my breath, and lifted the cover. A sweater. I tossed it aside. A blouse. I shuffled through tissue paper. Mittens. Socks. I looked at the tree, and tears fractured the lights into a million tiny crosses. I ran to mother. 'My doll,' and buried my face in her robe. She patted my head. 'Your father thought . . .'"

Bonnie stopped. "My first memory of an encounter with the male species."

"I wish I could tell you it gets better. Let's get on with the interview."

They began with the obvious—birth date and place, order of birth, siblings. Education, ambitions, career plans. One glass of wine led to another, and another. Bonnie hesitated, then leaned forward and pointed an accusing, if unsteady finger at Pearl. "Tell me about the priest," she said. "Tell me about your contemptible affair with the priest."

"I should be serious about this. But it's such a joke now. Times have changed."

Pearl sipped her wine, then tipped the glass. "I was a fourth grade teacher at Annunciation School, the only lay teacher on the faculty. The rest were Franciscan nuns. I must have been about your age. How old are you? We needed only two years at Normal School then to get a teaching certificate."

"Twenty," Bonnie said.

"Twenty what?"

"I'm twenty years old."

"Well, good for you. I'm 75. Anyway, I was decorating my classroom for Christmas one night when Father Moore, Father Antonio Moore, opened the door. He had a skeleton key which admitted him to any room in the school. And any room in the convent, for all I know." She emptied the wine bottle into her glass. "He locked the door after he entered. 'I saw your room lights from the rectory,' he mumbled. 'Working late?' He walked in, and I could smell booze, something tougher than altar wine. He clicked off the overhead lights. The only light in the room was the star above the Nativity scene. He grabbed my arms and pulled me toward him."

She stopped. "You have to understand the ground rules back then. Priests were God's representatives on earth. They were to be respected and obeyed. And in this case, I wouldn't have had much choice. He was a big man, reminded me of my dad. Heavy shoulders, big hands. I saw him pick up a basketball one-handed in the playground. 'Get on your knees,' he said. I thought he was giving me his blessing. *Hoping* that he was giving me his blessing. I closed my eyes and folded my hands in prayer, the way we did at Confirmation. He placed his hand on my head. I felt his other hand fumbling in front of me, heard a zipper open."

She emptied her glass. "You won't believe the next part. Talk about Divine Intervention. I heard keys rattling. The door opened, and the janitor switched on the lights and walked in, pushing a mop pail. I'll never forget the look on his face."

Pearl tilted her head, then lowered it in a shamed gesture. She stared into her twirling glass as if searching for her reflection. Something to prove that she existed. She sighed. "Funny, I still feel the embarrassment. I still feel the pain."

"And then?"

"Father Moore must have threatened the janitor with eternal damnation. He told me that I no longer taught at Annunciation. The next morning, I got a call from the Archbishop's office inviting me to report to the rectory. I expected to see him in vestments, his miter perched on his head like a stove pipe, a crosier in his hand, speaking from behind a smoky curtain like the Wizard of Oz. Instead, he wore a black suit and Roman collar. He chided me, humiliated me, blamed me for a priest's downfall. Said I lured Father Moore into sin. Me, a naïve twenty-year old country girl. 'You know it's a mortal sin to strike a priest, Miss Witte,' he said. I looked at him as if to say 'I didn't strike him.' 'No,' he said, 'you didn't strike him.' And I remember his exact words. 'Your sin was far more profound. You violated his priesthood.'

"I took the bus home that day. I couldn't tell my folks. They wouldn't believe me and, if they did, they wouldn't understand. You may not believe this, but I forgave him. In fact, I couldn't stop thinking about him. I was obsessed with him. I wanted to return, to give him a chance to apologize. Or to apologize myself." She stopped.

Had it been prudent of her to ask? Bonnie wondered. How could she lighten the conversation? "Violated his priesthood? He must have been talking about the priest's vow of chastity. Couldn't Father What's-his-name have saved you both the trouble and engaged in a little auto-eroticism?"

Pearl lifted her head and thrust her chin out. Her eyes sparkled behind the rose-tinted glasses. "He wasn't the type for manual labor," she chirped and slapped Bonnie's knee. "Let's open another bottle of wine."

Pearl poured two glasses. "I've been doing all the talking," she said. "What about you? Tell me another story about my boorish brother Carl."

Bonnie smiled. "Sure. It's payback time. You know Dad wanted a son. Mother said she offered to call me Carla, but what would that prove? I weighed nine pounds at birth, my mother's one and only. Dad said I tore the plumbing out of her.

"When I was six or seven, I tried helping him in the garage, handing him the wrong wrench, confusing clockwise with counter-clockwise, or holding a pipe with 'my other left hand.' I tagged along on fishing trips but couldn't remove a sunfish from the hook. I hunted squirrels with him and suffered a discolored shoulder. We watched television together, and I was shocked by the violence and bored by the predictability. Lots of frustration. For him and me."

She sipped her wine. "This is not fun. I feel like an ingrate."

"It's therapy. Continue."

"I enrolled in a summer swimming class in high school and discovered I had a natural buoyancy and a graceful, powerful stroke. My instructor praised me and encouraged me. I remember standing before him after the final class, dripping, shivering, my arms down and crossed. I wore a black one-piece suit with wide straps and ruffles around the hips. When the instructor placed his hand on my shoulder, I flinched. 'I hope you continue lessons,' he told me. 'You have great potential.'"

She hesitated, then rushed to the finish. "We had a swim meet for our families, and I won my division. I decided that summer to teach swimming to children with disabilities."

Bonnie opened her notebook. "I feel guilty, like I'm ratting on my family."

"Don't. They'd do the same for you."

"Time to be on my way. I have homework to do."

"No," Pearl said, "I want to hear more. Tell me you or some family member is preserving my tradition of impropriety."

"It's life as usual for me," Bonnie said. "Undergrad. Overweight. I'm still trying to shed my Freshman Fifteen." She patted her stomach.

"And your class work?"

"Doable, but not exciting." She backtracked and pointed to her notebook. "But this is."

"I'll bet you have a cute dorm room with matching drapes and bedspread right out of *Seventeen*?"

"Nope. A one-room efficiency off campus. I wouldn't recognize my neighbors."

"I'm searching," Pearl said. "Where's the spark that keeps you alive?"

Bonnie smiled and placed her empty glass on the table. "I have one," she said, her demureness trumped by the wine. She removed her glasses and twirled them by the temple tips. "A tryst. My lover and I. Every Tuesday afternoon."

"Well, good for you. I must meet him."

"I'm afraid we can't do that. He's my professor, and it's against college policy for faculty to date students. We can't be seen in public."

Pearl stopped, her glass half-raised. Bonnie's head drooped, her mousy brown hair providing convenient cover.

"Are you two in love?"

"I'm not sure. I know he likes me."

"What's the attraction?"

"I don't know. It just feels good to be with him."

"Where do you go on Tuesdays?"

"His friend has an apartment off campus. We use that."

"*Use*?"

"It'll be different at the end of the semester."

"Watch it, young woman. Some of my girlfriends made the most important decisions of their lives in borrowed apartments."

"He's very cautious about *that*."

"What's Prince Charming's name?"

"Scott Griffiss." Her courage from the wine dispersed. She looked at her watch. "I'd better get going. I have class tomorrow morning at eight. Can I come back later this week?"

"*May* I come back later this week."

"Go away," she says to the man sitting in the car outside the C-Store. "Get out of here. Get out of my life." She grabs a pen and holds it like a dagger. She places her finger over the panic button which summons the police. She won't talk to him if he enters, she'll scream at him, throw hot coffee on him, wound him, ruin him. She remembers security cameras are trained on the register, that her actions, present and planned, are recorded. She'll be fired for this. "I don't give a damn," she shouts.

He sits in the car, as if rehearsing a speech.

Final exams were two weeks away. For her Comp & Lit class, Bonnie would need to submit her biography paper. The conversation with Pearl had ignited an interest in her family history, in her genetics. She wondered if she was wired to suffer the same disappointments as Pearl.

She drafted an outline for her paper. She swam daily for practice, for relief. The paper stayed with her. She pulled a shift at the C-Store. The paper. Where would she start? She had biographical data—date and place of birth, birth order, nationality, economic conditions, religious affiliation, all that.

She knew of Pearl's father, responsible but indifferent, which sounded familiar. Her mother, dependent and ineffectual, also familiar. But the story began in the classroom at Annunciation. Where did it end? She made note of questions she would ask Pearl on her second visit Thursday night.

In Pearl's apartment, the sound of percolation trailed the aroma of brewing coffee. Bonnie opened her notebook and leaped into her questions. Where in Wisconsin had she taught? How long? What grades? Any boyfriends? Was she lonesome for home? What about the priest, Father Moore? Did she ever hear from him? About him? Bonnie began to feel the story was familiar, predictable. She focused on Pearl, keeping a distance from her own personal journey, not allowing Pearl's life to become her crystal ball.

"Nothing memorable about teaching Wisconsin kids," Pearl said. "Take that back. There was one memorable incident." She smiled a capricious smile. "The principal was a lesbian. I couldn't teach *Hans Brinker.*" She looked at Bonnie to gauge her comprehension. "You remember *Hans Brinker and the Silver Skates*? The story of the little Dutch boy who put his finger in the dike?" Her laugh was profanity.

She lingered over memories of students winning spelling bees, writing award-winning themes, earning scholarships later in school.

"How about your personal life?" Bonnie asked. "What happened after four? What happened on weekends?"

Pearl sighed. "Let's get the wine bottle out." She poured two glasses, twirled her own, sniffed it, twirled again. "Life as a school teacher is a life lived in a fish bowl. If you want to relax, have fun, act crazy, do stupid things, you have to get out of town. We, my girlfriend and I, drove to LaCrosse one weekend. We rented a cheap motel room and found a small bar where we didn't know a soul. Long story short, we got shit-faced, pardon my French. But it was the best therapy I ever had."

Pearl lifted her eyes to check Bonnie's reaction. None. "It got to be a regular thing," Pearl continued. "Every weekend. We met some of the regulars at the bar, found ourselves staying at nicer motels, drinking funky cocktails—Mai Tais, Singapore Slings, Black Russians. My weekend life started overlapping my weekday life. I found that I wore more makeup, a dressier wardrobe. The clothes were gifts from my weekend friends. I was more casual with my students, less demanding, less involved."

She paused, a sadness falling across her face. A ceramic clock with painted angels ticked a gentle rhythmic cadence.

"Fortunately, I was getting older. Not wiser, older. The regulars at the bars weren't as regular anymore. I realized that the whole education thing was a charade. Or was it the bar thing? I didn't know. Anyway, I quit the road trips and concentrated on my classroom until I retired." She drained her glass. "Enough about me."

"Were you curious about what happened to Father Moore?"

"Yes, I was. Maybe five years ago, I did a White Page search on Antonio Moore and found one in Muskegon, Michigan. I searched Franciscan Retirement Homes, and *voila*, there was one in Muskegon, Michigan. I drove there the following summer vacation.

"Father Moore, the very one, was in a wheelchair sitting in the garden when I asked for him. He was decrepit. He was wasted and shriveled. I was certain it was him by his size. His bony frame drooped in the chair. I introduced myself. He pretended to recognize me, to remember me. 'Ah, yes,' he said, shaking his head up and down.

"'Annunciation School,' I said. 'Pearl Witte. Christmas. And the janitor, remember?'"

He forced a limp smile and stared, his milky eyes unfocused.

"I realized then that the balance of power had shifted. I wanted to say, 'Get on your knees, you senile bastard.' Instead, I took his hand, still large but soft and feeble and trembling. Like holding a newborn puppy. He squeezed my hand, and lifted his other to give me his blessing. I stopped him. Those hands, those big hands. He should have been a carpenter or a farmer. And a father. A real father. Then, in a moment of total hypocrisy, I gave him *my* blessing." She paused. "I need coffee."

"So do I." Bonnie felt her blood pulsing. She needed respite. "Can I, *may* I tour your apartment?" She walked into the bedroom, her *boudoir*, as Pearl referred to it. The bedroom set was white provincial, the drapes rose antique satin, the carpet a pink plush. Tufts were missing on the pink chenille bedspread making it look like a maze. Beside the bed, on the lamp table, a rosary.

"Are you still religious?" Bonnie asked over coffee.

"I still believe in God. Say my prayers. And hope to spend life everlasting in heaven. I don't go to church regularly. I asked a priest about receiving the sacraments. He said the scandal value of someone like me taking communion precluded it. Whatever happened to *Forgive us our trespasses*? And what about you? Still say your prayers before bedtime?"

"You could call me a Proustian Humanist. You know, the Gospel according to Camus."

"Where did you learn that?"

"I studied Philosophy last year. Had a class in Abnormal Psych. Don't get me started on Freud."

"Not a chance," said Pearl.

Bonnie sensed a sliver of sarcasm. She pushed her coffee cup aside and poured two glasses of wine. "What's in this stuff? I haven't talked this much for years."

Pearl twisted her glass before the light, the wine sparkling like rubies. "It's a muscle relaxant, a mood alterative, a social equalizer, a conversation stimulant, an aphrodisiac. And a career blocker. But tonight, it's just a glass of wine."

Bonnie raised her glass in a mock toast. She referred to her notes, then sighed. "Do you regret never marrying? Never having children?"

"Hell, no. Most of my lady friends were married. After four or five kids, they were tired and overweight, and their husbands had girlfriends and drinking problems. In my forty-five years of teaching, I've had over a thousand children. I cheered at their ball games, applauded their band concerts, and shed tears at their graduations. Marriage? If I wanted a handsome, loyal, hairy-chested companion, I would've bought a collie." She laughed a tittering cackle and tipped her glass.

"Speaking of, I saw a picture of your *paramour* in the local paper this week. I saved it for you."

Bonnie braced at the hint of parental criticism. *Paramour?* Was this her joke? If not, how did she recognize him? What did she know?

Pearl handed Bonnie the newspaper, opened to a picture of a group of men distributing gifts to hospitalized children. Yes, it was Scott. The caption read "Members of St. Stephens Knights of Columbus spread Christmas cheer." They were identified. Scott Griffiss. The tall one. The one with the provocative smile.

"St. Stephens is only a few blocks from here. I've attended midnight mass there a few times. Sitting in the back row, of course. Would you like to do your old Aunt Pearl a favor and accompany her this year?"

"Sure," said Bonnie, happy to fold the paper. "I have to work Christmas Eve day and Christmas, but we can do it. And I'd like to show you the campus during Christmas break. Then, after my four-hour shift on Christmas Day, would you like to do your niece a favor and drive home with me to Mom and Dad's for Christmas dinner?"

"You've got a couple of dates," Pearl said. "When?"

"Wednesday, the twenty-second, the last day of finals, for the campus tour. I'll pick you up for lunch."

Wednesday came and, with it, black coffee, a rushed hike to campus, anxiety. Her last exam, exhilaration, doubt. Finally, relief. The ironies of Christmas, Bonnie thought as she walked home. Holiday banquets and food shelves; home for the holidays and homeless shelters; nativity scenes and abortion clinics. Enough. More than enough. At 11:30, she drove to Good Shepherd.

After lunch in a student diner, Pearl and Bonnie toured the campus—classroom buildings, the auditorium, the student union, the chapel, and the athletic building with ball courts and pool. "This is where I practice and compete and teach swimming to children with disabilities," Bonnie said. "Let's take a break."

They sat in the lobby of the athletic building and shared a Coke, breathing chlorine and condensation that fogged the lobby air. The sun, low at this time of equinox, shone through half-frosted windows. The snow had stopped and, through the windows, its fresh blanket beautified the campus. Bonnie walked to the rear door and scanned the faculty parking lot. The black Toyota with license plate *MR GRIF* was parked in the front row.

Bonnie felt apprehensive, then agitated. She sat half-facing the stairway from the men's locker room, listening for, glancing at each passerby. A group of four men climbed the stairs—Scott Griffiss and his racquetball opponents. Bonnie swiveled in her chair to hide her face. Pearl turned to look at these raucous athletes, red with heat and perspiration, swinging black grips, and trading insults. She recognized Scott from the photograph—tall, muscular frame, sandy hair, square jaw. She glanced at Bonnie, still looking away. "I'd like to meet him."

Bonnie shook her head, *No.*

Pearl stood. "Mr. Griffiss."

Scott turned in her direction. She heard a teasing mumble from the other three. "One of my non-traditional students," he said to them.

"I'm Pearl Witte," Pearl said, extending her hand. "Bonnie Witte's aunt."

Bonnie turned toward them, reluctant and embarrassed.

"Yes, of course," Scott said. "I'm looking forward to making your acquaintance in Bonnie's biography. I've scanned it, but I haven't read it. Hello, Bonnie. Do I get a preview of the character?"

Bonnie stood. "Aunt Pearl and I toured the campus. I wanted to show her where I swam." Mr. Griffiss was her professor again, not her *paramour.*

Scott seemed amused and gazed at Pearl as if she were a curiosity. He stood with his back to the sunlit window. The light shone through his dewy hair and cast his silhouette against the sunset. "You were in Education too, right? Bonnie says you have quite a library. What do you read?"

"I don't read contemporary American authors. I'm a Jane Austin fan. *Pride and Prejudice, Sense and Sensibility.*"

"Ah, a romantic."

"A romantic, yes," she said, "but a romantic realist."

"But don't all romantics believe they're realists?" Scott tossed it out in the meaningless banter style so popular among his peers.

"No," Pearl said with a hint of scold. "No. Often there's no intent of realism at all."

Bonnie finished her shift at the C-Store at 11 o'clock on Christmas Eve and drove to Good Shepherd. Pearl waited for her inside the door and walked to the car. Snow fell with a casual grace, covering the sidewalk and topping the handrails. A neighborhood house decorated with icicle lights broadcast "Silent Night" over loudspeakers. The streets leading to St. Stephens were empty and quiet, like a vacant cathedral.

"Getting a seat is likely to be a problem," Pearl said. "If you let me off at the door, I'll spot one for us."

The church was dark when Bonnie entered; the only lights were from candelabras along the center aisle. She craned to see a familiar face, a familiar head. Toward the front, she saw Pearl wave.

Bonnie hadn't attended midnight mass, hadn't attended any mass since she left home. The liturgy was familiar though, the hymns common and well-worn. She felt comfortable and relaxed, a folksy peace. The candles, the burning incense, the organ music intoxicated her. She felt a sensation of well-being that was familiar, but not recent. Perhaps in a previous life.

At the Sign of Peace segment of the mass, the priest turned to the congregation and asked them to greet their neighbors "in the spirit of the true Christmas." Bonnie hugged Pearl, grateful for her company tonight, and for her new friendship. She shook hands with the family behind her and looked ahead. Her eyes met Scott Griffiss's. He stood with a sleeping golden-haired child in his arms, her head lying in the crook of his neck. The woman beside him turned to shake hands with parishioners behind her. Her coat was buttoned down to a bulging pregnancy.

Bonnie stands paralyzed behind the counter at the C-store. Mr. Griffiss alights from his car, swings the door shut with a casual sweep, and lifts his head as if taking his first breath of morning air. He walks to the store entry and pauses to read an ad, then opens the door. "Good morning. Merry Christmas. I thought I'd drive over to talk about last night."

Bonnie clings to the counter.

"I called the store to get your hours," he says. "Cute antlers."

She swipes her head, sending the antlers to the floor.

Mr. Griffiss jiggles his keys. "What are your plans?" he asks.

She clenches her jaw. Her throat is dry, her stomach roiling.

"I must know your plans."

Bonnie holds his stare.

"If you don't have plans, perhaps I can counsel you. You must know the urban legend of small town girls coming to college and being smitten by the man at the lectern. The man who wears suits. The man who reads books. The sophisticated man who speaks in words longer than four letters. You must have noticed those girls gazing starry-eyed at their professor, sitting in provocative poses, and bantering with him after class. Doting on him to gain favor. Implicitly offering favor for favor."

Bonnie's knees weaken, her arms tremble.

"You must know the file cabinets at the Dean of Student Affairs's office proliferate with memos from staff regarding such conduct. Save-your-ass memos, we call them. Memos that profs file to protect themselves from harassment charges when these small town girls don't get their way." He fiddles with pennies in the junk change cup.

"Finally, you must know the faculty here is one small cohesive community. We stick together. It's not difficult for me to solicit letters from other professors documenting similar conduct. And don't forget. It's my word against yours. Save yourself the trouble." He heads for the door. "Oh, I nearly forgot. I need a gallon of milk."

The drive to the Witte home for Christmas dinner is quiet. Pearl breaks the silence. "It'll be good to see Wynetta and Carl."

Bonnie stares ahead.

"I don't remember this housing development. Is it new?" Pearl asks.

"Could you turn up the heat?" Pearl again. "My feet are freezing. Let's listen to some carols on the radio. It's Christmas. What the hell. Noel," she jokes.

She looks at Bonnie, her anger evident in her rigid posture, in her hands clenched around the steering wheel.

"You know, this whole experience could be your gift to yourself. You're young. Resilient. Able to move on. To move ahead. You don't have to suffer through the indignities I put myself through. And you don't have to be your mother's clone or your dad's disappointment."

Bonnie bites her lip. One more sermon.

"You have the opportunity for a successful career. I don't think it's in education, and I think you'd agree with that. Maybe working with children with disorders, disabilities."

Bonnie bristles at the words. They define her life.

"Breathe through your mouth," Pearl says. "You're going to drive us into the ditch. And for God's sake, loosen your grip on the wheel. I can see white knuckles through your gloves." She turns the radio on.

Have yourself a merry little Christmas.
Let your heart be light.
Next year, all our troubles will be out of sight.

Outside, the sun glows a huge orange above the western horizon. Bonnie reaches for her sunglasses. She takes a deep breath. Another. Another. Her shoulders relax against the back seat cushion. She flexes the fingers of her left hand, then her right.

"I knew he was married." Bonnie's voice is calm. "No proof, but I knew. I could have confirmed my suspicion with one phone call. But the forbidden fruit attraction . . . I wonder where I get that?"

"Happy to have been of help," Pearl says.

"I'm dropping Comp & Lit," Bonnie continues. "Part of me wants to stay in his class and glare at him. Part of me says what's the point? I thought about dropping out of North State completely, but that would be a win for him. I want him to see me around campus, around the Athletic Building. Want him to wonder what I'll do."

"Good plan," Pearl says.

"And I'm switching to Physical Therapy." She taps her fingers on the wheel. "Now I need a coffee break. There's a 24/7 truck stop ahead. I'll call Mother and tell her we're running a half hour late."

Pearl places her hand on Bonnie's shoulder. "The stuffed turkey and the mashed potatoes. That can wait."

"Yes."

"And the green bean casserole and the red and green Jell-O salad with a little dab of mayo. That can wait too."

"Yes, yes."

"And the cranberries and cloverleaf rolls and the pumpkin pie with a dollop of Cool Whip. All those can wait."

"Yes, yes, yes."

"And the football games blaring from the television. The pregame, the play-by-play, the post game with the replays and the analysis. All that can wait."

"Post game analysis. Very important. You gotta talk about it."

Bonnie pulls into the parking lot. In the side lot, semi-trailers align in diagonal precision. She parks beside pickup trucks in front of the building. Blinking Christmas lights run a chase around the café sign. An exhaust fan exhales the aroma of fried hamburger and onions.

Two drivers exit the café sucking toothpicks. They see Bonnie and Pearl and stop to hold the door. "Merry Christmas, ladies," one says and tips an imaginary hat. "Happy New Year," says the other.

In the entry, a stocky man leans into a wall phone, jeans riding below his belly, and wallet tethered to his belt by a chrome chain. He shouts, curses, and pounds the wall.

Inside, Bonnie asks, "What was that about?"

Pearl grunts, "Men."

Widow Maker

January 5, the anniversary of Woodrow's accident twenty-five years ago. He was 43 when he died, Woody's age today. A package rested against the door when Woody arrived home, a foot-square package posted from his mother Rayanna.

In the entry, he stared at the box on the table. So unlike his mother not to have called or written. He cut through the tape and tore the paper. An inner box was inscribed BOND CLOTHING COMPANY. Inside, a cellophane bag protected a brown felt hat, a fedora, with a contrasting band that held two small feathers, like flies in a tackle box. Woody lifted the hat to his face and inhaled. A faint scent of Vitalis released a string of memories.

Dad. The hat cocked over his right eye. He's in the woods, a logger in winter and dressed the part. Red and black plaid shirt tucked inside wool pants and wide red suspenders. Woodrow felled trees; Woody trimmed branches. At the end of the day after cutting four or five cords, Woodrow placed his arm on his son's shoulder, and the two would glow in sweat and admire their work. Woodrow would smile his signature smile. "Y'know your ole man loves ya," he'd say. "Your ole man's prouda ya."

Dad. He'd parlay that smile and say words that people loved to hear. They'd stop at the Broken Hart after a day in the woods. He'd unbutton his shirt cuffs and push his sleeves up and over his Popeye arms. Graybeards would sidle off their bar stools and buttonhole him to recount their *good ole days* in the woods. He'd smile, slap them on the back, and compliment them on their hardiness and derring-do. "Don't let those stories get away," he'd say.

Women would approach him, rest a sheepish hand on his arm, and offer small talk—the weather, the short days, the long nights. He'd smile and say something like, "Gosh, you smell good tonight." Everybody loved Woodrow. To not love him would be heresy.

Dad. Woody recognized several of his dad's signatures. His hat, his smile, his pickup truck. Woodrow was a modest man; his truck was the exception. International V8, cherry red, chrome wheels, dual exhaust, amber running lights. And a bed liner, because at the end of a day in the woods, they loaded the truck with firewood and delivered it to struggling families in the neighborhood. "Widows and orphans protected," he'd say.

Mondays, they'd stop at Widow Jensen's house, where Mrs. Jensen would burst out the door, coat sleeves dangling, yelling to the dog to shut up, calling the older kids to help. Woodrow would place the chainsaws on the doghouse away from the truck. He and Woody would unload firewood into a basement chute, under a frosted window where small faces peered through breath-melted circles. Sober, acquisitive faces that seemed to yearn, to envy Woody for having a father. Woodrow would wave to them; they'd stare motionless with an opaque expression. "Cute kids," Woodrow would say. "Must take after their mother." Back in the truck and halfway home, Woodrow would say, "Damn, I forgot the chainsaws. I'll pick them up later when I get gas."

Dad. On January 5, twenty-five years ago, Woodrow sawed into a forty-foot pine that hung up, nearly vertical, in a neighboring oak. It was late afternoon, the last cut of the day. A chill lowered from the dull winter sky and whipped in a north breeze from the clearing. A white wafer sun hesitated above a faraway tree line. Aromatic turpentine from fresh sawn pine permeated the icy air.

It was the first time Woody had seen his dad make that mistake. Woodrow had cautioned about it, calling the leaning tree a widow maker. He moved to where he shielded his son's view of the second cut, below the first. The saw wedged. He tugged. Twisted. Jerked. The pine rotated on its stump as if in a capricious game of tag. Woodrow ran left, then right, the tree shadowing him. He glanced up to gauge the tree's rotation and tripped on a branch. The pine dropped, true to its target.

Dad. Dad. Aw, shit. Dad. Dad.

For Woody, the events after his dad's death fade in and out of memory like a moon in fog. He remembers the constant telephone calls; the endless parade of hot dishes and cakes and bars; the suitcases of relatives staying at the house before the funeral.

Recalls his mother Rayanna standing at the cupboard, staring at a ham she was slicing for sandwiches. She mentioned her plan to Woody about how to present Woodrow for the review. A suit with white shirt and tie, she suggested, none of which existed in his wardrobe.

"Do that and I won't go," Woody said.
"We can't put him in a flannel shirt and jeans."
"Why not?"
"It isn't done, that's why. Don't make it harder for me."
"God damn it. Don't make it harder for *me*."
"Don't talk that way to your mother."

Woody strode to the door, grabbed a jacket off the hook. "Don't wait up."

He swaggered to his truck imitating his dad's gait, knowing his mother would be watching through the window.

Woody didn't recognize his dad lying in the casket at the review, didn't register the consoling pats on the shoulder and condolences: *You're the man, now. Take care of your mother.* The euphemistic laments: *He passed, he passed away. Too bad we lost him. He's gone to his Heavenly Father.* Words floated like a swarm of gnats. Escaping into a stall in the men's room for a cigarette, he heard a neighbor say, "Well, there goes *that* theory. I thought only the good die young."

At the casket, Rayanna combed Woodrow's hair with her fingers, perked the knot in his tie, and rested her hand on his. She greeted neighbors and consoled family, accepting their practiced compassion, their good intentions.

The focus shifted when Arnold Baxter entered the parlor. He strode up the aisle, creating a wake of murmurs through the muffled conversations. Neighbors reached to shake his hand. Church ladies, the Daughters of Martha, greeted him with respectful whispers. Raw-boned, red-faced men, naked without caps, grinned solicitous smiles, like ushers at offertory. "Good to see you, Arnold." "Hey, Mr. Lucky."

Arnold enjoyed celebrity status in the community when he placed in the State Lottery. "Got lucky twice in one month," he said. The *twice* reference, and the irony of the story, is that his divorce was granted days before his winning. "The ink wasn't even dry," he had said dozens of times.

The ex-Mrs. Baxter tried to reopen the proceedings, but failed. Folklore has it that he created a trust fund for his kids and future grandkids, bought a fishing boat, and returned to his job at the feed store. The grass widow became the butt of jokes among men folk. Women folk crowed she paid the price for her infidelity, that you don't have to wait to enter the pearly gates for justice. The ex-wife did the smart thing and moved to the county seat.

Arnold, his easy smile framed by a Fu Manchu mustache, approached Rayanna and embraced her with a shameless bear hug. Her shoulders relaxed, her body trembled, her head rested on his chest. He held her. She straightened and dabbed her eyes. Woody remembers the scene. Arnold holding his mother before the casket. A plaintive hymn drifting from the ceiling speaker. The aroma of coffee wafting from the kitchen. A metallic taste soured his mouth, like a new filling. He touched his dad's hand, unyielding like granite.

"Who's the guy in the suit?" Arnold pointed an elbow.

"We had a fight about that," Rayanna said. "The sport coat and tie are from the Thrift Store." She lifted the jacket. "The Levis and Redwings are authentic."

"I could've used those," Woody said.

"Other than that, how're you doing?" Arnold wrapped an arm around Woody's neck.

"Thanks for coming, Arnold," Rayanna said. Neighbors queued up behind them. "Please sit with us tomorrow afternoon at the service. I'll be glad when this is over. My sister Jonella is here and staying for a few days . . ."

"Good," Arnold interrupted. "You're in good hands. I'll get out of the way." He turned to Woody and led him by the arm. "Have you had supper yet? Let's go out for a steak. I need someone to leave with. I saw bad news outside, and I don't think either of us wants to see her."

In the parking lot, a horn honked, a Chevy Malibu with parking lights on. "I suppose I should say hello," Arnold said to Woody. He stopped. "Surprised to see you here."

The driver, a woman, puffed on a cigarette. A country western song twanged from the radio. She fumbled in her purse, then the glove compartment.

"It's almost eight," Arnold said. "Rayanna's still inside. They're getting ready to close the doors."

She tapped an ash out the window, took a last drag, and flipped the cigarette. "I can make it on my own, thanks."

Later, Woody asked, "Wasn't that your ex in the parking lot? Cookie?"

"Yup. Don't know what she was doing there."

They sat in a far corner booth at the Back Forty, a steak house and sneak spot, favored among Woody's crowd because of the farsighted bartender who, at the sight of a young patron, lifted his glasses, scanned the patron's drivers license, but couldn't read the date of birth.

Moose, deer, and elk heads stared from high knotty pine walls. Tables and chairs were crafted from de-barked aspens, and the bar was decorated with red and green balloons which popped from an occasional cigarette and caused shrieking, then riotous laughter. A holiday party occupied the bulk of the bar, the ladies in sequined-sweaters and stretch jeans, sipping pink drinks with red umbrellas. The aroma of fried chicken merged with cigarette smoke and beer. The juke box played a Bonnie Raitt song, and three or four couples danced, holding their drinks and cigarettes.

"I'll miss your dad," Arnold began. He carved into his steak. "He was a good man and a good friend." He paused, a bite of steak raised and waiting. "He had his weaknesses, but he was a good man."

"Weaknesses? Like what?"

Arnold looked at Woody. "You're eighteen years old." He stopped. "This isn't the time to discuss that. I expect that sooner or later all the dirty laundry will be aired. And what people don't know, they'll guess. Let me say that he was a good man." Arnold chewed his steak. "Did you know he apprenticed with me in the woods when he was about your age?"

Woody pushed his plate ahead and rested his arms on the table. "A lot of what I'm hearing tonight doesn't make sense. A guy in the latrine made some comment about the good not dying young. Your ex-wife is in the parking lot, and you don't want me to see her. Now I'm hearing about Dad's weaknesses."

"You're going to have to sort this out for yourself. But I'll give you a clue. Your dad carried a small ledger. He recorded his hours, his deliveries, his expenses. And a few other things. His *little black book*. Find that and save your mother a big embarrassment."

Arnold drove Woody home to a driveway filled with cars, the house lit, his mother visible through the window milling in the kitchen amid sisters, neighbors, friends. Woody edged to the garage, to the red pickup truck. He touched the door handle and felt his dad: cold and unyielding. He searched the console and glove compartment, behind the seat, the tool box, above the visor, under the floor mats. He checked the console again. In the cover, inside a pocket, he felt a small rectangular shape, a book. He held it—warm, alive, pulsing. He checked the pocket again. A folded magazine. He checked the garage door; no one there. He opened the magazine, a tawdry cover: *Minnesota Singles*. A letter inside was addressed to Woodrow McLeod, with a P.O. box address in Morristown, fifteen miles south. Woody slipped the magazine and book under his jacket and scrambled to the house.

The kitchen smelled of Italian sausage and oregano. The crowd parted; the chatter hushed. Rayanna emerged, wiping her hands on an apron. She hugged him. "We're making pizzas. Ready in a few minutes."

"No thanks, Mom. Arnold and I had supper." He eyed his extended family.

Rayanna opened her arms to the room. "Have you said hello to everyone?"

"I think so. I'm tired, Mom. I'm going to bed."

Coats and jackets were piled on the banister and railing. Woody threaded his way through nodding aunts and uncles and climbed the stairs.

The black book. He held it, uncertain. Inside the front cover were three numbers: 12-6-18. The magazine dropped to the bed, the envelope beside it. The envelope had been opened, a jagged tear across the top. He pulled the letter out and smelled a faint perfume.

Dear Paul,
I know you're looking for a Blue Ox, but would you settle for
a Red Fox?

A snapshot slid from between the pages. A busty red head, frontal nude, a mocking coyness to the downward tilt of her head. Woody stuffed the letter and photo in the envelope. He thumbed the magazine. Women seeking Men. Men seeking Women. Alternatives. In Men seeking Women, he read the bold print before the ads. Romeo Seeks Juliet. Take a Chance on Me. You're Gonna Like What U See. A page of ads. Another page. And there:

Paul Bunyan Seeks Babe the Blue (F)ox. Young 40s, outdoorsy guy, seeks fun-loving female. I'm stocky, cocky. You're wild but discreet. Married/single.

Woody read the envelope again and tucked it and the book in his jacket pocket.

"I'm having breakfast with my friends." Woody stood in the kitchen the next morning while Rayanna stamped baking powder biscuits out of a cloud of dough. The coffee pot gurgled its last breaths. A pale pink sky promised a cold November day. An unfamiliar woman sat at the kitchen table.

"Have a cup of coffee with us before you leave."

"I'd better get going."

"Be back in time to be dressed for church at noon then."

Woody drove to the Morristown Post Office and scanned the empty lobby for the mailbox listed on the envelope. He tried the combination printed in the book: 12-6-18. Inside were three letters, addressed to Woodrow McLeod. He walked to the postal window.

"You can close Box 303," he said. "It was my dad's. He's dead."

"Well, I'm sorry about that. I'll close it right away. Do you have a forwarding address for him?"

"No. Just mark any letters *Return to sender.*"

"If they're first class mail, I can forward them without a problem."

"I don't think you can." Woody walked out.

Memories, conversations, suspicions juggled in his head. His dad's struts into the Broken Hart. His sweet talk. His forgotten chainsaw at Widow Jensen's. The black book. The magazine. The letters. The unexplained, abbreviated phone calls at home. The incongruous sweet fragrance in the truck. The showers before bed when he arrived home late.

Woody held the evidence. Privileged, incriminating, damning evidence. It aroused an instant, heady authority in him, an ace in the hole. An authority he would have traded, just as instantly, for ignorance. He had to talk to Arnold. Arnold Baxter, Dad's hunting and fishing partner, now his friend. Woody had helped him move to Good Shepherd last month. Arnold could still drive, cook a decent meal, manage his finances, but the doctor advised against living alone. "You survived the first time, but who knows if you'll be lucky enough to have someone around if you have another stroke?"

Arnold's apartment at the Good Shepherd was a work in progress. Boxes piled on boxes. Bare furniture. Bare walls. A coffee pot on the kitchen counter; a mug on the table. Unread newspapers, magazines, advertisements littered the couch. A table lamp lit his leather chair. The television blared the morning news. Bare windows welcomed the mid-morning sun, its winter white light casting harsh, triangular shadows. "I'm not in a big hurry to settle in," Arnold said. "Not sure the transplant will take." He cleared a spot on the couch. "Coffee?"

"I found the book," Woody said, and patted his jacket pocket. His head dropped. He choked. "Now what?"

Arnold poured coffee and lowered the volume on the television. "Your dad had a weakness for women," he said. "There's a line in *Zorba the Greek* he used to quote. 'A man will burn in Hell if a woman goes to bed alone.' Or something like that. Either he believed it or he used it as an excuse. He seemed to think it justified his behavior."

Woody held the mug, watching dust particles wander and weave in shafts of sunlight.

"He had a lot of friends," Arnold continued. "Opportunities for infidelity popped up like weeds. It wasn't his fault that women were attracted to him. He didn't discourage it either. He generated excitement in women. Excitement they hadn't felt since high school."

He hesitated. "I don't know why I'm sharing this gossip with you, but my ex-wife fell into his trap. He never violated our friendship while the Mrs., the ex-Mrs., and I were married. I don't know what happened after that, but I have my suspicions. She thought *he'd* leave your mother when *she* left me." He paused. "Why would he change? Your dad was a talented juggler. He could keep a dozen balls . . ."

"I saw her name in the book," Woody interrupted, his eyes focused on the eddy of coffee in his twirling cup. "Cookie Baxter, followed by a couple lines of hash marks."

The muted television flashed static images. Arnold dropped into his chair like a winged bird. He rested his head in his hands, collecting his composure.

Outside, an engine fired, exhaust pipes roared. Woody's concentration shifted to his dad's truck at home, the red International pickup. It always felt incongruous. Their house was modest. Their tastes simple. Their lives commonplace. But the truck. His trophy. His signature. Brazen, ostentatious, expensive. And his dad's furtive visits. Didn't the lusty dual pipes, the brassy color by day, the gaudy lights by night, didn't they betray him? Or was discretion trumped by confidence? Now, the truck resided in the garage. Woody's truck butted against a shed, a horse blanket over the hood.

"He could keep a dozen balls in the air," Arnold repeated. "He may have put them down, in time. But he never let them fall.

"You may have suspected this," Arnold added. "The temptation is to see the good side and sweep the crap under the rug. Better for you to know your dad now. Then at the church, before they close the casket, let him know how you feel." He paused and sipped his coffee. "Have you ever flown in an airplane?"

"Our senior class made a trip to Washington."

"Remember looking out the window after liftoff? Remember how neat and orderly the landscape was? Roads following section lines. Rectangular fields. Homesteads tucked at the end of driveways. Buildings squared. Fields cultivated. Trees aligned. But when you see that homestead from the ground, the house needs paint, the yard's a mess, the barn roof sags. Mother needs surgery. The kids need shoes. That's reality. My intuition says that you worshipped your dad from afar, not aware of his imperfections. Allow him some."

Woody rotated the cup in his hands. He opened his mouth to speak. Nothing. He lifted the cup to his lips and saw his hands tremble. He put the cup on the table and took a deep breath. "And what should I do with this?" He patted his jacket pocket.

"Here's what I'd do. Right before they close the casket at the service, slip it in beside him. You're rid of it then. Nobody will question what you're doing. Just a grieving son saying goodbye to his dad." Arnold cracked a smile. "And I wouldn't be surprised if he doesn't thank you for it."

The pews were filled; ushers clanged metal chairs and placed them in the rear of the church and narthex. The organist stumbled through a doleful prelude. Whatever was said, whoever said it, Woody didn't recall. After the service, he, his mother, and Arnold followed the casket down the aisle to the narthex.

From her pew, Widow Jensen wiggled a finger wave at him, her string of kids repeating the gesture. The older kids, fair-skinned blonds, tall and thin. The youngest boy, dark and stocky. The parade of mourners halted at the back row of pews, waiting while the pallbearers lifted the casket off the rollers. Beside them, a woman with large rose sunglasses sobbed, her shoulders quaking.

At the cemetery, Woody asked Arnold, "Wasn't that your ex?"
"Yup."

For Woody, the following week dragged in slow motion. He yearned for companionship and craved solitude. Hunger gnawed at him, but at dinner, he picked at his food, pushing it around the plate with his knife. He soaked in long, hot baths, stood in steaming showers, hoping to scrub away his anxiety. Exhausted, he couldn't sleep, but rose at three to brew a pot of coffee. He walked in a haze, went through the motions of life, feigning remorse from well-intentioned neighbors with their constant phone calls. "How're ya doin'?" "How's your mom?" After a week, he tired of the doldrums, felt like it was time to break the emotional logjam, time to get back in the woods.

Woodrow's hat hung on a hook by the mirror at the back door. Woody donned the hat and looked in the mirror. He cocked the hat over his right eye and smiled a flirtatious smile. Damned if he didn't resemble his old man. Nearly his size. A few years to accrue the dark beard, the bull neck, the broad shoulders. Rayanna stood at the sink, her back to him, peeling potatoes for supper. He approached her and placed his hands on her waist. "Hello, Gorgeous," he whispered. She jumped. The potato flew. She spun around, glaring, and pointed the knife at him. "Don't ever do that again."

Neighbors regaled them with casseroles, cakes, salads. That, and incessant phone calls. Rayanna developed a few trite responses that got callers off the line. A call came the day after Aunt Jonella left, and Rayanna listened. She didn't say anything after *Hello*, just listened. Listened and reddened. After a few minutes, she slammed the receiver.

"Who was that?" Woody asked.

She stood silent for a moment, deciding whether or not to respond. "The ex-Mrs. Arnold Baxter," she said. "She called to ask my forgiveness. No mention of the cause for her request, as if I didn't know. Said she was overcome with grief. Her therapist said that to deal with it, she had to call and ask my forgiveness." Her shoulders stiffened. She choked back a scream and pounded up the stairs.

Arnold and Woody went ice fishing the next day, a three day trip to Canada. Rayanna had encouraged them to go. "I need some time," she said. "You do too."

When they returned, Rayanna greeted them at the door, wearing a different, maybe new, sweater. She hugged Woody, then Arnold. She surveyed the catch and invited Arnold to stay for dinner. "Relax. Take a shower if you want," she said. "Then join me." She lifted a brandy snifter. She tapped Woody on the shoulder and motioned him toward the garage. "Take a look."

The truck was gone. The space created was filled with a lipstick red Thunderbird.

Widow Maker

Now, Woody rubs the cold from his fingers and trembles as he holds the old man's hat. He lifts it to his face and inhales the thin whiff of Vitalis. Sweat, his dad's sweat, has leached out and darkened the band. He fingers the feathers, the soft felt, soft like a woman's shoulders. He walks to a mirror, closes his eyes, and in a slow deliberate motion, places the hat on his head and cocks it at the jaunty angle. A tingle courses through him. A rush of heat. A transformation. He smiles, and opens his eyes to a squint, like the old man's. A golden, vaporous aura envelopes him. It exhumes memories: the little black book, the names, the numbers, the hash marks. He stands weightless, mesmerized. The aura assumes Woodrow's form. It disperses an endowment, a consent, a legacy. "You will leave a note for your wife," it murmurs. "Tell her not to wait up for you."

"Yes."

"Tell her you're taking Arnold out for supper." The image in the mirror laughs. "Y'know your ole man loves ya," it says. "Y'know your ole man's proud."

Johnny

Joshua Cushman was baptized on St. Valentine's Day—a tiny, wriggly infant with a shriveled face like a dried cranberry. The priest poured water on his contorted head, still scarred and ruddy from birth, and his black hair, mussed and curled around his ears.

"Joshua Cushman," the priest pontificated, wiping the squawking baby's head with the arm of his cassock. "He has the same initials as Jesus Christ."

Godfather Uncle Merle scrutinized the kid, the black hair, the jaw skewed in a tight scowl. "J. C. I was thinking Johnny Cash."

The moniker *Johnny* stuck. Although Mrs. Cushman, a devout Christian, had named her children for Old Testament stalwarts, those biblical patriarchs and matriarchs were no match for secular contemporaries. Aaron became Hank. Ruth was Baby Ruth until she showed an affinity for softball, when she became Babe. Mrs. Cushman acquiesced when she registered Joshua for kindergarten.

"Joshua," the teacher said. "I thought that was a tree."

Johnny

Johnny is thirty-four, teetering between *up and coming* and *down and out*. If there's no promotion to management this year, his career at Wal-Mart is toast. He knows that; that's the downside. The upside is that retail management is not his strong suit. Johnny is an entertainer. It started on his sixteenth birthday when Uncle Merle gave him a guitar and a Johnny Cash songbook. He adopted the black wardrobe, kept the skewed jaw, and experimented with grass and hooch, full of confidence that a June Carter would appear in his life as savior. And the other half of his duet.

June is Sue Ellen, a nursing supervisor with a full plate of career responsibility and mild intolerance for Johnny's show biz fantasies. "We treat people with psychoses like yours," she says. "And no, I won't tailor your shirts. No, I won't dye your hair. No, I won't sing 'Jackson' with you."

With Sue Ellen working evenings at the hospital, Johnny has uninterrupted hours to practice singing and playing, to mimic his hero. He drops his chin to his chest to lower his voice. "You're about an octave higher than Cash," his guitar teacher told him. "Why don't you try Wayne Newton?"

Johnny works on articulation, phrasing, guttural harmony. "You need work on your timing," his teacher said. "Listen to everyday rhythms—your heart, the ticking of a clock, your windshield wipers clacking. Count out the beat. Do it until it's natural."

One, two. One, two.

Johnny clocks the beat of coffee percolating, a nuthatch pecking.

One, two. One, two, three.

Sue Ellen walks in the door at midnight, in a drab hospital smock, without makeup. She throws her coat over the chair and collapses on the sofa. She's a tall woman, tall as Johnny, with blond hair that curls to her shoulders. Johnny stares at her, wondering how he won such a beauty.

"I think I've got it," he says. "'Ring of Fire.' Wanna hear it?" He stands with his guitar, grinning.

"Not tonight, Johnny. I want to soak in a hot bath and then hit the sack."

"I'll run water for you, and play it while you bathe." He scurries into the bathroom.

Sue Ellen eases into the warm water, the bubbles from bath crystals expanding to fill the tub, the aroma of eucalyptus transforming the bathroom into a spa. Johnny rests one foot on the toilet stool and, counting, taps his toe to the beat of the introduction.

Love is a burning thing, and it makes a fiery ring.
Bound by an old desire. I fell into a ring of fire.

"That's good, Johnny. But it's fire, isn't it? Not fa'ar."

I fell into a burning ring of fire.
I went down, down, down, and the flame went higher.
And it burns, burns, burns, the ring of fire, the ring of fire.

"June wrote that song. You could write one too."

"Please. Give me ten more minutes to soak. Then come in and help me out."

He strums a few chords in the bedroom, then lifts Sue Ellen from the tub. He dries her back and kisses her shoulders.

Later in bed, Sue Ellen tightens her arms around him and sighs, "Johnny, you're counting."

"How do you feel, Mother?" Sue Ellen asks as they visit Grace at Good Shepherd. Grace is a prim, petite woman who wears starched white blouses, her silver hair waved in meticulous geometry. The apartment is tidy, the dishes English bone china, the tablecloth creased linen. Philodendrons and ferns and dieffenbachia crowd the windows. Grace motions for them to sit, offers to pour coffee. She ignores Sue Ellen's question as if it's medical small talk, not daughterly concern. Sue Ellen digs for her blood pressure cuff.

"And how are you, Johnny?" she asks. "How are the guitar lessons?"

Johnny smiles. "They're coming."

"I want to hear you play," she says. "The entertainment committee is looking for a musical act for our Valentine's Day party. About a half hour. I suggested you." She consults her appointment book. "Friday, February 14. One o'clock."

Johnny stumbles, looks at Sue Ellen for validation, sees none. "I guess I could play a couple songs. Gotta start someplace. Would you like to audition me? I have my guitar in the car."

Sue Ellen throws him a scowl and places the cuff on her mother. "Hold still."

Johnny leaves the apartment and hustles to the parking lot. *What shall I play? How many songs can I learn by Valentine's Day? Can I take a day of vacation from Wal-Mart?*

Back in the Gathering Room, he nudges a resident with his guitar. "Pardon me," he says.

"Any day," she replies. "You must be Grace's son-in-law. I understand you're playing at our Valentine's Day party. I'm Grace's friend Pearl. You certainly do remind me of someone."

Johnny lifts the guitar to his chest, drops his chin, and says, "Hello, I'm Johnny Cash."

"Of course," says Pearl. "Will you be singing 'Heartbreak Hotel'?"

"I think that was Elvis Presley's song."

Pearl touches his sleeve and puts a finger to her lips. "Of course," she says. "I'll see you at the concert."

"Looks like the word is out," Johnny says to Grace. "I met one of your friends in the Gathering Room."

"Never mind her. Let's hear you play something."

Sue Ellen counts out medications and places them in a Sunday-through-Saturday pill box.

"I really appreciate this, Grace," Johnny says. "I only have three or four songs under my belt, but I could have thirty minutes' worth by party date."

He straps on his guitar, places one foot on a hassock, and plays.

Sue Ellen opens the cupboard doors and shakes the cereal box. She opens the refrigerator and checks the expiration date on the milk carton.

"I'm going to need a dry run for this gig," he says to Sue Ellen in the car.

"It's not a *gig*. It's an act of charity."

"I don't want to embarrass your mother. I'd like to try out my songs before I sing to the Good Shepherd audience."

"It's not an audience. It's a bunch of old people who don't know Johnny Cash from Jimmy Carter."

Johnny is quiet. "The Broken Hart has karaoke on Friday nights. I could try there." He recalls karaoke nights, the boisterous dice games at the bar, the rude disregard for performers. "I'll call them tomorrow."

"It won't be a pretty picture."

Friday night, Johnny sits at a side table in the Broken Hart nursing a Coke and holding his guitar. The D.J. calls the name Jesse, and a lanky cowboy slams his beer bottle on the bar. "It's show time," he says. He steps to the mic and listens to the intro to "New York, New York."

"Here's to all the lovely ladies," he says, and smiles a toothy smile.

"Start spreading the news . . ." he groans in gravely voice, searching for the right key. "I'm leaving today." Up and down the scale. Can't find it. Gives up. Concentrates on reading the lyrics. "If I can make it there . . ." he finds the key. "New York, New York."

The bar crowd hoots and hollers as Jesse leaves the stage. "Ladies and gentlemen," the D.J. yells. "Let's hear it for Jesse." Jesse's buddy hugs him and lifts him off his feet. "That was really horseshit," he says.

"This might be easier than I thought," Johnny mutters.

"And now, Johnny," the D.J. yells. "Looks like we've got Johnny Cash for you tonight."

Johnny takes the stage, slinging the guitar over his head. He hears the opening bars to "Ring of Fire." Something's wrong. He hears the song played in a different key than he learned. He tries to strum and gives up. He wrestles with the lyrics, tries to remember the body language, taps the guitar.

For a moment, the crowd is quiet until someone yells "Does anyone know 'Clancy Lowered the Boom'?" A drunk at the end of the bar starts, "Oh, that Clancy . . ." Johnny sings louder. He should have chosen an upbeat number. He looks around the bar; no one is listening. He looks at the D.J.; she sorts request notes. When the song is over, he lifts the guitar over his head. Someone at the bar yells, "Nice job, Slim Pickens."

"That had to be the longest three minutes in show business," the D.J. whispers in the mic.

Johnny walks to his table and guzzles the Coke. He looks for a rear exit where he won't walk by the bar crowd. The D.J. says, "Okay boys, here's what you've been waiting for. Anita, you're on!" A Dolly Parton look-alike bounces to the stage in mini-skirt and western boots. She opens her arms and takes a deep bow. "Careful, girl," the D.J. says as the crowd hoots.

Johnny feels a tap on his shoulder. "Can I talk to you before you leave?" Johnny turns to a tall woman, black pants suit, a black coat over her arm, not a local. "I'm Melinda Foster, manager of the Country Western Tribute Band."

Johnny has heard of the band, a group that plays in the style of legendary CW performers. "My Johnny Cash left the show," she says. "Had a sex change and now books her act as Joanie Cash. I'm looking for a new Johnny. You're the best one I've heard. Matter of fact, you're the only one I've heard. Can we talk?"

Johnny stammers. "You're serious? Let's go outside. I've got to get out of here. Talk about a lesson in humility . . ." He slips into his jacket.

They stand on the deck outside the bar, the muffled strains of "Nine To Five" permeating the wall. "You need practice, but I think you could make it as my Johnny," she says. "You got the right look, and that's half of it. Gotta work on your confidence, your conviction. I've never seen Johnny Cash embarrassed. Until tonight."

"She didn't play the song in the key he recorded it in."

"You did the right thing," Melinda says. "Put down the guitar and just sing. That was a rough crowd. I think the real Johnny would have had a problem. Let me give you my card." She searches her purse. "I must have left it in the car." He follows her to the parking lot, to a black Cadillac El Dorado. She reaches for the glove compartment, the dashboard, the side pocket. Then back to her purse. "Here's my card. Call me tomorrow. We'll schedule an audition."

"How'd it go?" Sue Ellen asks, hanging her coat and turning out the porch light.

"Good and bad."

"Let's hear the bad first."

"I bombed."

"And the good?"

"The manager of a tribute band asked me to call her to audition. She's looking for a new Johnny Cash."

Johnny

Sue Ellen stops. She leans on the kitchen archway, folds her arms, and tilts her head. Her blond curls sprawl across her face. "Are you serious? You're not going to call her, are you?"

"Of course I am. This could be my big break." And then, "Don't you think that's good news?"

"I don't know if it's good or bad. Who is this manager, this *she* manager, and how do you know she's legit?"

"I don't know how legitimate she is, but she's obviously successful. She drives a big black Cadillac."

"If that's how you measure success, there are many ways for women to be successful. Not all good ones."

Johnny rotates Melinda's business card in his hand, the edge catching the calluses on his fingertips. His lower lip protrudes in a fake sob.

"I'm too tired to discuss it tonight," Sue Ellen says. "Let's pick it up tomorrow."

"I'll take it one more step. I'll call her. We'll talk about it tomorrow night."

"Well, just don't quit your day job yet. You know, one of these days, we're going to have to talk about starting a family." She walks to the bathroom, without the usual sway of hips. "And I'm too tired to discuss that tonight too."

"You're bouncier than usual this morning," Johnny's Wal-Mart co-worker says. "Must have scored last night."

"You could say that," Johnny says. "Cover for me. I have to make a phone call." He retreats to the employee lunchroom.

"Melinda, this is Johnny Cushman," Johnny says in the phone. Silence. "We met last night. Johnny Cash. Remember?"

"Sure, now I remember. I'm glad you called. Interested in scheduling an audition?"

"Yes. When and where?"

"The Tribute Band meets at my place on Thursday evenings. Eight o'clock. We rehearse for the weekend shows. You'll meet Glen Campbell and Garth Brooks. And me; I'm Patsy Kline."

Johnny straightens his tie and returns to the floor. The assistant manager gives him a stare. "Better check that hair length," he says. "You're at least an inch longer than regulation. And those furry sideburns? Uh-uh."

Thursday evening feels like an eternity away. An eternity until Johnny realizes he has only three songs in his repertoire—"Ring of Fire," "Walk the Line," and "Jackson." He tries "Folsom Prison Blues" and "Rock Island Line." He listens to recordings. He stumbles through chords on the guitar, memorizes lyrics, concentrates on phrasing and body language. He likes the upbeat treatment of "Daddy Sang Bass." Patsy and Glen and Garth can be backups. That's what he'll sing at audition. He'll get them involved.

Thursday evening sneaks up on Johnny. He writes himself a note to remember his guitar. He wears a freshly pressed black shirt, slicked hair, and a crooked smile. On Melinda's street, he looks for her house number. A car horn honks. The driver rolls down his window, shakes his fist, and yells, "Watch where you're goin', asshole."

Johnny waves an apology.

He finds Melinda's address, an apartment building in a neighborhood of single family houses. He parks the car and jumps the curb. "Settle down, boy," Johnny tells himself.

He juggles the guitar case and pushes the button beside M. FOSTER. The door buzzes. Down the hall, he sees Melinda, a glass in one hand, a cigarette in the other. "Hey, Glen and Garth, h-e-r-e-'s Johnny!"

Johnny

Glen is twice the girth of the original with a bad blond dye job. Garth looks old enough to be the original's father. Melinda has taken no pains to look like Patsy Cline.

"Pour yourself a drink," she says. "Let's hear what you got to tell us."

"Can I have a glass of water?" he asks.

"Help yourself in the kitchen. Glasses are in the cupboard."

Johnny walks to the kitchen, eyeing the contemporary furniture, the decorator accessories, the showroom-look of the place. He opens the cupboard doors. Four white plates, four matching cups, bowls, and salad plates. Another door full of crystal—highball glasses, beer steins, wine goblets, champagne flutes. He pours a glass of water.

"I hope you weren't expecting to see homemade bread and beef stew in the kitchen," Melinda says. "I haven't cooked a meal since I moved here."

Johnny straps the guitar around his neck and strums a few chords. "I'm gonna do 'Papa Sings Bass.' And Patsy, at the chorus, you sing *Mama sings tenor*, and Glen and Garth, you sing *Me and little brother would join right in*."

Patsy drinks a deep gulp. "We got it," she says.

A couple hours later, Johnny walks to his car with Glen and Garth. "That was fun," he says. "You guys are great."

"Aw, shucks," Garth says.

"I'm looking forward to Saturday night," Johnny says. "Melinda was noncommittal. What do you guys think?"

Garth looks at Glen and laughs. "How do we tell him, Glen?"

Glen takes Johnny's sleeve. "You're not in the act until you pass the confidence test. Melinda has a 'personal audition' (he makes quotation marks with his fingers) with each of her performers. Once you pass that, you're in."

"Shall we save him some time and identify her erogenous zones?" Garth asks.

"He'll find out for himself. I'm freezing. Let's go."

Friday at Good Shepherd, Johnny tunes his guitar in Grace's apartment. "I've got to tell you about last night," he says. "That Country Western Tribute Band is a hoot. Patsy Cline, Glen Campbell, Garth Brooks, Johnny Cash. What a line-up. They back me up on guitar, and Glen plays the harmonica. I have my first performance with the band tomorrow night. At Cranberry Pines, no less. Fifteen dollars a ticket. Can you believe it?"

"Johnny, that's marvelous," Grace says. "I'm glad we booked you while we could still afford you. Aren't you excited, Sue Ellen?"

"Let's just say I'm in a state of disbelief. I'll wait until the jury returns."

"You're not very supportive, girl. He's having fun. It's a harmless venture. How will he know whether or not it's the right thing unless he tries it?"

"Listen, Mother," Sue Ellen says. "If you know the Johnny Cash legend, it's not his wife June Carter who steers him; it's Maybelle his mother-in-law. That's you. Have at it. Now, let's take your blood pressure while we're all relaxed."

"We don't have much time," Grace says. "The show starts in fifteen minutes. And I have my hair to do."

"Hello. I'm Johnny Cash." He stands in front of the residents. "And I have a few songs for you." He leads with "Rock Island Line." The chairs in the Gathering Room are arranged around him. A perky lady in pink velour, the one he met earlier, taps her foot. Sue Ellen sits by Grace in the front row. Director Mrs. Fitzgerald stands in her office door. Johnny finishes the song, and Grace leads an enthusiastic applause.

"Thank yew," Johnny says. "Are any of you Johnny Cash fans?"

Johnny

A lady raises her hand.

"And what's your favorite Johnny Cash tune?"

"'Cool, Cool, Water.'"

"You're right. That's a great song. I think the Sons of the Pioneers recorded it too. I'm gonna do 'A Boy Named Sue' for you."

When he finishes, the entire group applauds. Mrs. Fitzgerald and Mary, the nurses' aide, applaud from the doorway. A man walks into the Gathering Room.

"There's a chair up front here," Johnny says. The perky lady pats the seat beside her. "Come on in. Join the party. I'm Johnny Cash."

"And I'm Frank Sinatra." The crowd chuckles.

"I'm gonna ask my wife Sue Ellen to help me on this next song. And any of you who want to sing along are welcome to." Sue Ellen shakes her head, *No*. Grace nudges her. "In the refrain, I'll sing *Papa sings bass*. Sue Ellen sings *Mama sings tenor*. And the rest of you sing *Me and little brother would join right in*. Got it? Let's go."

Sue Ellen is tentative in the first stanza, sings louder in the second, stands and claps time with the music in the third. Grace leads the group in *Me and little brother*. Johnny smiles and raises his arms when he finishes.

"I don't know that Johnny Cash wrote any of his own songs. But if he did, it might sound like this one. I wrote it and dedicate it to my wife." He nods to her. She gives her mother a *what next?* look.

It's a shame, but it's a fact.
Opposites, they do attract.
And you're the big attraction in my life.
I knew something I was missin.'
All your huggin', all your kissin'.
Now I'm proud to say that you're my wife.

Sue Ellen waves him to stop, stop.

"I think I'm embarrassing the lady," he says. "There's more stanzas that talk about opposites, but they'll have to wait for another day." The crowd applauds.

"I understand we have a piano player in the group," Johnny says. "Maxwell, would you join us in a group sing-along? Something everybody knows. How about 'You Are My Sunshine'?"

An old man maneuvers to the piano and plunks out a one-finger rendition. Johnny strums and sings. The crowd joins in.

The half-hour show ends quickly. Grace hugs Johnny. Sue Ellen smiles and shakes her head.

A lady stands behind Grace. "Thank you, Mr. Cash. That was very nice." She winks. "And could I have your autograph?" She hands him a napkin. "Sign it *For Thelma*."

Grace nudges Sue Ellen. "He's a star."

Sue Ellen looks at her watch. "I've got to get going. I'm on duty in thirty minutes." She gives Grace a hug and kisses Johnny's cheek.

In Grace's apartment, Johnny walks to the refrigerator, walks to the window, back to the refrigerator. "That was fun," he says. "I wish Sue Ellen could enjoy this as much as I do."

"She's concerned about what happens next."

"So am I. For the time being, I wish she would at least humor me. Sometimes she treats me like a child prodigy—fascinating for a few minutes, then a bore, then an irritation. I don't feel her high expectations."

"What are your expectations?"

He stalls. "I don't know yet. Ask me after this weekend. See how the Country Western Tribute Band goes."

"You can't ask her to buy into your plan until you've bought into it yourself. I say go for it, although there's a difference between a vocation and an avocation. Playing for a living could take the fun out of it. You don't have to decide this minute." She gives him a hug. "Let's go back and join your fans for coffee and cookies."

Sue Ellen stirs her Saturday morning coffee and glances at the newspaper. "I have to admit, you wowed the Good Shepherd folks. And you obviously were having a great time."

"You ain't seen nothin' yet. Wait 'til tonight at Cranberry Pines."

"I won't be there, Johnny."

"You won't?" He stops with a spoonful of cereal halfway to his mouth.

"I want you to do well. I want you to have your fun. But I can't buy the idea of you in show biz. I'm afraid you'll fall hook, line, and sinker. And God knows, a Johnny Cash wannabe can't support a family. That's what I want to talk about. A family. I'm not getting any younger, you know. I have enough seniority at the hospital to get an extended leave. A pregnancy leave. Maybe two. We'll need a stable, dependable income while I'm off work."

"I want a family too. And I'm sure I'll get satisfaction out of fatherhood. In the meantime, all I have is Wal-Mart. *Welcome to Wal-Mart. Thank you for shopping at Wal-Mart.* That's my day. Every day. You have nursing to fulfill you. I had nothing. Until now."

"I understand." Sue Ellen folds the newspaper. "And in a perverse sort of way, I'm excited. I just don't want you to give up your day job."

"Promise," Johnny says. "Let's just string along with this for a while. I'm not the only Wal-Mart employee that moonlights."

"By the way," she says, "when we have this family, our first son will not be named Sue."

"Glen, you lead off with something upbeat. 'Rhinestone Cowboy.' 'Gentle on My Mind.'" Melinda is driving the Country Western

Tribute Band to Cranberry Pines Country Club. "Garth, you follow with a lovey dovey set. 'To Make You Feel My Love.' Something else slow and syrupy. If they start dancing, keep singing. I'll give them some pure Patsy. Then, Johnny, you come on with 'Rock Island Line.' Another one, if that goes well. End with 'Papa Sings Bass,' which brings us all front and center for your choral backup. And then, thunderous applause, modest bows of gratitude, the end of the first set. Got it?"

Melinda lights a cigarette. "During intermission, we'll ask for requests. Don't worry, Johnny, if someone asks for a song you don't know. I won't read that request. I'll read the name of a song you know." She signals a turn into Cranberry Pines. A gentle snow falls, blanketing the cars in the parking lot. "This is a dinner show, so the crowd is already inside finishing their meal. Does anybody know 'My Funny Valentine?' That would be sweet." She parks the car. "Read the crowd. After requests, we'll end with whatever's appropriate. Any questions?"

"You guys were great," Melinda says on the way home. "Johnny, I'd hug you if I wasn't driving. Damn near stole the show."

"That was an easy crowd," Johnny says. "They actually listened. Not like another place I sang."

"Forget that. You don't have to sing karaoke anymore. I made a few mental notes of things to work on. You look at your guitar too much. Gotta look at the audience. But that off-center grin is perfect. Don't you think so, Glen? Garth?"

"Perfect," they say.

"We'll post-mortem the performance Thursday night. Jot down your thoughts. Johnny, I'd like you to join us."

Melinda parks her car in the apartment garage, and Glen and Garth open the doors. "Johnny, can you and I have a little private talk?" she says. "Good night, guys. See you Thursday. Johnny, come up here in the front seat." She lights a cigarette. "I think you're off to a great start. But you're singing too much with

Johnny

your head. Johnny Cash sings with his heart." She taps a finger on his chest. "More heart, understand?"

The car's engine idles, the heater blows, the radio plays. Johnny feels heat around his collar. "You'd better shut off the engine. Carbon monoxide, you know."

"Don't be so practical. The garage door is open anyway. Of course, you'll have to learn more songs. My old Johnny Cash had hundreds of them. Are you free any night next week? Monday? Tuesday? Drop by my place and we'll practice." She snuffs out her cigarette, cocks her head, and eyes him. "Will you do that for me?"

Johnny is tired. He doesn't stay up past eleven-thirty, when Sue Ellen comes home. Sue Ellen. He hasn't thought of her all night. She'll worry if he doesn't get home soon. She knows what time the bars close. He's tired. And now this talk of a practice session. Is this the "personal audition" Glen and Garth joked about? And the cigarette smoke. He'll have to hang his clothes outside. And her perfume. Heady stuff. Feels like it's clinging to him.

"Well, Johnny, will I see you Monday eve? Six o'clock. We'll have dinner. I have some Johnny Cash songs we'll listen to. Together. Okay?"

"Yeah, I guess so. I gotta run. My wife will wonder."

Once home, Johnny removes his jacket, his shirt, his trousers and hangs them in the garage. The clock is striking two. He tiptoes to the bathroom and runs the shower. Out of the shower, he sees light from the bed stand lamp. "Where are your clothes?" Sue Ellen asks. "And why were you taking a shower?"

"My clothes smelled like a smokestack," Johnny says, "and sweat from all the excitement, I guess. I hung them in the garage."

Sue Ellen sits up in bed. "How did it go?"

"Great. We all did encores. Got a standing ovation at the end of the act. Garth sounds great. Glen has all the right moves. The ladies loved him."

"And you?" She pulls the blanket up and over her arms, hugging it close.

"I was satisfied. The guys said I did well too. They did a great job backing me up on guitar. And Glen plays harmonica. Nice train whistles on 'Rock Island Line.'"

"You're only talking about the guys. Isn't there a woman? Patsy Cline? What about her?" Sue Ellen narrows her eyes and clamps her jaw.

"She was fine."

"Wait a minute. You walk in the house practically naked. You take a shower before you come to bed. You skip over any discussion about the female manager of this group. Why do I smell a rat?"

Johnny digs in the dresser for a pair of shorts.

"Oh, damn. I can't believe I'm acting this way," Sue Ellen says and reaches to touch his arm. "All night long, I thought of you. Hoping all was going well. You won't believe how close I came to driving to Cranberry Pines."

"Honest," Johnny says. "I was a model husband. Had only two Diet Cokes. Lots of offers for free drinks. Lots of smiles. Could have been a few offers. But here I am."

"I was being totally selfish this morning," Sue Ellen says. "I have no business defining your happiness. If you want to be Johnny Cash, be Johnny Cash. I'll come along and enjoy the ride."

"This is pretty heavy for two o'clock in the morning," Johnny says. "Let's call it a day. Right now, all I want to be is your husband."

Three o'clock, and Johnny is still awake. He lies on his side, away from Sue Ellen. He knows from her regular breathing that she sleeps. He replays the night. The songs. The applause. The laughter. The party atmosphere. The slap on the back by Glen when it was over. The handshake by Garth. The hug by Patsy. Patsy. Her perfume clings to his brain like Velcro. She didn't defer

Johnny

to Glen and Garth like she did to him. And she invited him to dinner. Maybe he still has that same old charm. Maybe. And maybe he'll accept her invitation. See what happens. Maybe.

Monday afternoon, he returns from Wal-Mart, takes a shower, and shaves. He never showers or shaves in the afternoon. He splashes aftershave on his face. He never uses aftershave. He wears a black cashmere sweater that begs to be touched. He combs his hair in a style that allows a curl to drop over his forehead, like Dean Martin. He hears himself singing. He checks his image in the mirror. Great for thirty-four. Great for possibilities tonight. Just be sure to be home before Sue Ellen finishes her shift.

He walks by the wine rack. He drinks reds; Sue Ellen drinks whites. He has a gift bottle of Merlot that he's been saving for a special occasion. Sue Ellen won't miss it. He takes the bottle and slips it into a wine sock.

Johnny parks his car on Melinda's block and walks to her apartment. He's nervous. He's excited. He doesn't do this often; he doesn't do this at all. The cool February air exhilarates him. He passes small front yards in front of modest bungalows. Warm yellow lights glow; the homes are animated with bits of conversation and television sound trailing outside. In one yard, two boys stand by a snowman. The older one piles on snow; the younger one holds a toy truck. The door of the house opens, and Johnny catches an aroma—roast beef, gravy. "Supper time," the man in the door calls.

The smaller boy looks at Johnny. "Truck," he says.

"That's his Christmas present," the man says. "And he hasn't put it down since."

A woman walks to the door and ducks her head under his arm. "Who are you talking to, Hon?"

Johnny stares at the man, the woman, the kids. This is what he wants. A wife beside him. Kids. Roast beef and gravy. He stammers. "Would you like a bottle of wine to go with supper?"

"Well, sure," the man says. He extends his hand. "I'm Mort. And this is my wife Ellie." He points to the boys. "That's Mort, Jr. and that's Will."

Johnny shakes his hand. "Cushman," he says. "Josh Cushman."

Familiar Quotations

Annette didn't know Drew Deardon existed, would never have known if her dad Wayne hadn't spotted him picking his way along the snowy sidewalk on crutches and crossed the street to avoid him. "Bad news," Wayne says. "Stay away."

"He's a loner, a braggart," Wayne explains when pressed for details. "I don't like him. Only comes to town for staples—groceries for himself or feed for the livestock." Wayne chuckles. "From the crutches, it looks like he also makes trips to the clinic."

"That's enough reason to dislike him?" Annette asks. "What else? I'm curious."

"Curiosity killed the cat," he says. "Trust me."

Annette finds herself in a disliking mood lately. Today she dislikes her dad. He also has become a loner, holing himself up at the assisted living center and treating her like a servant or poor relation. "I don't need you today," or "Take me to the clinic Thursday." Berating her with his sarcasm. "When are you going to lose some weight?"

When the clinic administrator asks Annette if she'd consider taking Drew Deardon as a home health care client, she says yes. Maybe out of spite.

"Wayne and I were friends in high school," Drew reveals at their introductory visit in the clinic. "We joined the Army when we were eighteen."

"Recurring service injury?" Annette asks, pointing to his hip.

"No. Slipped on the ice." He offers that he survived a tour in Korea as a medic and returned home to farm. Wayne re-enlisted and opted to be a lifer.

To Annette, it doesn't make sense. Why would Dad do that?

The drive to minister to clients is difficult, and now the weatherman forecasts more heavy March snow. But as her dad would say, "Nothing ventured, nothing gained."

Drew Deardon farms a woodsy quarter-section south of the city limits. The townspeople thought the area undesirable once, with its creeks and hills and valleys. With rezoning next spring, it will be sold as sites for hobby farms and weekend villas for city people. Drew will be a rich man.

A crooked street sign marks the minimum maintenance road that leads to Drew's farm. Without the County's wing plow, the snow is drifted and rutted with tire tracks. At the end of the road, a bridge signals Drew's driveway. On either side of the bridge, upright railroad ties stand like sentries with red reflectors.

His house nestles on the south slope of a treed hill, dwarfed by the barn and machine shed. The garage is tethered to the house with orange electrical cords. A German shepherd rises from a lean-to doghouse to greet her, sniffs the tires, and walks her to the porch.

The house is faded white with once-red trim, its base surrounded by snow-covered bales. Plastic sheeting over the windows is nailed with lath. A screen door hangs by one hinge.

Not trying to impress anybody, Annette thinks.

The porch overflows with piles of newspaper, bins of recyclables, and firewood stacked to the ceiling. She steps over a dog dish, a plastic bag of garbage.

"C'mon in," she hears from inside. "Any trouble with the drive?" Drew asks.

"Piece of cake," she says removing her coat and digging through her bag.

Drew sits in a one-room open area—living, dining, and kitchen combined. The dining table, strewn with magazines, newspapers, and junk mail, is cleared on one end and set with a bowl and mug.

"You farmed out here since you were discharged from the Army?" Annette asks.

"Yup. Be it ever so humble . . ."

"You and Dad enlisted in the Army together, right? You served one term and were discharged. He re-enlisted. Why do you think he chose the military?" She slides a thermometer under Drew's tongue. "And why the MPs? I expected those guys to be brutes. Six feet tall. Three hundred pounds. A hundred pushups, one handed."

Drew shrugs his stout shoulders, looking larger in a thick gray sweatshirt with sleeves pushed up. His fleshy jowls are ruddy and crusted with week-old beard; his thick brown hair is indented in a ring from his cap.

Annette removes and reads the thermometer. She startles when a ferret appears from a pile of unfolded laundry and watches her from the table.

"Groucho, meet Annette," Drew says.

"Dad must have weighed all of a hundred and fifty pounds. Smaller than Mom," Annette continues. "And he practically collapsed at the sight of blood."

Drew nods and reaches for the ferret.

"It wasn't like our family had a history of military service. Dad was the first to serve. Grandpa was too young for World War II. Or too old. Or too many kids."

The room, and Drew, smell of horses, cows, barn, and a musky smell she can't identify. Her clients will complain. She will schedule Drew the final visit of her day.

"Wayne wanted to break out of Dodge," Drew says. "Wanted to join the Army and see the world. Pity he never had a chance to see combat." The ferret climbs to his shoulders. "Tough to prove you're a hero when you're stuck twenty miles behind front lines. The closest he ever got to action was a food fight in a Hanoi mess hall."

"Then why did he re-enlist time after time?"

"Have you asked him?"

"I asked Mom and got the feeling there was a reason he feared civilian life. Something more than the small man syndrome."

Drew slides his shirt sleeves down and pets Groucho.

"Then, when Mom died, Grandma gave me Mom's letters," Annette continues. "Letters she had written while Dad served stateside and overseas. In the letters, she talks about her worry, her problem. Comments like, 'I hope we can come back someday.' or questions like, 'Does anybody talk about it anymore?' I wonder what the *it* is. Any ideas?"

"Maybe," Drew says. "Ask Daddy Wayne. He's still in the nursing home, isn't he?"

"It's not a nursing home," she informs him, "it's assisted living."

Good Shepherd is a half-hour drive from Drew's farm. Since Annette's social life ranges from limited to nothing, her weekly visit to Dad fills a void. Try as she may to like him, she walks away uncomfortable after seeing him, and feels his discomfort in seeing her. Their conversation is forced. She's an intruder in his routine—television, meals, naps, television. There's no one to talk to about relationship issues, no one to ask.

Why should she, his only daughter, his only living relative, need a reason to visit? She doesn't know, so she relies on a self-assigned obligation to provide nursing care. And occasional chauffeur duty.

She's curious about his Army career, and Drew challenged her to ask. Whatever reason she concocts to chat after she takes his vitals will be deceit. Just a lame excuse to question him. He'll know that and clam up. He's fond of military books, and she found a history of the Civil War and a dog-eared paperback of *The Uniform Code of Military Justice* at the town's Thrift Shop.

"Dad, I saw these books and thought of you."

"Leave them on the table, Dearie. I took my meds a few minutes ago and I feel them kicking in. It's lights out for me."

"You don't get drowsy for a half hour."

He's wearing his usual attire—Army fatigues, starched jacket and pants with sewed-in pleats, olive drab socks, and slippers. His face shines a slick, shaved red.

"Pull up a chair and tell me what's going on," she says. "Any groceries you need? Any interesting phone calls?"

"No and no, Dearie. I'm going to bed." He walks into his bedroom. "Take the garbage out when you leave. And mail the bills."

She stands with the books, passing them hand to hand, then sets them on the table and follows him. He opens a closet door and lifts a folded afghan from the shelf. His clothes hang in military precision, two fingers apart, all hangers facing the rear. Shined shoes are aligned toe to toe. She feels an urge to pull half the clothes out and toss them on a chair, cram the rest in one end, and mix up the hangers.

Instead, she follows him to the bed. "Tomorrow's your day at the barber shop. Want a ride?" She sits beside him; he lies with his back to her. She rubs her hand across his short crew cut, bristling like she remembers it as a child, tickling her palm. He pushes her hand away.

"I need the exercise. I'll walk."

"I feel sometimes you're hiding something from me, that you don't trust me. Honest, Dad, my concern is real, my intentions are good."

"The road to hell . . . You know the rest."

She sits on the bed, kneading her hands, struggling for conversation.

His room is spare—a bed with patchwork quilt, a dresser with his portrait in uniform and white helmet liner, a bedside table with alarm clock and a jar of pennies. The closet doors are mirrored, and her reflection glances back. Stringy brown hair needing a cut, light blue eyes behind plastic rims, shoulders sloped to arms that inflate her smock. Mom's daughter, for certain; Dad's arms are half of hers.

"Sometime I'd like to talk about Mom." She rubs his back. "I miss her." She waits. "I read some of her letters to Grandma. I don't mean to intrude, Dad, but there are things I want to know." She looks at his head on the pillow. His eyes are locked shut, his breath is slow and regular.

"I'm just curious, Dad." She feels an urge to take his pulse, his blood pressure, his temperature. Any reason to touch him. She watches him as she walks away. The door lock clicks behind her.

"I presume you're Wayne's daughter," a resident says in the hall. "I'm Thelma. We don't see much of your dad. Anything we can do?"

Annette shifts gears from her dad's ignoring her to the neighbor's asking to help. "Yes and no. He's getting all the attention he wants. Maybe more. He has multiple medical issues which are being addressed."

"I see you're carrying a medical bag. Are you a doctor?"

Annette smiles and shakes her head. "No. I'm a home health care nurse. All I dispense is TLC."

"That's often enough. That plus aspirin and cough medicine."

"I can help you with those. We have samples at the clinic."

"Now I am glad we met. I'll try to keep an eye on your dad."

"How's Daddy Wayne doing at the nursing home?" Drew dog-ears a book page, the author's name Havelock Ellis prominent on the cover. The ferret curls around his neck.

"He's temperamental and I never know what to expect. He watches a lot of television, reads war stories."

"I can imagine him telling war stories, not reading them."

Annette ignores his sarcasm. "His list of maladies is long as your arm—emphysema, type 2 diabetes, rheumatoid arthritis, eczema, high PSA. Everything but his heart. Doc Provence says he has the heart of an eighteen year old."

"Probably because he never used it for anything but pumping blood. I wonder what keeps him going."

"I think he's waiting for me to find Mr. Wonderful and present him a grandson."

"Hope you have a better reason to marry than that. It's wonderful when it works. But for every marriage made in heaven, I'll spot you a dozen made in hell."

"Dad and Mom made it work. Of course, we lived off base, and he always had an excuse for not being home. You can't fight if you're not in the same room."

"Lots of interesting things to do on base," Drew chuckles with a wink.

Annette pumps the cuff to take his blood pressure. "My theory is that Mom suspected Dad was messing around. She was always covering for him." She pauses to listen and scribbles numbers on the chart. "I don't think she would have handled the truth very well."

"Truth. Interesting topic. And what do you think it is?"

"The way she avoided my questions. The way she got nervous when I asked. The way she broke into tears, I think she knew something terrible."

"Does that trouble you?"

"Of course it does. Her pain certainly affects my decision to marry." She removes the cuff and tugs the sleeve down his arm.

"If you knew the true story, would that make it better or worse?" He stares at her with Germanic blue eyes.

"I could handle it. It's deception I can't handle."

"What if I were to tell you? Tell you the truth?"

"Try me."

Drew rises from his chair, hobbles to the table, and reaches for a mug. "Coffee?" he asks. The room is humid from clothes drying—underwear on the backs of chairs, shirts on hangers suspended from doorframes. A week's worth of dirty dishes is stacked in the kitchen sink. Windows are frosted and patterned in opaque lace, with a yellow glow of yard light shining through.

He hands her a mug of coffee, then sits in his chair and stirs his. The ferret returns to his shoulders. "Doesn't sound like Daddy Wayne is long for this world. Doesn't seem like he's likely to tell you his story, if he hasn't done so already. In a way, I feel I'd be ratting on him if I told you what I know."

He stands and hobbles to the stove door, the ferret clinging to his shoulder. Tobacco spit stains the belly of the stove. The wood fire creates shadows that dance around the room and redden his face. She watches him stare at the flames, biding time.

"When your dad and I were eighteen, we were young and stupid. One night, a late winter night like this, we were driving around, going nowhere, having fun, doing nothing. We used to play a game where we'd pull alongside another car and roll down the window. We'd point to the tires and make circular motions with our fingers, like the tires were going around. The driver usually waved a thank you and pulled over to the shoulder, thinking he had a flat."

Drew sips his coffee, and the ferret stretches his neck toward the mug. "This one night, we pulled alongside old Einar Stockman. Einar was an old geezer. Used to weave down the middle of the road ten, twenty miles an hour. We gave him the signal, and he stopped and stepped out of the car. We watched him in the rear view mirror. Hilarious. Mission accomplished.

"Then a vehicle behind him didn't see his parked car, didn't see him bending over the tire. We didn't hear brakes. We heard a crash and saw something, someone flying through the air. We put the pedal to the metal, as we used to say, and got the hell out of there."

Drew sits. The ferret balances on his shoulder, then snuggles on his neck and watches Annette with inquisitive eyes. "Daddy Wayne didn't stick around to be questioned as a suspect. No one could have seen our license plates. There's no way we could have been found out. But he felt guilty. He was nervous.

"Back in those days, if you joined the Army, you were granted a sort of immunity to criminal charges. We knew there'd be talk. There'd be speculation. There'd be finger pointing. Wayne wasn't a good liar. Guess he felt he'd be identified."

"Did Mom know this?"

"Your mother was no stranger to misbehaving. I suspect she knew everything. Tough to keep the lid on gossip in a small town. In fact, we heard some old wags cackling in the grocery store that they bet kids were involved.

"If the authorities knew anything, they never came after me or him, as far as I know. We were considered heroes for going off to war."

Annette knows the Stockmans. Einar's son is her client, his grandson still runs the family farm north of town. Drew's story needles her, sticks in her mind like a dirty joke. Dad a killer? And she's surprised? What other conduct should she expect of a thirty-year Army veteran? No killing? No wounding? No torture? But Mom's cover up. How could she live with that?

She stops at the county courthouse on her day off and checks the death certificate for Einar Stockman. With the date, she searches the local newspaper in the library for the editions after his death. His obituary appears and a short clip in the Sheriff's News column, mentioning the department had responded to a traffic fatality on County 20. No mention of an investigation.

She juggles the information, uncertain and afraid. Her dad will deny everything, probably get angry. Probably have a heart attack to shame her for meddling. To hell with him, she concludes, and drives to Good Shepherd.

She stands at the door of his apartment, knuckles poised to knock. The air smells of warm dust. Yellow candle bulbs in wall sconces cast a jaundiced pall over the flocked wallpaper. Inside, she hears the drone of television and pictures her dad asleep in the recliner, a beer on the end table, at peace for the moment. Instead of knocking, she tries the knob and opens the door.

"Who's there?" she hears from the bathroom and then the toilet flushing.

"It's me, Dad."

"Didn't anyone teach you to knock?"

She looks at him, as if seeing him for the first time. His erect carriage she once considered commanding, now looks brittle. His eyes once narrowed by a ready grin, are feisty cracks. His thin mustache once debonair, now looks affected, like a villain in a silent movie. She opens her medical bag. "I was in the neighborhood and thought I'd drop in and take your vitals. Everything okay?"

"It was until now. I'm in the middle of my program. I don't need my vitals taken."

"Dad, I have some questions for you."

"Well, I have some questions for you too, Dearie."

"Dad, what do you remember about Einar Stockman?"

"Never heard of him."

"That's strange. The Stockmans were your neighbors at the home place."

He stands, hands parked on hips, and glares at her. "I don't know what you're talking about."

"What do you know about him being killed in a traffic accident?"

"I said I don't know what you're talking about. Now, get out of here."

"Dad, I want to know. Is that why you joined the Army? And did Mom know? How could you both live with that all these years?"

"What you don't know won't hurt you, Dearie. Now get out of here, damn it. Out." He snaps a quick nod and hustles to the bedroom, slamming the door. On the television, three panelists rant and yell simultaneously.

She opens the bedroom door. "Dad, please."

He jolts up from the bed, rests on one elbow, and wags his finger like an angry school teacher. "You've been talking to Drew Deardon, haven't you? That lying son-of-a-bitch. He's crazy. Too much time alone. Never married, and there's a reason. Don't listen to him, and for Christ-sakes, don't trust him."

Mrs. Fitzgerald is at her desk talking to nurse Betty Brockett when Annette passes her office. "May I come in?"

She motions to her and asks her to sit. "You're Wayne Merkel's daughter, yes?"

Annette hesitates and nods. "Yes. I'm concerned about him. Is he contrary only when I'm here?"

Mrs. Fitzgerald reaches for his file. "He's had no other company. According to his application, he spent his youth in this area, then left for most of his adult life. Are there siblings, cousins, family members?"

"No."

"I see he's widowed. Any friends from back when? School friends? Neighbors?"

Again she hesitates. "No."

"He doesn't associate with any of the Good Shepherd people," Nurse Brockett says. "Often eats alone reading a magazine. Hasn't joined in any social gatherings. I've thought about contacting you to get your opinion on whether a visit with Dr. Provence would be appropriate."

A woman appears at the door. "Excuse me, Mrs. Fitzgerald."

"I'm busy now, Pearl. Can you come back?"

"I only need a second. Can you contact one of the male residents and ask him to help me with a stepladder?"

Mrs. Fitzgerald looks at Annette as if to say *Wayne?*

Pearl stands in the doorway dressed in pink, her blond hair piled high, pink toenails peeking through heeled pink slippers.

Annette shakes her head, *No.*

"I didn't expect to see you today, what with the snow and the forecast. If I thought you were coming, I'd have opened the driveway with the horses." Drew dog-ears another book.

Annette glances. Masters and Johnson.

Groucho climbs off Wayne's shoulder and sidles to her medical bag. Annette smells wood smoke and meat and onions cooking, thinks of asking what's for supper, but doesn't.

"I'm making goulash," Drew says. "In case I have company."

She pretends not to hear. Groucho stands on his rear legs and looks into her bag.

"He's curious," Drew says. "He won't hurt you. Might chew your rubber gloves. Might hide in your boots." He wobbles to take her coat. "Did you talk to Daddy Wayne?"

"Yes and no. He figured I'd been talking to you. From the fuss he's making, there has to be more to this than Mom's being an accomplice to an unintentional homicide."

Drew sits at the table where she takes his vitals. He deals a hand of solitaire, keeping his eyes on the cards, snapping them three at a time, snapping three more. "My talking to you shouldn't bother him if his conscience is clear." Drew sucks a toothpick. "Maybe he has something to hide."

She fumbles through her medical bag for a thermometer, always facing Drew. She glances at him, the scruffy beard, the flannel plaid jac-shirt with long underwear sleeves protruding, the grubby jeans tucked in felt boot liners. A loner, for certain, as Dad had described. She recalls his admonition. "Don't trust him."

"You know why he calls you *Dearie*? It's not a term of endearment, as they say."

Dearie is Dad's nickname for her, a name he gave her as a young girl, never spoken in front of anyone but Mom. She wonders how Drew knows about it.

He ambles to the cupboard and grabs a bottle. "Want a shot of brandy?"

She shakes her head, *No*.

"He won't tell you that either." Drew eyes her. She looks at her coat, her boots, the door.

"Why don't you ask him? And let me know what lie he tells you."

She grabs a chair to steady herself. "Let's get these vitals taken. It's getting dark and snowing. I'd better get moving."

"No big rush. If you get snowed in, you can stay. Anyway, I want to tell you how you got your nickname *Dearie*. You want to know, don't you? And it's a lead pipe cinch Daddy Wayne won't tell you."

"Lots of fathers call their daughters *Dearie*." The smell of wood smoke chokes her.

"Right. But you're *Dearie* as in *Deardon*." He pauses. "Wayne accused your mother of cheating on him when he was in the Army. He came home on leave from basic training about a month after me. A couple months later, your mother jumped on a train and headed for Ft. Campbell where he was stationed. She was pregnant and wanted to get married."

He sips his brandy and eyes her. "Your mother and I went steady in high school. She said I made the perfect boyfriend but wouldn't make the perfect husband. Not for her. She didn't want to be a farmer's wife, and she knew I'd end up on the farm."

"Dad thought that you and Mom . . . ?"

"He did the math after you were born, and either you were an awfully big premature baby, or you weren't his kid. I was flattered that he credited me. So Daddy Wayne isn't so much lovingly calling you *Dearie* as he is rubbing your mother's face in her infidelity."

Annette struggles to the kitchen sink for a drink of water. She remembers as a teenager calculating the number of months between her parents' wedding and her birth and concluded there was a reason other than love for their marriage.

But Drew . . . ? And Mom . . . ? She realizes she never knew her mom. Never knew her as capable of misbehaving, with enough passion to get pregnant before she married. And later always living in her husband's shadow. Living wherever he moved her. Bending to his demands. Shrinking from his threats.

And her own relationship with Dad. His sarcasm. The sneer that accompanies the term *Dearie*.

"Look at us," Drew says. "Same hair, same eyes, same build. You don't resemble Daddy Wayne at all."

She stuffs the blood pressure cuff in her bag and reels, her heart pounding in her ears, her head about to burst. "I have to get going. I have to get home."

"I have an idea," he says. "When you take Daddy Wayne's temperature, take a swab of his saliva. Spend the money for a DNA test. Then I'll give you a swab of mine."

She pulls on her boots.

"If we could clear that up, I might have good news. You heard about the proposed zoning ordinance, haven't you? This area will be zoned recreational and hobby farms. I've had a couple real estate agents call me wanting to subdivide my farm and list it in five-acre parcels. They figure megabucks per site. A hundred and sixty acres. Do the math. Could be over a million bucks."

She checks one final time that she's not forgetting something in her bag.

"I probably won't live long enough to spend all that. It would be nice to do some estate planning. With next of kin."

She slips into her coat.

"Hey, look at it snow." Drew walks to the window. The yard light is bathed in a warm yellow corona, lighting snowflakes that hover and freefall. The dog howls from the lean-to.

Drew glances left, then right. "No one there," he says. "Could be he saw a rabbit. They're out on nights like this, foraging for food to last them through the storm. Owls know that, and they're out too."

She pulls gloves from her pocket and reaches for keys.

"You'd have to be suicidal to drive in this. Or do you have to visit Daddy Wayne? That poor old bastard. Always a corny saying. *A stitch in time saves nine. You can lead a horse to water, but you can't make him drink.* He should have been a preacher, all that sermonizing and speaking in parables. I told him *Speech is silver, silence golden.* That shut him up for awhile."

"I have to get home."

"One more thing. Ask Wayne about the results of his fertility tests. Ever wonder why you never had brothers or sisters? We know your mother was fertile." His voice is sinister, teasing. "Maybe tonight would be a good opportunity for us to get acquainted." He stirs the brandy with his finger and licks it. "Just father and daughter."

"I have to go home."

Drew leans against the window frame. Flames from the woodstove door reflect in his eyes like fireflies. He lifts Groucho to his cage and grins. "Your call."

She looks at the door, and looks at Drew.

"Do what you have to do. But we have lots to talk about. Look, it's chore time for me. Put the horses in the barn, feed the beef cattle, milk the Jersey. Think about staying. Take the goulash out of the oven. Set the table. I'll be back in a half-hour." He slips into his Sorels, jacket, and cap, grabs the milk pail, and hobbles out. The door slams behind him.

When the barn lights go on, Annette grabs her bag and scurries out.

The shepherd shuffles up, brushes her side as he walks her to the car, wagging his tail. She pats his head. "Goodbye."

The driveway is drifted, but the downhill slope allows her to gather speed. She plows through loose snow, the windshield wipers struggling. She should have allowed time for the car to warm, the defrosters to clear the windshield.

"I will not visit this place again," she says aloud. "I will call the clinic tomorrow and tell them that."

Concentrate on your driving, she murmurs. *Concentrate.*

Dearie. How stupid. She'll ask Dad about the nickname. No, she won't. If only she could ask Mom. Mom.

She's preoccupied, she knows. Planning and practicing every word with Dad. Telling him she must know the truth. Telling him that she will no longer minister to Mr. Drew Deardon. This is her last visit. She'll never see him again.

The car has momentum now. "Keep it," she says. "Keep it 'til I get to the highway."

A reflector glows on the bridge post to her right. Where's the left post?

A form explodes in the headlights. A flapping form. Golden eyes. An owl. She cranks the wheel. The car leaves the ruts. It catches soft snow on the sloping shoulder. Pulls it down. Down the embankment. Tipping. Tipping. Sliding on the roof. Down, down through saplings, down, down.

When she wakens, she's hanging in her seat belt, stomach pressed against the steering wheel, face before the shattered windshield.

Her shoulder aches. She tastes blood.

Stay calm, she whispers. *Stay calm. Turn the ignition off. Release the seatbelt. Open the door.*

She lowers her right hand to reach the key and feels a numbness, a disconnect between elbow and fingers.

Her arm dangles on the dashboard like a broken stick. She extends her left hand. It reaches the steering wheel. Inches from the ignition key. Inches from the seatbelt clamp.

Stay calm. Stay calm.

She raises her left hand to her face and feels a blush of clammy warmth. She strains to focus her eyes, her mind.

Steam rises off the warm engine like threatening smoke.

The buried headlights burrow through the snow and reflect back on the windshield. Patterns. Shapes. Eyes. Golden eyes.

The ache in her right arm eases and she feels a disarming calm, like a warm blanket wrapped around her.

Stay awake. Stay awake. Stay awake and stay calm. Stay calm. Stay . . .

Mom. Mom. Is that you, Mom?

The shepherd trots down the drive from the house. He stops at the bridge, then crawls down the stream bank to where tail lights shine red in the snow. He circles the overturned vehicle until he reaches the windshield, sniffs, and howls a low guttural wail. He struggles up the bank, up the hill, to the lean-to where fresh straw is tucked against the house. He bites frozen snow from his paws, then curls and sleeps.

Garden of Eden

Adam leans against the window, squinting at a morning sky drained of light. Outside, a huddled Good Shepherd caregiver bends into an April bluster. The bell on the Catholic church tolls. Six o'clock.

"Mother, bring my robe," Adam says, then cocks his head and drops his eyes. He is alone. He shuffles to the closet, steadying himself against the piano, the back of the sofa, a chair.

He retires to the recliner, stuffs a pillow in the small of his back, and fingers a small diary. The television in the next apartment hums through the wall. A mantle clock tick-tocks in boring monotone. With eyes closed he says, "Mother, brew me a cup of tea."

He braces himself against the chair, rises, and navigates the living room, the kitchenette for tea, back to the living room, to the piano. After flexing his fingers and cracking his knuckles, he pages through sheet music—Beethoven, Mozart, Schubert. He runs his fingers against the glassy top of the piano, stopping at a framed portrait, Adam and Eva. They sit on a porch swing at the lake house. Smiling, together, alive.

Today is their wedding anniversary. Fifty years.

He turns to reach for the diary. The grief counselor at the hospital suggested he record his feelings, his emotions every day for a year. Then weekly, monthly, review them and celebrate his progress. He reads *Sorrow. Shame. Guilt. Disgust. Betrayal.*

Three weeks prior, Eva sat erect at the head of the Country Club dinner table, her hands clasped, the menu resting on her plate. Adam sat beside her, turning the pages of the menu, forward and back.

"Is anyone else coming?" Eva asked. "If not . . . Waiter," she called, "you may remove the extra place settings."

"Mother, is this a meeting or a meal?" daughter Martha laughed.

Eva ignored her. "I think I made it clear that you and your brother could bring a guest tonight. Your significant others, if you will. But since it's just the four of us, we'll proceed." She glanced around the table with a matronly smile. "First, I'll order wine."

Dominic leaned toward his sister. "I don't miss this."

Eva motioned to the waiter and selected a pinot noir from the wine list.

"To what auspicious occasion do we owe this celebration, this display of parental beneficence?" Martha asked. "Cranberry Pines, no less. Pressed white linens. Fresh flowers. Dad in a tie, albeit a remnant from his faculty days."

Adam looked at the tie and stroked it. "It's my favorite. I want to be buried with it."

"Adam, don't be morbid."

The waiter displayed the wine bottle, opened it, and poured. Eva inhaled, sipped, and swirled it on her tongue. "Perfect."

"For those of you who don't remember special occasions," she pointed her glass at Martha and Dominic, "in April your father and I celebrate our Golden Wedding Anniversary." She smiled her bridge club smile.

Dominic raised his glass in a toast. "Married fifty years, Dad? To the same woman? I'm impressed."

Adam rolled his tie in a coil. He nodded.

"Wish I would have inherited your marital perseverance," Martha cut in. "And they said yours wouldn't last. Cheers."

"Thank you for your sentiments, charitable or otherwise," Eva said. "Now I remember why we delayed having children. However, to celebrate the occasion, I'm booking passage for all of us on the maiden voyage of the cruise ship Garden of Eden. Adam and Eva on the Garden of Eden. Isn't that too perfect?" She smiled and raised her glass in a toast, awaiting her family's validation.

Diners at scattered tables ate in dark silence. Adam turned toward the windows where lighted candles reflected on dark, snow-covered fairways. The hostess led couples to their tables, past Eva, who smiled and fluttered her fingers. From the swinging doors of the kitchen, the wait staff marched to a table across the room carrying a cake with sparkling candles.

Adam folded his napkin into the shape of a ship, then unfolded it. He glanced at his son and daughter. "Your mother thinks of everything. Don't be surprised if she . . ."

"The Garden of Eden, Mother. How appropriate," Dominic cut in. "Nude walks through a pastiche apple orchard. Talking snakes. Huge leaves on fig trees. How delightful."

Martha waved a dismissive hand at him. "How delightful and how sweet, Mother," she said. "Do you have a date in mind?"

"The Garden of Eden departs Miami on April 12. Ten days and four ports of call later, we return to Miami. Now, all I need is a headcount. Martha, your father and I have discussed this, and he has agreed, reluctantly I might add, to allow you to bring Jim even though you're engaged and not married. Isn't that right, Adam?"

Adam shrugged his shoulders and concentrated on the versatile square of white linen becoming a helmet, a sword, a dunce cap. "As if my opinion makes a difference."

"Mother . . ."

"We thought it might be a pre-honeymoon," Eva continued.

"Mother, Jim and I have split. We've called off the wedding. We decided to save the pain and price of divorce and not get married in the first place."

Adam's chin rested against his chest. He lifted his eyes, peering over glasses. He glanced at Eva who steadied the wine glass with both hands, then lifted and drained it.

"I can't take this on an empty stomach. Can we order, Mother?" Adam asked. "I haven't eaten since lunch."

Martha interrupted. "However, this would be a great opportunity for you to meet Mike. I've known him for years. I can't believe it's taken us this long to get together. You remember him, don't you? We worked together at the ad agency."

Eva motioned to the waiter and tapped the wine bottle. "We'll discuss that later. Now, how about you, Dominic? Will you surprise your mother by announcing you've found your one and only true love? Someone you'd like to introduce us to on the cruise?"

"Yes, Dominic," Adam said. "Introduce some sanity to this discourse. It's beginning to sound like a banal television show."

Dominic balanced a fork on his knife and tried adding a spoon. He looked at his sister.

"Go ahead," Martha said.

"Yes and no," Dominic said. "I don't believe in one and only. Or true love. And I'm not sure that a cruise is the proper venue for you to meet Derek."

Adam jerked his head up to meet his son's eyes. "Wait a minute," he squeaked. "What am I hearing? Who's Derek? And Martha, who's Mike? I don't know these people. And you want to bring them, these degenerates, on a cruise? This is the Garden of Eden we're talking about, not the Sodom and Gomorrah." He cocked his head toward the ceiling, as if scolding the chandelier. "You're not living in sin on my nickel."

"Adam, hush," Eva whispered. "Children, this will require a discussion with your father. I'm surprised, maybe even disappointed. But it's your life to lead."

"Sure it is," Dominic whispered.

"Let's drop it for tonight. Waiter," she raised her hand and snapped her fingers. "Could we order, please? And more wine." She perched her glasses on the end of her nose and held the menu like a diva soprano holding an operatic score.

"Mother," Martha said, "let's not drop it. I think it's a great idea for you and Dad. But inviting me and Dominic? That's a recipe for disaster."

The waiter returned with a bottle of wine. "May I recite the evening's dinner specials?"

Adam quieted him with a wave of his menu. "Martha, the recipe for disaster is your flitting from man to man. And you, Dominic." He pointed to his son with a steak knife. "Your conduct is reprehensible. I don't understand." He held Dominic's stare for a moment, then glanced at the windows, the fireplace, the incoming diners.

"I'm not asking you to understand. I'm asking you to accept. What I'm hearing is that you don't." Dominic tossed his napkin on the table. "No point in perpetuating this one big happy family fantasy. *Bon voyage*."

"Dominic, come back here." Eva slammed the menu against her plate. "Sit down. I won't stand for this."

"Let him go, Mother. Let some of the emotional dust settle. The good news is that you're previewing ten days of cruise behavior without paying the extra fares. Save yourself the anguish. And the money. You and Dad go."

"I'm not giving up that easily." Eva sipped her wine. "Adam, say something."

"I can't believe what I'm hearing. I have one son, and he's what? Gay?" He lifted his knife and feigned a chest stab.

"Dad, welcome to the twentieth century. You must have known about Dom, or at least suspected it. How many of his lady friends have you met? How many men friends?"

"None. Lots. But I didn't know he was gay. Eva, did you know?"

Eva sipped her wine, then finished the glass. "Yes," she said. "I knew. The way a mother knows about her children." She looked left, then right. "At first, it was intuition. Then, I intercepted a couple phone calls. Yes, I knew."

"Why didn't you say something? Maybe we could have helped him. I can't believe you shut me out of such a critical decision."

"Dad," Martha said. "You're angry, and that's understandable. But don't take it out on Mother."

"It's okay, Martha. I'm used to it."

"I'm not going to let this drop," Adam said, straightening in his chair. "What other family secrets are you hiding? Is there a second shoe to drop? A third? A fourth?"

"Dad, I said *stop*. You're making this sound like it's Mother's fault."

"You stay out of this, young lady." Adam pointed his knife again. "I don't need your Dear Abby advice." He turned to Eva, still pointing his knife. "What kind of children did we raise, Mother? Four years of college for Dom, a degree in business administration. We bankroll his two business ventures, and what does he do for a living? House sits and walks other people's dogs."

Adam turned to his daughter and poked the air. "And you, Martha. How do you justify your adulterous life style? I'm embarrassed. I'm appalled."

"Adam, shut up," Eva snapped through clenched teeth.

"Mother, this is going nowhere. If it's okay with you, I'm leaving. But please, don't give up on the cruise. Ten days of pampered distraction is probably what the old fart needs."

"Martha . . ."

Martha stood and snapped her purse off the table. "Bye, Mom."

"Will the young lady and man be returning, Mrs. Douglas, or should I remove the place settings?" the waiter asked.

"Take them. Take mine too. We will not be eating dinner. Adam, finish your wine or I will."

He handed her the glass.

"I feel a severe headache coming on. If we wait any longer, you may have to drive home."

"I don't drive after dark, Mother."

"Don't call me *Mother*. I'm your wife. Remember?"

"Martha, this is your father," Adam spoke to a telephone answering machine. "It's after midnight. Your mother had another headache. I called 911, and she had an ambulance ride to General Hospital. Give me a call when you get this. Room 4200. And call Dominic too."

Eva lay in the bed, sedated and sleeping. Adam shifted in the reclining lounge chair, positioned his pillow, tucked the blanket around his neck. "Mother," he whispered, "get me a blanket for my feet." Mother. Eva. He listened to her labored breathing, watched her fingers twitch, her arms writhe. He turned in the chair to lie on his side. "Mother," he whispered. "Let's go home. Martha's coming. She'll take care of you."

The door opened, and a shaft of hall light shone on Adam. "Time to check vitals," the nurse said. "Are you resting well, Mr. Douglas?"

At seven-thirty in the morning, Martha arrived. "Where's Mom?"

Adam struggled from the lounge chair and ran fingers through his hair. He flattened and smoothed his shirt and tightened the tie from last night's dinner.

"They're doing a full body scan. The brain scan last night was inconclusive."

"What do they suspect?"

Adam watched Martha in the doorway, twirling keys, and glancing at passersby in the aisle.

"Could be a brain tumor, they say, based on her history."

"What history?"

"She's had these severe headaches for a month or so. They come, they go. This one didn't go."

"Had she seen her doctor?"

"No. You know your mother. Always reaching for high drama. I have to admit, I never thought this was more than a ploy for attention."

"You mean you didn't encourage her to check in at the clinic?"

"Well, I . . ." Adam looked at his daughter, and realized that in heels, she was taller than he.

"You thought that if she were hospitalized, she wouldn't be there to care for you. Is that what you thought?"

"Well . . ."

"Dad," Martha said and stopped. A gurney approached, wheeled by a cadre of attendants in blue scrubs. They continued past her. "I hate to leave without seeing Mother," she said, "but she'll likely be sedated when she returns. I'll check at the desk and call from work."

When the orderlies wheeled Eva into the room, she stirred, glanced at Adam, and said nothing. They lifted her onto the bed, her face and arms faded as white as the linen. A doctor stood in the doorway. "Are you Mr. Douglas?"

Adam nodded.

"I'm Dr. Marshall. It's definitely a brain tumor. We need to run a biopsy to determine whether it's benign or malignant. We'll have results in twenty-four hours."

Adam tilted his head and dropped his chin. His body trembled.

"Prognosis? Too soon to tell," the doctor said. "If it's benign, it may be operable. If it's malignant . . ." He spread his hands.

"Doctor, I'll have to sort this out. I mean, how can I . . ."

"Would you like me to schedule a conference with your family? I see that you and Mrs. Douglas have a son and a daughter."

"You'll likely be hearing from my daughter. I'm going home. I'm exhausted. Where can I call a cab?"

"Good morning, Mr. Douglas, this is Dr. Marshall. Did I wake you?"

Adam shook his head and glanced at the clock. Seven a.m. He sensed what the doctor would say, felt an urge to capture the moment. This moment, the last before the tragic pronouncement. This moment. Late March sunlight peeking through window blinds. The hum of warm air from the furnace. The down comforter and fluffy pillow.

"Mr. Douglas, are you there?"

"Yes, you caught me in a deep sleep."

"Are you coming to the hospital today?"

"From the tone of your voice, it doesn't sound good for me. Or for her."

"I can see you at ten o'clock. Can you be here?"

"The suspense is killing me, Doc. Can we talk on the phone? Now? I don't trust myself driving in the state I'm in." His pulse quickened. He held the receiver with a sweaty hand and steadied its cool plastic body against his cheek.

"If that's what you prefer. Mrs. Douglas has a malignant brain tumor. Inoperable. Untreatable. Lethal. I estimate she'll survive a week, maybe two. Mr. Douglas, do you want me to continue?"

"What is there to continue? Bottom line: my wife is dying."

"Bottom line: she has a few precious days to live. You need be aware, however, that she will experience incoherent intervals. We may have to restrain her. But we can't restrain her voice. Patients have been known to speak unpredictably. Hurtful and fallacious accusations. If you hear that from her, remember: it's the tumor talking, not your wife."

"I wish I could believe that," he whispered.

"Excuse me?"

"Nothing. The kids will wonder how she's doing. I'll take a cab and be there within the hour."

"She's sedated now. She may be sleeping when you arrive."

Adam called a cab and dressed for March weather. Clement overnight temperature had given way to wind and sleet. Adam searched for his overshoes, his parka, his gloves, his keys. The taxi honked in the driveway.

The door to Eva's room was ajar, and Adam slipped through the open space, not wanting to wake her. She slept, breathing a steady, sonorous snore.

Adam approached her but stopped outside her reach. IV tubes dripped, dripped, dripped. An instrument on the headboard blinked a digital readout. A call button was snapped to the bed sheet near her hand.

Eva. Strange to see her without makeup. Her hair damp, matted, awry. Her face mottled, taut, crisp as parchment. Her face. A death mask.

Weeks later, Adam hears a knock at his Good Shepherd apartment. "Come in. The door's open." He maneuvers toward the door in his walker.

"Good morning. I'm Thelma Ritts, your neighbor across the hall. I haven't seen much of you at meal time or any of the social grab-ass functions." Thelma extends her hand to shake his. She's a petite woman, smaller than Eva, her animated eyes at a level with Adam's. Black rimmed glasses hang from a braided lanyard around her neck.

"It's not easy to get around with this."

"You think you got problems. You should have met the guy who lived here before you. Maxwell. Dead now, God rest his soul. I'd say you'll survive."

"Thanks for the encouragement."

"The reason I stopped is that I'm tired of seeing I'M NOT OKAY hanging from your doorknob. None of us is okay. You call *wolf* too many times, and no one will take you serious. By the way, what happened?"

"This?" Adam points to his walker. "I fell on the hospital sidewalk after visiting my wife."

"I heard she died. You got kids? I haven't seen them."

"Word gets around, doesn't it?"

"Let's just say no one has secrets. Now get some shoes on, and I'll take you down for coffee."

Adam wheels the walker to the bedroom.

"Nice piano," Thelma calls. "You play?"

"I taught piano at the University for thirty-five years." He hears her play the scales, a few chords, the opening bars of "Fur Elise."

"Piano needs tuning," she says.

Adam reaches for his slippers and sees his tie, his favorite tie. He runs his fingers over its fine silk fabric. "I want to die and be buried with this tie."

In the dining room, Thelma pours two cups of coffee and leads Adam to a table where Stella sits with a young girl, attentive, chatty, and cheery. Stella's crutches lean against the chair. "Let me introduce the newest member of our family," Thelma says. "We haven't been introduced ourselves, but his name is Adam. Adam Douglas. Apartment 107. He's recently widowed, and he has kids but they don't visit."

"I'm Stella and this is my niece Mimi."

"Grand niece," Mimi corrects her.

Stella nods a scowl at Mimi. "Adam, I see you have transportation issues too."

"Temporary. I fractured a hip."

"Better than being kicked by a horse." Stella points to her crippled leg.

"Adam plays the piano," Thelma says.

"Yes, I saw them move the piano into his apartment. You play too, don't you, Thelma?"

"You play the piano?" Mimi interrupts and claps her hands. "I love piano."

"Do you play?" Adam asks her.

"I'm a second year violin student. Next year, piano."

"Maybe we should teach piano here at Good Shepherd," Stella says. "You taught too, didn't you Thelma?"

"Yes. But Adam taught at the University. I taught snotty-nosed kids who had to be paid to practice." She sips her coffee. "The piano in the Gathering Room is a piece of crap. But with Adam here, I'll bet they repair it. If they don't, he'll have to change his repertoire to play it." She sips her coffee. "Are you visiting your great aunt today?" Thelma asks Mimi.

"She gets extra credit in Social Studies for helping an old lady for half a day," Stella says.

"It's our Assist the Elderly program," Mimi corrects her and returns the scowl. "And I don't need the extra credit."

"So what assistance are you providing?" Thelma asks.

"Already today, we've baked a batch of peanut butter cookies, sorted the recyclables, and started scrap booking," Stella laughs. "I must have ten shoe boxes full of pictures, birthday cards, invitations, prayer cards, newspaper clippings, stuff."

"I'm looking for pictures of my dad," Mimi says. "And my grandmother, Great Aunt Stella's sister. I found a picture with my grandparents at Great Aunt Stella's wedding. It's setting on the television now."

"And what do you do when you're not playing the violin or baking cookies or scrap booking?" Adam asks.

Mimi sits erect in her chair holding a glass of juice. "I'm on the junior varsity swim team. I'm a girl scout, and I get a merit badge for helping her." She points to Stella. "I study Latin and French. I have a stamp collection. And I have two pet gerbils."

"Have you ever sat down and watched a full hour of television?" Adam asks.

"No."

Stella shifts in her chair. "Who else have you met here, Adam?"

"No one. Just Thelma and you."

"Well, let me preview the tribe." She turns. "That fake blond making all the noise? That's Pearl. A live wire, but she gets on my nerves. The handsome hunk next to her? That's Arnold. Scuttlebutt around here says that she has her eye on him. The elegant looking one at the next table is Grace, Princess Grace. She raises the bar at Good Shepherd for etiquette. She's talking to Hazel. Acid tongue. Don't get on her wrong side.

"Not everybody shows up for coffee. There are twelve of us here. Maxwell died, you moved in. Maxwell, he lived in your apartment."

Adam scans the room and settles on Arnold, notices he's the only one not wearing a sweater or jacket. Notices he's conspicuous by his healthy mien, commanding by his easy smile under a Fu Manchu mustache. "Good to know I'm not the only man."

Stella taps him on the arm. "Tell me about your music, Adam."

"He has this beautiful classic baby grand," Thelma says. "Ebony. Shines like a you-know-what. An impressive array of sheet music too. I hope to hear some Mozart coming under the door soon."

"In time," Adam says. "I've been told my piano needs tuning."

"My friend tunes pianos for the Symphony. I'll see when he's available."

After coffee, Thelma and Adam return to his apartment. "I want to hear you play," she says.

"Nothing doing. Not with this leg."

"You have two feet. Come on, let's hear something. And while you're playing, I'll give this place a little attention." She stacks half-finished crossword puzzles on the lamp table and swipes a finger across the piano. "Where's the furniture polish?"

Adam sits at the piano, cracks his knuckles, and stares at the sheet music. He hasn't played since . . . Strange, because he thought music would rescue him. He plinks out a few bars of "Fur Elise," the piece Thelma sampled. "You're right," he says. "It needs tuning."

"It sounds great," Thelma says. "More."

He plays the opening bars of a Chopin etude, the first movement of a Beethoven sonata. He raises his arms and flexes his hands.

Thelma leans on the piano, her fingers touching the portrait of Adam and Eva. "Beautiful," she says, "but don't you ever play to the final note? Play more, please, while I reclaim your kitchen."

Adam shuffles through sheet music, selects one, and plays. Thoughtful, soulful. He stops.

"That was touching," Thelma says.

"'Fur Elise.' I couldn't finish that one either. It was Eva's favorite." He touches the portrait. "I wish I would have done things differently."

"Save it for another day," Thelma says. "You're a powerful guy, but you're not powerful enough to have saved her. I loaded the dishwasher. Put *soap* on your grocery list. And for Christsakes, dump your garbage. You'll stink up the whole building. I have errands to run. I'll call my friend about tuning your piano. See ya." She turns at the door. "By the way, you'd better water those plants before they croak."

Those plants, remainders of Eva's memorial service. Dozens of plants only a few of which he kept, the little WITH SYMPATHY gift cards tucked among the leaves. He taps the soil around the Norfolk Island pine. Dry. The jade. Dry. The fern and Boston ivy. Dry. The cactus garden, an unusual choice he thought, when he checked the card at the memorial service. *Dominic*.

Eva's memorial service. An awkward memory, clumsy and painful. The mortuary parlor buzzed with bridge club ladies, book club friends, garden club members, neighbors, people he didn't recognize, didn't know until they introduced themselves. He suffered through their clichéd condolences: "So quick, so hard to believe"; their brief remembrances: "Such great memories of the weekends at her lake place"; their well-intentioned advice: "She'd want you to be happy." Clumsy and painful. Adam remembered their eagerness to desert him, to return to their friends.

Martha and Dominic arrived together, late. Adam leaned on the table that held Eva's portrait and the urn of ashes, twisting his tie, his favorite tie.

Martha approached holding Dominic's hand. "Too bad Mother isn't here. She would have loved the party." She hugged him, waving to a neighbor.

"I'm feeling weak," Adam said. "I'd better sit."

"I'll get you a chair." Dominic hurried off.

"So many of Mother's friends to talk to," Martha said. "Let me know if you need me."

Adam doesn't remembering seeing them the rest of the night.

"That sounds one hundred percent better," Thelma says the next afternoon. "What did he charge you? It sounds great."

Adam sits at the piano chording. "I thought I'd never play again. Other times, I expected to return to teaching. I can't do either. Too many memories among these scores."

"I see you have sheet music for piano four hands. Did your wife play?"

"No, my daughter played. Incidentally, she called last night. Said she'd drop over today after work."

"Schubert's 'March Militaire.' Did you and your daughter play that? I played that in competition. If you know the *secondo*, I know the *primo*." She sits at the piano next to Adam and opens the sheet music.

Adam slides away from her, creating space between them. He scans the notes and flexes his fingers. "Ready?" he says, and starts to play.

Thelma enters on cue, raising and lowering her hands, swaying her body, crossing over his hand, leaning until their bodies touch. She glances at Adam concentrating on the music. She plays with dramatic flair, her head bobbing, her torso rotating, her free hand high above the keyboard.

They finish and sit without speaking. Thelma looks at Adam and offers her hand to shake.

Adam slumps, sighs, and closes his eyes.

"That wasn't bad," Thelma says. "If you were my student, I'd give you a B minus. Next time, pay attention to tempo. You missed a couple of decrescendos. And you know what *pianissimo* means, right?"

Adam jerks his head up and stares over his glasses. "I haven't had that harsh a criticism since seventh grade."

"Get used to it." Thelma pages through more sheet music and stacks it beside the portrait. "This picture looks recent. Last summer, I'd say. Where was it taken?"

"At our lake house, not far from here. We shopped in town on our weekend visits. That's how I knew about Good Shepherd."

"Do you still spend time there?" She picks up the photo and stares at it.

He hesitates. "No, not since last fall. It was her idea to buy it. I'm not a tree hugger or a fisherman or a boating enthusiast. Eva wanted a lake place. Her friends had second homes up north. She wanted to join in the conversation about how expensive they are to maintain." He runs his fingers over the ivory keys.

"Do your kids spend time there?"

"They helped us move furniture and fell in love with the place. They'd rotate weekends coming up. My daughter Martha is a poet, when she's not auditioning significant others. My son Dominic wants to be a landscape artist when he grows up, which won't be in this lifetime. They come up for inspiration. Do their best work up there, they say."

"What about your wife?"

"Eva liked to host her bridge club there on weekends. Paid a local fellow to plow the drive in winter and mow the grass in summer. And spray the apple tree. That tree clinched the sale for Eva. 'We'll call the place Paradise,' I remember her screaming to the delight of the selling agent. 'Adam and Eva and the Tree of Knowledge.' And didn't she play that to the hilt with her bridge club friends. Adam and Eva in Paradise. She wouldn't have married me if my name was Fred. One helluva high price for a bit of trite humor, I'd say. Tree of rotten luck would be more apt." Adam toys with a finger exercise.

"Who's your favorite composer?" Thelma asks. "Play something of his. Make you feel better. I'll brew coffee."

Adam touches the keys in a melancholic reading of a few bars of "Clair de Lune." Thelma returns to the piano bench.

As Adam plays, there's a knock, and the door opens. "Dad," Martha says. "I heard you playing." She looks at Thelma, bewildered. "Oh, excuse me. Have I interrupted something?"

"No," Thelma says, rising from the piano bench. "I'm Thelma, Adam's neighbor across the hall. It's remarkable how music lifts his spirit. He seems genuinely passionate about it."

"That's the first time I've heard anyone use my dad's name and *passion* in the same sentence."

"Well, I'll leave now," Thelma says. "Nice to meet you. There's fresh coffee in the pot."

"That didn't take long," Martha says when the door closes.

"I could remind you of someone else who changes partners faster than she changes socks. But I won't. She taught piano too," Adam says. "She was being a good neighbor."

Martha inspects the kitchen, the bedroom, the bath. "What kind of place is this? An old folks home or a senior dating service?"

"It's an assisted living facility, Mother. It's . . ."

"Hold it. I'm not your mother. I'm your daughter." She taps her foot on the floor.

"I'm sorry. Mother: Martha. Martha: Mother. It's an honest mistake."

"Forget it. Coffee?" She heads for the kitchen. "I want to talk about Mother. I miss her." She pours two cups. "Not that we were close. I just miss her. You won't believe the times I reach for the phone to call her."

"I know the feeling."

"I hear her voice chastising me every time I eat a brownie or have a cigarette or wear colors that she considered clashing." She sets coffee in front of Adam.

He sits, chin drooping to his chest.

"I need to know more about her illness. When did she suspect she had a problem? Did she talk about it? I can't imagine her suffering in silence."

"I didn't know. I don't know."

"You don't know, or you don't care? Oh, for Christ's sake, scratch that. I don't want to sound accusatory, Dad."

"Martha," Adam said. "I'm sorting this stuff out myself. What I know is that we lost Eva."

"We didn't lose her. She died," Martha declares, clinking the spoon in her cup.

"All right. She died. I have to accept that and move forward. I'm hoping this baby can help me make the trip." He pats the piano. "Did I tell you I had it tuned, Mother?"

Martha stares at him. "Stop that."

"I apologize. I'm sorry. My mistake."

Martha rises to leave. She looks at her watch. "I have a long drive back and a busy day tomorrow. Good night, Dad."

"I thought we'd have dinner together. And have you heard from Dominic?"

"No and no. Bye."

"How'd the visit go?" The following morning, Thelma carries a tray with a plate of caramel rolls and an urn of coffee.

Adam pulls the blanket to his chin and huddles in his chair. "Terrible. She walked out on me. I've lost everything. My wife is dead. My daughter is estranged. My son is . . . Did I tell you he's gay?"

"What happened with your daughter? Martha?"

"I made a stupid mistake. I called her *Mother*. Slip of the tongue. I called Eva *Mother* when the kids were small, and never got over it. And Martha sounds like Eva. Looks like Eva. Reminds me of Eva."

Thelma hands him the plate of caramel rolls. "Didn't Eva resent your calling her *Mother*?"

"If she did, she never mentioned it. Not until the night of the pre-cruise dinner." He sighs and takes a cup of coffee, and bites into a caramel roll.

"It sounds to me like your family has relationship issues. Your son doesn't visit, so working on that is remote for the moment. Better to mend that fence through your daughter." Thelma perches on the edge of the piano bench.

"I don't feel up to that."

"You're one miserable old man. Nothing to look forward to. Nothing to be thankful for. Maybe you should just pull the plug." She waves her coffee mug in front of him. "Listen," she says. "Kids grow up. Once upon a time they needed you. Now the roles are reversed. You need them. Not financially, not physically, but emotionally."

"Once upon a time, I had everything." Adam sets the caramel roll on a napkin and fiddles with fringes on the blanket, braiding them, unbraiding them.

"Once upon a time, you had the same nothing you have now. Get used to it."

"But Martha's my daughter. Dominic's my son. I'm their father. They must need me for something."

"They don't need you as badly as you need them. Let's drink our coffee. It's a beautiful spring day, and I'm up for a drive. Care to join me?"

"After the scorching my daughter gave me? Probably not." He lifts his coffee, inhales, and sets it down.

"That shouldn't surprise you. Typical daughter response. Doesn't want anyone substituting for Mom. Get over it. Take charge of your life. Do something for yourself. She'll respect you for it someday. Now, how about that drive?"

"I could show you the lake house now that I've shed my walker."

"Great. I'll have the car in front at ten." She gathers the tray and coffee urn. "By the way, are you planning to finish that caramel roll?"

Snow melts on the south side of the lake house. The sun-warmed earth smells of spring. Spikes of tulip leaves stab through clumps of brown leaves. Tight-fisted ferns punch through last year's growth.

"This is it," Adam says.

Bright yellow-green branches droop from weeping willows. The dogwood is wine-red. Blackbirds trill in reeds along the lakeshore.

"April in Paradise," Thelma says.

Newspapers are rubber-banded to the doorknob. Melting snow trickles down the walk along yellow budding forsythia.

"I'll open the place up, then I want to see the lake," Adam says. "The ice is going out, and the west wind piles it on the shore."

"You're in charge," Thelma says.

They walk through the house, the temperature chilly. Adam pokes through a pile of mail and tosses it in the wastebasket. He walks in the living room and picks a magazine off the floor, then in the bedroom and straightens the bedspread and pillows. Thelma follows and drags a finger across a dusty bookcase.

"It feels cold," Adam says. "Empty. Dead. Depressing." He walks out the lakeside door onto a screened porch that overlooks a garden, a path, the lake. Beside the garden, the apple tree stands, waxy buds about to burst. Around its trunk base, a circular bench tempts passersby to sit, relax, converse.

"This is it," Adam says. "The Tree of Forbidden Fruit in Paradise. I prefer the new translation of the Hebrew text: The Tree of

Pleasure in the Garden of Desire." They walk outside, down to the dock that winters on the shoreline.

"I'm ambivalent about this place," Adam says. "It never was mine. But it was a great place for inspiration. I composed a few pieces sitting in front of this lake, in that garden, under that tree."

"What kind of pieces?"

"Fragments of large works that never got larger." They startle when ice on the lake cracks.

"Did you share those with your family?"

"Yes. They said I was a better composer than I was a pianist. And I was."

"Is that what you want in your obituary? Is that what you want from life?"

"What I want from life is to be cared for."

"What you want from life is to be cared *about*."

Adam scans the lake. A cold wind blows off stacks of ice boulders and musses his hair. Thelma shrugs her coat around her shoulders.

"I have to admit, I'm not accustomed to your candor," Adam says.

"Forget it. Do you feel the muse sitting on your shoulder? Now?"

"No. In fact, I want to leave. This place unsettles me."

"Your call. It'll probably still be here next week."

Back in his apartment, Adam sits at the piano and stares at the keyboard. "Eva," he says, then waves his hand as if to say goodbye, or dismiss her. "Martha," he says, and buries his face in his hands to protect himself from her caustic tirades. "Dominic," he says. The scene at the Country Club replays. Maybe it was a hoax, a misunderstanding. Eva and Martha's idea of a joke.

"A good day for a drive," Thelma says at coffee a few days later. "I have to drop off the car for an oil change. We could borrow one of their clunkers and drive to your lake house."

"I'm due for a change of scenery," Adam says. "And I'm feeling an unusual creative urge."

"Bookmark that page," Thelma says. "I'll pick you up at ten. Bring pen and paper."

New leaves shimmer since their last visit. Crocuses bloom through last year's leaf drop. Remaining snow hides in shadowy corners. Ice floes on the lakeshore look gray and porous. Adam reads the thermometer on the porch. Sixty-four degrees and climbing.

"I'll sit outside and see what happens," he says.

"I brought magazines and my knitting. If I tire of that, I'll spiff up the house a bit. I think I can find cleaning supplies."

"Have at it."

"We'll have coffee at noon. I brought sandwiches and apples."

Adam walks down the steps to the lake, past the Tree of Forbidden Fruit now budding pink blossoms, down the path to a pair of Adirondack chairs tipped upside down for the winter. He hears Thelma open windows, then close doors and drawers. He sits and waits. And waits. Blackbirds trill. A squirrel chatters from a bare oak tree. He waits. *Bookmark that page*, he remembers, and begins to write.

"Time for a break?" Thelma asks. "It's noon." She stands beside him sitting in the chair.

Adam closes his notebook and turns away from the lake. "Sure."

"Did you say your kids still use this place? How long has it been since they were here, with or without you?"

"They both have keys. They could have been here anytime."

"Do you offer the house to anyone else? Friends, neighbors, family?"

"No. What are you getting at?" Adam frowns, confused.

"I found some sex toys in the bookcase. But I also found these." She fans a handful of composition books and offers them to Adam. He flips through one, then another.

"What do you know about them?" Thelma asks.

"What do I *remember* about them? Nothing."

"From my perspective, they're definitely out of the mainstream."

"That's probably why they were hidden in the bookcase."

"Who said they were hidden?"

Adam stammers. He scans a book with the notation *Random Fragments, Large Works*. "Eva wouldn't have understood. Not at my age. Not from a respected interpreter of classic composition."

"But she understood your son Dominic."

"Wait a minute. Are we talking about the same thing?'

"I think we are."

Adam hands the books to Thelma. He braces against the armrests to rise and shuffles to the lake, hands in pockets. He shuffles through slush, litter on the shore, remnants of winter.

He stops, facing the frozen lake, and spreads his arms. From the center of the lake, ice cracks in a thunderous roar. Gale winds ruffle his hair, balloon his jacket, and teeter him. He leans into the wind, screaming.

"Eva, I've betrayed you. Please forgive me.

"Martha, I've shamed you. Please forgive me.

"Dominic, I love you. Please forgive me."

He drops his arms and places his head in his hands.

From behind him, "And Adam?"

He raises his head. "Adam. I've betrayed you, I've shamed you. I love you. Please forgive me."

He waits, expecting an echo response. "Is it too late to change?" he screams.

He hears, "Never."

He stares at blue ice far out on the lake. "I could keep walking, keep walking."

"Yes, you could." He hears a choked chuckle. "You could. Go ahead."

He stands, confused.

"I'm not worried," she says. "You never finish anything you start."

Icy water seeps through his shoe. He shudders. It seeps through the other shoe. He lifts a foot and steps backward.

May Day

Interesting, isn't it, we recall where we were, what we were doing when history is made. John Glenn's earth orbit in Friendship 7, President Kennedy's assassination, the Beatles' appearance on Ed Sullivan. Our family's move to Burdock was triggered by such an event. When my mother Adeline was asked why we moved to the Burdock farm, she always began with the story of Dad working at the Ford plant in Minneapolis during the war. At three, he'd ride the Selby-Lake streetcar home, and since radios were banned at the plant, it was just another spring afternoon for Dad.

"Once home," she'd continue, "we sat at the kitchen table, Henry and I, listening to the news. The two of us. It was a Thursday, and Victor was in school. Violet was napping upstairs." She'd point to an imaginary staircase. "I can tell you where I was when Franklin D. Roosevelt died," she'd say. "It was April 12th. I was sitting at the table . . ." That's where Mother was when that historic event occurred.

May Day

I won't venture to guess which event was more historic for her—the president's death, or her family's move that it generated.

Dad had uprooted us from the country, moving to Minneapolis when the United States entered the war. For the time being, he was deferred from the draft, him being married and supporting two kids, a third on the way. Big defense plant wages, he surmised, would allow him to accumulate a nest egg and buy a larger farm when the war was over. That was his plan.

Dad quoted Edward R. Murrow lamenting the President's untimely death and the war news in Europe. "We have the momentum now. The end of the war is in sight." Mr. Murrow closed with, "Good night, and good luck."

Time to move back to the farm, Dad concluded. The Big City stint was never meant to be permanent.

Funny how conversations repeated enough tend to sound scripted, repeated word for word. I must have heard Dad's rendition of the move saga a hundred times. Mother nodded at the same point each time she heard it, a smile thrown off to the side. I liked Murrow's word *momentum*. My sister Violet would mouth *good night, and good luck*.

Dad kept the United Farm Agency catalog on the kitchen table in the Minneapolis house, monitoring prices of small farms within a couple hours' drive of the city. His job at the defense plant was a "critical occupation," and he didn't have the option to leave. But his family could. He spotted a farm in the brochure—forty acres, house and barn, an hour's drive to the city, river view, rent with option to buy. "I could move you out there," Dad said, "and live here in the city until the war is over."

"It's only April." Mother placed her hand on my shoulder. "Victor has another month of school."

She may as well have spoken to the wall.

On Sunday, Dad rode the train to the town of Burdock to meet the United Farm agent and owner Guy Stearns.

When he returned, he reported the house was a white two-story, 1920s design, with a porch extending across the front. He had only peeked at the interior. The barn had stanchions for a dozen cows, stalls for two horses, an attached calf pen. No hay mow or silo, no granary or machine shed. Behind the barn, an outhouse. There was an abandoned orchard, he said, with apple trees, a few prickly plums, and overgrown grape vines that strangled a windmill. The *river view* mentioned in the catalog was a creek that meandered through the pasture within view of the house.

"I should ask a higher price, this being river-front property," Dad quoted Guy as saying. "The creek never floods, and next fall you can hunt ducks right in your back yard."

They discussed the $2,500 asking price, the monthly rent payments, the interest rate. "Immediate occupancy," Guy had chirped.

Dad recalls scribbling a few numbers in his pocket notebook and saying, "I'll take it."

Back in the city, Dad stripped the garage walls of tools and fishing tackle. Mother and I stood in the doorway, her twisting a handkerchief and asking questions. *How many bedrooms upstairs? How much cupboard space? Wood floors or carpet or linoleum? Will the kids walk to school? Ride the bus? Where will we go to church?*

Dad kept packing. "It'll all work out."

I followed her to the house, both of us confused. She grabbed cardboard boxes off the back porch for pots and pans and dishes, whispering questions to herself. I remember her stopping at the kitchen door and shrugging her shoulders. Then she proceeded, humming as she packed, resigned to making another new home and finding a new parish.

By the end of the day, dishes, groceries, clothes, and bedding were packed and stacked in the kitchen. What we couldn't carry,

May Day

Dad would keep in the house until he finished work at the Ford plant.

"There's a mission church in town," Dad said over a sandwich supper that evening. "Our Lady of . . . something. You could walk to it. I met the priest in the café and told him we planned to move. There's daily mass and two on Sunday." That satisfied her.

Dad bought a three-quarter ton Chevy truck from a defense plant buddy and rented a trailer. On moving day, six hours and six flat tires later, we limped into the new driveway on the seventh flat. Dad said to hell with it. Mother crossed herself. Her first words when she saw the house interior, "I hope no one visits us for a few months."

With Dad in the city, Mother learned to start the truck, straight stick with a slippery clutch. She jerked it into gear and the engine killed. She restarted it and steered it down the driveway. She was pregnant with Vanessa, although I didn't know about pregnancy and wouldn't have recognized it. After a few hours of practice, she declared herself ready for her first trip into Burdock. My five-year old sister Violet and I braced against the dash. The truck jerked, the engine killed. I sat next to the door, ready to abandon ship if she headed for a tree. It was late April, and Mother planned to enroll me in school.

"We just moved into the Thompson place from Minneapolis," Mother said to the elementary school principal in Burdock. "Victor here is in first grade." She handed him my report card.

The principal scanned the card, looked relieved to see good grades. "No need to register him for one month of school," the principal said. "We'll put him in second grade in the fall." He chucked Violet's chin. "And the little girl in first." She buried her face in Mother's dress.

Dad continued to work at the Ford plant Monday through Saturday noon, and caught the Soo Line to Burdock at one, arriving at three. Violet and I waited at the depot among small assemblies of locals, some of whom would be in military uniform. The train hissed and squealed to a stop, muffling the sobs of mothers, wives, and girlfriends. Dad was first to detrain.

"What did you get done this week?" He was refreshed from a nap and eager for news of the farm. He walked with the characteristic slump-shouldered farmer gait, as if carrying a 90-pound milk can in each hand. He wore his factory clothes—gray shirt and pants and black cap. Outside the factory, he removed the UAW pin from the cap's visor. "Don't need R. J. Thomas or Walter Reuther," he proclaimed. "I can think of better ways to spend those union dues." I carried his laundry bag; Violet carried his lunch pail, knowing it held a treat.

"The Germans came and hoed the pea patch," I said. The contract Dad had signed allowed seller Guy Stearns to plant and harvest this year's crop, giving Dad time to finish his work at the plant and buy horses or a tractor. "They were P.O.W.s."

"That's prisoners of war," Violet added. "They had guards with them. With rifles. We weren't supposed to talk to them or take pictures. Mom did though, through the kitchen window."

"Was Guy Stearns there?" Dad asked.

"Yeah. He bossed them around and then went to town for lunch meat and bread. Mother made sandwiches."

"Keep an eye on Mr. Stearns," Dad said. "I don't trust him."

May, the month of the Blessed Virgin. Mother cleared a lamp table in front of the parlor window and prepared an altar. Lacey curtain panels flared down to a white-draped silverware chest. Bouquets of plum blossoms on either side scented the room. Between the blossoms, atop the chest, stood a statue of the Blessed Virgin, arms at her side, face down, a faded blue veil with a gold stripe along the border. In front of the statue were two votive candles.

May Day

Dad took a three day vacation from the plant, time to spruce up the farm, think about his future, and relish the new life he had created. The morning burst with spring life—phoebes building a nest in the eaves, buds on the apple trees, rhubarb leaves as big as kites. The peas, about five acres of the forty, were four or five inches tall, standing in neat, weed-less rows. An adjacent ten acre patch was plowed, disked, and harrowed, ready for corn planting. The earth was warm and black and friable. Dad sifted a handful of dirt through his fingers. "My cornfield," he said. "Probably a hundred bushels an acre."

He replaced a window in the barn and hammered together a pen for chickens that Mother had ordered. He reclaimed barbed wire and a few posts from a former pasture and fenced in a yard for the milk cows he would buy. Mother grubbed out a garden. I worked with Dad; Violet sat in the dirt near Mother. Occasionally, I would hear Mother singing, her bird-like voice in the still morning air.

On this day, O beautiful Mother,
On this day, we give you our love.

Mid-morning, Violet carried a jar of coffee to Dad and me in the new pasture, weeds up to her waist. Dad set the posthole digger aside, poured coffee into the blue enameled mug, and handed it to me. He drank from the jar. I'll never forget that moment. Or the taste of the coffee—lukewarm, sweet, and creamy.

When we finished, Dad eyed the fence and declared it straight, the corner posts supported, the pasture small but adequate. He cut weeds from under the barn eaves and dragged a stock tank to catch rain water. He oiled and nailed hinges on the barn door.

Mother had reclaimed enough space for a row of potatoes and onions. After planting, I saw her stand and place her hands on her stomach. Then she sang.

*On this day, we ask to share
Dearest Mother, thy sweet care.*

Neighbors up the hill, the Borks, had kids our age. Mrs. Bork, a fleshy lady with a thick Germanic accent and bowed legs, brought a hot-dish down for supper. Her husband, she said, was a blacksmith, and a good one. He had a shop in Burdock and would be pleased to weld our machinery or shoe our horses. "He's a self-taught preacher," she said. "And he fancies that someday, he'll get the call. A big congregation in a rich town. All he'll do then is save souls." She laughed. "In the meantime, he works over the forge all day and comes home black except the whites of his eyes."

That night, we heard a knock on the door. Dad was listening to "The FBI in Peace and War" and Mother paged through a seed catalog. Violet and I played pickup sticks, all of us content, happy. Mother looked at the door, then glanced around the room. Boxes of wedding china, linens, crystal and silverware, winter coats were stacked in the parlor. "Oh my goodness," she said. "Not company, I hope."

Dad opened the door. The porch was empty, but on the doorknob hung a basket. A folded paper basket with flowers—lilacs and apple blossoms. The basket sagged when he lifted it. Four pieces of fudge wrapped in wax paper. Fudge. With sugar a wartime rationed item, this was a rare event. I remember the wrapper's crinkle when I opened mine, the aroma of chocolate, the taste of fudge melting on my tongue. Someone outside yelled, "May basket."

Dad looked across the yard. No one. "I know you're out there," he called. "Come on, kids. Let's find them."

I hadn't seen Dad in a playful mood, never before saw him running, jumping over the red coaster wagon, reeling off the pump handle, swinging from clothesline poles. The Bork kids surfaced in the orchard and scattered. They sprang from their hiding places as he approached, running, laughing, screaming. When he neared one of them, he swung in a circle and headed for another. They scrambled through the yard, down the driveway, and home.

Dad ran into the plowed field, scooped a handful of dirt and twirled, the dirt sifting through his fingers. Violet and I, mimicking his gymnastics, ran behind. Mother stood at the porch. "Be careful, Henry. Be careful, children." She picked her way through the dark, holding her stomach and lifting her skirt. "Oh, children, look."

A wedge of moon lit the warm night. Mother stopped at the edge of the plowed field. I circled her, Violet behind me. Dad whirled in and out of view, a dancer on a plowed stage, scooping the fertile earth, releasing it through his fingers like stardust. Behind us, the house was a black silhouette with warm yellow rectangles of light. The farmstead was framed in shades of gray—dark oaks still bare, a skeleton windmill, the black barn beyond. Above it all, the moon lit a pale gray sky. I don't remember more of what was said, only how I felt.

Wednesday, I rose early to walk Dad to the depot to catch the morning train to Minneapolis. He gave me a verbal to-do list and cautioned me to look after Mother and my sister while he was gone. He didn't commission me, didn't impose the power of commander-in-chief, but I felt a transfer of responsibility. And authority.

Later that day, Guy Stearns drove up the driveway, stopped to inspect the peas, and approached the house. "Your dad home?" he asked. "I'm going to wire some electric outlets in the kitchen and I don't want you kids hanging around. Dangerous. Okay?" It seemed reasonable. Mother had complained about not having a place to plug in the toaster. Plus, I had jobs to do, and only three and a half days to do them before Dad returned. Weeds to swathe in the orchard, dead apple tree branches to prune, grape vines to trim. Violet must have been in her bedroom.

The orchard was alive with honey bees, buzzing in low harmonic frequency. Weeds fell in wide swaths before the scythe, creating a carpet, a clearing. Severed apple tree branches oozed a fruity pungency that mixed with the fresh ozone aroma of country air and chlorophyll.

Mr. Stearns walked out the back door as I approached the house. "You better check on your ma," he said. "She's acting kinda weird. Maybe had a stroke or something." He slumped into his truck and spun out of the driveway.

In the house, Mother stood by the sink, her hair mussed, fingering a button on her dress. She said nothing, didn't ask how I was doing, didn't ask if I was hungry, didn't offer me a glass of water. I knew there was a problem. I didn't see new outlets. She stood there, buttoning and unbuttoning her dress, jerking her head from side to side. Then, for the first time, she looked me straight in the eye. "Who are you?" she said. "And what do you want?"

The days, the weeks, the months that followed are a blur. I recall that Dad came home, threatened with arrest for quitting his job. He confronted Guy Stearns on Guy's next visit. I remember Dad's approach. I expected a fist fight.

"What're you talking about?" Guy said. "Is your old lady pointing the finger at me?"

She wasn't. She wasn't pointing the finger at anyone. She wasn't talking. Dad yielded. "The sooner I'm done dealing with you, the better," he said.

"Well, the feeling is neutral," Guy said, and hopped in his truck. I think he meant *mutual*.

Mrs. Bork cared for my little sister Violet at her home. Mother roamed the house as if trying to orient herself, trying to remember who and where she was, and who we were. When Dad brought her to the local clinic, the doctor diagnosed her condition as chronic fatigue. Prescription: bed rest. Prognosis: this too shall pass.

May Day

Japan surrendered in August ending the war, and our world celebrated. Horns honked on Main Street. Henry Johnson, proprietor of Johnson Drugs, offered ice cream cones to all kids. The Last Chance poured free beer. Dad drove Mother to Our Lady's.

Violet and I started school in September, and Vincent was born in October. When presented with the infant, Dad reported that Mother looked surprised. "What have we here?" she asked.

Mother stayed in the hospital and was transferred to the psych ward. Dad defended his decision to move to the farm in a session before a counselor, with Mother, Violet, and me present. "I did the right thing," he insisted. "The city was no place to raise kids. She," he pointed a nervous finger at Mother, "had allergies to smoke, and we lived a stone's throw from the railroad switch yard. She was afraid of bums who drifted over from the tracks offering to mow the yard in summer or shovel the sidewalk for a sandwich. I never thought she'd get the wits scared out of her, out there in the country."

Mother sat, twisting her robe belt, her head down, her hands quivering. Her hair, frizzled from home permanents, sprouted gray roots from the center part. She pinched her ear when she listened, or touched her chin. Never had eye contact with the counselor, Dad, even with us kids.

She stuttered a nervous laugh when asked a question, as if creating time to remember. She didn't disagree, didn't argue, didn't respond.

Back in her hospital room, she crossed herself in front of the statue of Mary, bowed her head, and prayed.

At the social worker's recommendation, Dad offered Vincent up for adoption. My aunts and uncles had all the kids they wanted and more than they could afford. Dad must have known he couldn't raise a baby; Violet and I would be challenge enough. I haven't seen Vincent since he left that October morning in the social worker's car. Mother was in and out of hospitals, institutions, and clinics. She even tried a chiropractor. Nothing. A faith healer pulled in the drive one morning—suit, tie, hat, a male driver beside him. Said he had heard of Mother's plight from a prayer list at First Methodist. Would she consent to his Laying On of the Hands?

"Absolutely not," Dad said. "And I hope you remember the road you came in on."

For years, I didn't marry, didn't feel the confidence to give myself to another. Never was certain Mother's condition wouldn't be mine. Or my children's. Caring for her and Dad provided a credible excuse. Mother was in and out of hospitals, mental health clinics, treatment centers. Dad was torn between obligations, trying to patch a life out of caring for Mother and caring for the farm.

I met Jeanine in the psych ward of Jordan Memorial Hospital during one of Mother's stays. She exemplified tender loving care and treated Mother as if she were her own. Within six months we married. We joked about her caring more for Mother than she cared for me.

"There's a world of difference between caring for a patient and caring for a husband," she said. "And your mother's more of a challenge."

Mother's stays at home between admissions grew shorter. Meantime, Dad's arthritis affected his farm chores—lifting milk cans, harnessing the horses, and cleaning the barn. Mother had added a few pounds, what with her new life being sedentary, and needed help rising from the bed and sitting on the commode. Dad didn't trust himself to lift her. She was no longer an obligation; she was a burden. He didn't discuss it with me, but I read his weary eyes. "Sell the livestock, Dad," I said. "We'll find a nursing home for Mother."

Jeanine knew of Good Shepherd from former patients who were transferred there. She called for an appointment. No vacancies, they said, but we'll put you on the list. They called soon after, and in April Mother's apartment was ready for inspection.

Without routine and family or farm responsibilities, Dad's wanderlust reignited. He consulted the United Farm Agency catalog again, and found a *farmette* in south Texas that appealed to him. "No more winters for me," he said, "no snow tires, no mackinaws, no wood splitting." Violet, also single, accompanied him and shared driving. In Texas, she took a part-time job as a motel maid to finance her trip home. Instead, she fell for the manager, and they married within weeks.

At Good Shepherd, Mother was reclusive at first, but grew to accept, even anticipate the structure, the routine. Breakfast at 7:30, crafts at 10, lunch at noon, bingo at 3, dinner at 5:30. Jeanine continued to treat her as her nurse, not her mother-in-law. "We were sitting in the Gathering Room today," Jeanine told me, "looking at a magazine photograph of an orchard in full bloom. Your mother stared at the picture, then murmured, 'Plum blossoms, Violet.' She thought I was her daughter. She called me *Violet*."

Days later, Good Shepherd's ad hoc social director Pearl met me in the lobby. "We have a tradition here of monthly entertainment days. That's next Wednesday. Part of the entertainment is celebrating patients' birthdays. Your mother's birthday is in May, isn't it? We'll sing to her, give her a small gift. Can you join us? Good." She held my arm. "I'll walk you to your mother's apartment. By the way, the entertainment this month is tea leaf reading. The Old Bones Woman is coming, and we're excited." We stood at Mother's door. She patted my arm. "You can decide what to tell her. And when."

Jeanine had bought a dress for Mother, a frilly dress appropriate for a birthday party. When Mother opened the box, she said, "Oh, Violet. You shouldn't have." She raised her head, expressing surprise at speaking five words. I choked. Jeanine unfolded the dress and held it in front of Mother. She turned her toward a mirror on the closet door. "Pretty," she said. Mother admired her reflection. "Pretty," she repeated.

Jeanine and I sat on either side of Mother in Good Shepherd's Gathering Room. Pearl stood in front of the residents and their guests and announced the day's program. "But first," she winked, "we have a birthday to celebrate. Happy birthday, Adeline." She clapped her hands; the audience followed. Mother dropped her head and turned, her fingers toying with her mouth.

"Adam," Pearl continued. "Will you do us the honors?"

Adam, a dwarfish curmudgeon with wispy white hair and a cocky sneer, ambled to the piano. Once his fingers touched the keys, he tilted his head and transformed, became animated and joyful. He began with a coloratura's trill up and down the keyboard, the melody tainted with unintended sharps and flats. He followed with an improvised introduction, then struck the keys hard at *Happy birthday to you*. The crowd sang. Mother wore the gold cross necklace Dad had given her and twirled it around her finger. She blushed at the applause. Jeanine accepted the gift from Pearl.

"And now," Pearl announced back in front of her audience, "we have this month's entertainer, the Old Bones Woman." She pointed to a woman who stood in the doorway behind us. Grandmotherly, with silver hair, a generous smile, gypsy shawl, a long skirt. And a necklace of bones. "The Old Bones Woman will read your tea leaves. Won't that be exciting?" Pearl asked. "The birthday girl will be first. While the rest of us are waiting our turn, we'll play bingo."

Mother clung to Jeanine's arm as they walked to the kitchen. There, the Old Bones Woman unpacked cups and saucers of fine china in a variety of patterns, all the cups with wide diameter bowls. "The better for distribution of tea leaves," she said. She poured water in a teapot and placed it on a burner. "Happy birthday, Adeline. Why don't you sit there, and I'll sit here." She pointed to a small table near the door. "You two are welcome to stay if you wish."

I wished, but Jeanine said, "We'll wait in the dining room, if that's okay with you, Mother." Adeline tossed a desperate glance at us, then smiled. We stood at the door.

"My, what a pretty dress," Old Bones Woman said.

"Pretty," Mother repeated. "From Violet."

"Would you like to select a tea cup?"

Adeline stared at a cup and saucer of translucent coppery color and a soft blue outer band. "My wedding china," she said.

The teapot whistled.

"What we'll do is pour a cup of tea." The Old Bones Woman spooned tea leaves in the cup. "I'll ask you to drink it down until the leaves slosh in the bottom. Then we'll tip the remainder into the saucer. The leaves in the saucer will tell me about your past. The leaves remaining in the cup will tell me about your future." On her tablet of paper, she drew two circles intersected into quarters. "The position of the handle is at the bottom. That represents today," she said. "Moving clockwise, we'll read your leaves in weekly, monthly, or yearly intervals, whatever you'd like."

Adeline looked at us standing in the doorway, looked as if asking for help. She twirled her cross necklace.

"We'll read whatever the leaves suggest," Old Bones Woman said.

Adeline sipped the tea.

"A heavy concentration of leaves in any position suggests heavy activity," Old Bones Woman continued. "No leaves, no activity. A scattering of leaves suggests motion. Small particles of leaves suggest small objects, trivial events, or children. Large particles are large objects, important events, adults." She glanced at the door and saw Jeanine and me watching, listening.

Mother swirled the final remaining tea, placed the saucer over the cup, and inverted it. Old Bones Woman oriented the cup's handle to the bottom and diagramed the pattern of leaves in the saucer onto the paper. "Interesting," she said. "Much activity a long time ago. Not much recently." She did the same with the cup, diagramming the pattern of leaves.

She held the saucer at eye level and studied it. "From this heavy concentration here at the beginning, the leaves tell me that many years ago, you witnessed a significant life-changing event. I see adults. I see children. I see motion. People moving fast, running. It feels like night, but I see light. It feels like outside." She paused and studied the saucer, then the diagram. "After that, the tea leaves are layered. I can't see through them. Does any of this make sense? Children? Moonlight? Running?"

"Violet," Mother cried. "Victor." She reached for the children.

"And the motion? The running?"

She raised her hand to her forehead, as if recalling a faint memory. "Henry. Be careful, Henry. Be careful, children." She massaged her stomach and rocked in the chair. "Oh, children. Look."

"And the light? Is it moonlight?"

She raised her head. "The moon. The May Day moon."

When relating this story after she regained her voice, Mother would add, "I looked up and saw the moon. Beside the moon, two stars flickered like votive candles. And there in the moon's shadows, Our Lady of May, face looking down at me, hands at her sides, open palms. Looking down at me, telling me of her sorrow, the sorrow of all mothers."

Cameo

Back then, the Avalon movie theater, a rococo style building on the corner of Main and Elm, dominated Main Street. Small yellow lights of the marquee raced up and down the vertical standard where AVALON was backlit in red. Around the canopy that extended over the sidewalk, FORREST GUMP was backlit in green. Teenagers mingled under the canopy watching cars pass, staring at those they didn't recognize. Early summer rain was falling, and reflections of the marquee and stoplight on the wet pavement fascinated Elaine.

"Isn't it beautiful? It looks like Christmas." She was driving with Mason to their new home in Browns Prairie and had wondered aloud whether the movers had set up the master bedroom and placed the box of linens in a conspicuous spot as she had requested.

"Avalon," Elaine continued. "Isn't that where Sir Lancelot went to die?"

"King Arthur," Mason said. He slouched in his seat and stared out the window.

They continued on Main to Hickory Avenue and turned toward their new home.

"It looks different at night," Elaine said in front of the house. "Smaller, more secluded." They removed a few pieces of luggage from the car and walked up the sidewalk. Elaine unlocked the door, took a breath, and stepped inside. The house was warm and damp. Musty. She turned lights on and adjusted the thermostat, then walked through rooms sidestepping furniture and moving boxes. "Are you hungry?" she asked from the kitchen. "I'll fix a light snack."

Mason stood in the hall, scanning the interior.

"If you're tired, I'll make the bed," she said.

Mason continued to stand, as if seeing the house for the first time.

"Let me help with your medications," she said. "You must be worn out."

"Quit treating me like your hospice patient," Mason snapped. "I didn't return here to die. I returned to rejuvenate."

Elaine reached for his hands and nodded. She knew his rationale for relocating. To escape critics and editors and students who crowded his life. To grant him unfettered time and space to create poetry. To escape every demand except his contract with *The Poet* magazine. He would honor that.

"But your internist's diagnosis. His prescriptions," Elaine reminded him.

"To hell with him. I've written my own prescription for a hiatus out of the spotlight."

Mason had spent his youth here in Browns Prairie and left to enter the university, always proclaiming his disdain for small town life, his intention never to return. For the magazine, he had developed what he called the Smell Test. If his poetry was clear enough to be understood by anyone in this rube town, he rewrote it to a higher criterion of obscurity. Elaine, a fellow lecturer at the university, read his monthly submissions before sending them to the publisher. His article, "The Last Word," appeared inside the back cover.

"That third stanza," he'd say, "it's trite in its clarity. Obfuscate it."

Elaine had always read his poetry, although it didn't appeal to her. She understood an occasional line or stanza, but she found his poetry affected. His disregard for cadence, his archaic language, his bizarre subject matter alienated her.

She had begun writing poems of her own, with no intention of publishing or sharing them with Mason. She'd note a phrase or line he had edited out that resonated with her and create a context for it, soften the impact, and combine it with a figure of speech.

She could see a poem in reflections on the wet street, the soft curve of a red umbrella bracing into straight-line rain. But Elaine would defer to Mason, regarding him as the resident poet. She accepted his privilege of gender.

Their new home, or temporary relocation as Mason preferred, was two blocks from Main Street on Hickory Avenue, the avenues named alphabetically for trees—Ash, Basswood, Cottonwood, Dogwood, Elm, etc. as was common in the Midwest. The house had been built in the rush of residential construction after World War II, and had been updated and restored for resale. It had a small yard, aluminum siding, and combination windows, all designed for minimum maintenance. Elaine was sold when she discovered the back screened porch rendered private by a curtain of ivy.

The doorbell rang early on their first morning while Mason slept. Elaine, with no idea where to find her robe, slipped a windbreaker over her nightgown. She opened the door to a woman with an elaborate coiffure—spit curls and a blond chignon under a spray of pink rosebuds.

"Good morning. I'm your next-door neighbor, Verna. Call me Verney. Welcome to Browns Prairie." She handed Elaine a plastic-wrapped plate of cinnamon rolls and a business card. "I'm the town hair stylist, and your first visit to Salon Chic is courtesy of the management."

"Well, thank you. Which house is yours?"

Verney pointed. "The man-less looking bungalow that needs paint. The one with the ruby red Cadillac in the drive. Beside me is Betty Brockett. Her daughter just enlisted in the Army. We get together for coffee on my day off. You'll have to join us."

"Thanks. I'd like that."

Days later, when Elaine called Salon Chic, Verney said, "Come on in this afternoon. I only take appointments for Friday."

Elaine brought the telephone to the upstairs work area she had organized for Mason—his desk, chair, writing pads and pens, reference books, all waiting. The desk in front of a window faced a dying apple tree. Mason joined her.

"I'm going to get groceries and have my hair done. The phone and the salon number are on the table if you need me."

"Looks like a bird built a nest," Mason said, pointing to the tree and tapping his pen against a blank page.

"That's a robin. Robin, apple tree, nest. Man, new home, creation. There's a metaphor for you."

"Maybe in an earlier life."

Salon Chic nestled between Our Own Hardware and Main Street Family Shoes, its display window decorated with mannequins sporting hairstyles and wardrobes never seen in Browns Prairie. Inside, Elaine whiffed the alkaline smell of permanents.

"Good morning. Come in. Have a seat," Verney said. "I'm rinsing Rosalie's beautiful silver tresses." Rosalie, with her head leaned back into the sink and eyes clamped shut, wiggled her fingers in hello.

"Nice shop, Verney," Elaine said. "Tasteful décor. Is that a Renoir behind you?"

"Yes, 'Combing Girl.' You're the first person to identify the artist. It's a nod to the French heritage of the establishment, Salon Chic." She fluffed a towel over Rosalie's head. "Rosalie and I are catching up on the town gossip, what little there is. And what we don't know, we guess." She giggled. "Right, Rosalie? Most of the sinners in this town have worn themselves out."

Rosalie nodded her head.

Elaine sat on a yellow plastic chair with chrome arm rests. A country western music station played from ceiling speakers.

"And the saints," Verney continued. "What's the point?"

"Saints?" Rosalie said. "Name one."

"Well, Pastor Granquist was. Until the youth camping trip. And Sheriff Harkness was. Until he negotiated a plea bargain with Mrs. Krupp in his squad car. And the high school librarian. Until she was caught buying porn with district funds. You're right. We're short on saints."

Elaine laughed at their easy conversation, watched Rosalie chuckle and give Verney a thumbs-up. She fingered a stack of hairstyle magazines, then selected a dog-eared *People*.

"Are all the snowbirds back in your neighborhood?" Verney asked Rosalie.

"Back and bragging about the good life at Villa del Sol. I've seen pictures of those trailer parks. Twelve-foot trailers on sixteen-foot lots. Reach out and touch someone."

"Come on, Rosalie. You're jealous. What could be more fun than beading all morning and backgammon all afternoon?"

Elaine looked up from her magazine, smiling at their easy repartee.

"And I've heard the traffic lights stay green for ten minutes so the old geezers can make it across the street. Five mile an hour speed limits. With speed bumps. No thanks."

Elaine dug for her grocery list and wrote *Snowbirds, beading and backgammon, speed bumps.*

Back home, the house was quiet. Elaine walked upstairs. "How is the August submission progressing?"

"What are you talking about?" Mason sat in a wing-back chair reading a book.

"Your submission to *The Poet*. It's due to be mailed Monday, June tenth."

"I don't know what you're talking about. Where's my sweater?"

Elaine found a sweater in the closet and handed it to him. "Have you started anything?" She walked to his desk by the window. Crumpled sheets of paper littered the floor. The writing pad was scribbled with scratched-out lines and torn, as with the point of a pen.

The Poet paid a handsome fee for Mason's articles. In them, he chose an arcane poetry topic, illustrated its use with a published poem, deconstructed it, and offered a contemporary example of his own poetry. The letters to the editor gushed with praise for his scholarship. Names of his published books appeared at the end of the article, keeping sales active and royalty checks arriving quarterly.

Elaine glanced at Mason huddled in the chair. She would have to write the article, select the example, and find a poem by Mason to illustrate it. Or create one of her own. She picked up his pad and walked from the room.

At the kitchen table, she stared, recollecting last year's columns. For the August topic, she selected Free Verse and Robert Frost's "Out, Out" as her example. There must be fodder in

Browns Prairie for a new poem, she reasoned. The man-less house on Hickory Avenue. The modest bungalow with the ruby red Cadillac in the drive. Everyone in Browns Prairie would identify the subject, but that would not be a problem.

On Monday, Elaine mailed her article to *The Poet* after a perfunctory reading to Mason. "Frost," he huffed. "Common poetry for common people."

Elaine was gratified with her effort, felt the article had sufficient gravitas to pass for a Mason original. It asked rhetorical questions about associations she couldn't answer. More important, it piqued excitement in her own poems dealing with ordinary themes of life in Browns Prairie.

"I close my salon Mondays," Verney said when she called Elaine. "Betty's coming for coffee this afternoon. Betty Brockett, our next door neighbor. Join us."

"I will. I finished an important task this morning and I feel like celebrating."

Verney answered the door and swung her arm. "Welcome to my kitchen." Sunshine yellow cabinets with blue countertops wrapped around the room. At the far end, a table set with cups and saucers and covered with a red-checkered cloth snuggled in an alcove.

Elaine hugged Verney. "Neighbors," she said. "It's been a long time. What a cozy spot. Is that Fiestaware?" Three plates in primary colors hung on trellised ivy wallpaper.

Betty tapped the door, walked in, and introduced herself. "Welcome, Elaine. I'm Betty," she said, extending her hand. "Are you unpacked and settled in?"

"I'm not sure where we'll put all our stuff," Elaine said. "We could furnish two houses."

"I thought the same thing when I watched the men unload the moving van," Verney said. "Please sit. By the way, if you decide to sell the red velvet settee . . ." She pointed to herself.

"I haven't seen your husband," Betty said.

"He's recuperating. He'll be out walking soon, I'm sure."

"Not that we see a lot of men on this block," Verney said. "We call this Grass Widow Row."

The coffee pot gurgled to a climactic finish and flooded the kitchen with an inviting aroma.

"About your husband's recuperation," Betty said, "I'm an RN at Good Shepherd Assisted Living. If you need help, call me."

"And if you need advice, call me," Verney said.

"I understand your daughter joined the Army," Elaine said to Betty, sipping from a pink Melmac cup.

"Yes. Helen's in advanced basic training at Fort Campbell. Electronics and Computers. It's all Greek to me."

"I have a daughter too," Verney said. "Desiree. Got some of her mother's bad habits, I'm afraid. She's an instructor at Arthur Murray Dance Studio in the Cities."

"Your husband's condition," Betty repeated. "What's his diagnosis?"

"His internist suspects early onset of Alzheimer's. It may just be fatigue."

"Memory loss? Depression? Mood swings?"

Elaine nodded.

"Trust your doctor. Alzheimer's is the geriatric malady of choice these days. We have brochures, if you're interested."

Elaine shook her head, *No*.

Betty placed her hand on Elaine's arm. "Let me know if you need help."

"Let's lighten the conversation," Verney said.

"Let's," said Elaine. "There must be a story behind that ruby red Cadillac."

"Do you want the true story? Or the one I've been accused of?"

"Both."

"Well," Verney stalled. "How about a fresh cinnamon roll with your coffee first?"

At home, Elaine scribbled notes from their conversation and wrote:

> *Ruby red Cadillac*
> *In waiting by the bungalow*
> *While Her Highness preens*
> *Bleached blond hair piled high*
> *Beneath sunglass tiara*
> *Then taps stiletto heels down the walk*
> *To lounge in leather throne.*
>
> *Whose ruby red blood spilled*
> *For Coupe de Ville extravagance?*

By August, when Mason slept through breakfast and had to be wakened for lunch, Elaine called Betty at Good Shepherd. "I've accepted Mason's limitations. Now I have to accept mine. Please come." That afternoon, after her shift, Betty arrived.

"You offered to help me with Mason." Elaine stood in the kitchen with Betty and poured tea. "He's upstairs. I told him you were coming. I'll ask him to join us. I'm curious what your diagnosis will be."

"Impression, not diagnosis," Betty said. "Lord knows I've seen enough of them to diagnose. What are the latest developments? What will I see and hear?"

"He quit writing. He has a contract with a poetry magazine for a monthly article which he's ignoring. I started covering for him. Three articles. So far, so good. In fact, I'm enjoying it. Started writing my own poetry."

"And Mason?"

"He sleeps a lot. Often stays in his pajamas all day. Talks to himself. Scribbles a few lines, then crinkles the paper. Walks from window to desk to bed. Only leaves to use the bathroom. Hasn't shaved for a week. Talks lucid one minute, irrational the next."

"This sounds more like floor duty than a coffee break. Ask him down. And don't coach him."

Elaine walked to the stairway. "Mason," she called. "Betty's here." The door opened, and Mason appeared wearing a burgundy silk smoking jacket. He descended the stairs, dapper as a Hollywood star.

"Good morning," he chirped. "How nice of you to come. So you're interested in my current opus. You teach, I understand. The university, I presume. You must know my friend, my confessional poet friend John Berryman."

"I haven't read him. Welcome home, Mason. I'm your neighbor Betty Brockett."

"Well, isn't this a lucky coincidence. For you and me. Serendipitous, wouldn't you say? The poet in one house, the professor in the next. I presume my collections are in your every syllabus."

Betty threw a lost look at Elaine.

Mason sat in a leather chair and motioned Betty to sit. "Welcome home, you say. Thomas Wolfe be damned. You *can* go home again. 'It was the hour of twilight on a soft spring day toward the end of April . . .' Such genius. Makes a man proud to be a fellow writer."

"Mason, would you like tea?" Elaine asked.

Mason nodded. "A spot of tea would be fine." Elaine walked to the kitchen. She heard Betty ask, "Where did you live in Browns Prairie in your youth?"

Elaine handed the cup to Mason.

"On the east side. My father was a man of the cloth. Presided over the Presbyterian flock. Well educated. Well read. A fish out of water here, I'm afraid."

"The town must have changed since you left."

"We returned occasionally. My first wife was from Browns Prairie. Her father was president of the bank. They had a summer home on Spirit Lake. We weekend-ed there."

Elaine cringed. She sat opposite Mason, eyes fixed on him.

"Spirit Lake is beautiful," Betty continued. "We often . . ."

"Are you a Browns Prairie native? You may have known my father-in-law, my ex-father-in-law, Paul Sinclair. I married his only daughter, Natalie. A sweet girl, charming but plain. Not *to the manner born*, as they say."

Elaine lifted a hand to her forehead, closed her eyes, and shook her head.

"I don't recall either one of them," Betty said, tossing a glance at Elaine.

"Paul was rightfully placed in a small town, a very small town. He could negotiate a crop loan but was frightfully wanting when it came to high finance. But perhaps I shouldn't be so critical. After all, he financed my doctorate."

Elaine watched Mason tip the cup to his lips, watched him sip his tea and study Betty. "You look familiar," he said. "Did I deliver the keynote for a poetry symposium you hosted at the university?"

"I'm sorry. I don't teach at the university. I'm a nurse here in town at Good Shepherd."

Mason jerked forward, spilling his tea. "You're not a professor? You don't know my poetry? Well, what are you? An imposter? What am I to make of this fraud you've perpetrated?"

Elaine rushed to Mason, took his cup, and held his arm.

"An honest mistake, Doctor," Betty said. "You made an erroneous assumption from the start. You . . ."

"*I* made an erroneous assumption? *I'm* at fault? *I* acted the dilettante? Get out of my house, you charlatan. A nurse, for God's sake. And at an old folks home. How pedestrian is that?" He stood. Elaine struggled to steady him while balancing the cup. He shook her off and tromped up the stairs.

Elaine accompanied Betty to the door. "I'll call you when he settles down."

"He may have lost his manners, but he still has his vocabulary," Betty chuckled on the porch step. The early summer air was still, like the quiet after the storm.

"Words are his stock in trade."

"You asked for my diagnosis. I promised you my observations." Betty took Elaine's hands in hers. "He has issues. It may be the onset of Alzheimer's. It may be another form of dementia. Some are treatable. I suggest you see a physician."

Elaine looked at the yard, the hosta garden, the apple tree. "Mason won't agree to that."

"You're right. So his condition will degrade." She squeezed Elaine's hands. "My advice to you is take care of yourself. You won't be doing him any favors if your condition degrades along with his."

"I can do that with poetry." She felt lightened by the word, held back a smile.

"I've heard writing is therapeutic. Perhaps poetry can be your therapy. Is it true that beginning poets write only about birth, death, and falling in love?"

"None of that in my poetry. I only write about things I know. Interesting that Mason doesn't appear in any of my poems."

Betty hugged her. "Keep writing."

"Do you give senior discounts? I have my AARP card." Elaine stood in the doorway of the Salon Chic, pretending to flash a plastic card.

"My rate schedule has your discount built in, neighbor. All my ladies are eligible. Come on in. You're sounding chipper today."

"It's been a productive morning." Elaine collapsed in a waiting room chair.

"Betty says you're writing poetry. Good for you. And how is the Professor?"

"She mentioned him too? No change. He sleeps late and waits for me to bring him breakfast. At least I don't have to worry about him boiling oatmeal and burning the house down."

"You remember Rosalie, don't you?" Verney gestured with a comb. "She was here when you had your first styling."

Rosalie wiggled her fingers. "Hi."

"Rosalie and I were talking about the tourist trade in town. All that big city money. Guess the girls in the café are getting tips for a change. And the Antique Boutique is bustling. Gotta clean out a few more basements and stock up the place."

Elaine thought of boxes of vases, wall hangings, table lamps that decorated their city house that were not unpacked at the new smaller house on Hickory Avenue.

"I heard an Aunt Jemima pitcher brought seventy-five dollars," Rosalie added.

"Those tourists," Verney said. "They fall into two groups. First, there's the cheapies from Iowa who drive their motor home full of groceries and tow a motorboat full of gas and bait. They plunk down by a lake in the county park, then leave a week later with every cent they brought." She motioned to Elaine. "That's a fact."

"That's not true," Rosalie said. "They send their kids to scrounge aluminum cans out of dumpsters and sell them to the recycling center before they leave."

"You're right. I forgot about that. Then there's the second group. The *noblesse oblige*, if I may impress you with my French."

"The what?" Rosalie asked as she watched Verney in the wall mirror.

"The *noblesse oblige* of the *nouveau riche*."

"Oh, now I get it," Rosalie said and shrugged her shoulders.

"Funny how a couple issues of *Elle* improves one's French. Anyway, as I was saying . . ."

"Hold it. Hold it," Elaine interrupted. "Let me make a few notes. I feel a poem coming on."

"I hope I don't show up in any of your poems," Verney said.

"You may recognize a few references. Rest assured, I change the names to protect the guilty."

"As I was saying, the second group are the moneyed set who find us amusing, but dumb." She shook her head, then handed Rosalie a mirror. "They walk into the antique shop and wave a cast iron frying pan at Marcie." She grabbed the mirror back and dangled it by the handle. "'How much for this old used pan,' they ask, knowing full well it's a Griswold and worth every cent she's asking for it."

"Remember the two that came here in skinny jeans last week?" Rosalie asked. "Wanted fingernail polish."

"Not fingernail polish, Honey, fingernail lacquer. And not only fingernail lacquer, but OPI fingernail lacquer. Sorry ladies. Could I interest you in some Avon? Then one said, 'Oh, I just must buy something. This shop is so cute, so quaint.'"

Elaine shrugged her shoulders. "That's one of my discoveries about life in the city and life in a small town," she said, paging through an old *Redbook*. "Many of my city friends are sugar-coated, but they can be sour inside. When they want to get rid of me on the phone or in the checkout lane, they say, 'Let's do lunch, soon,' knowing full well it'll never happen." She glanced at Verney. "My small town friends go about their own business and pay no attention to me. But when I need them, they're there. They'll do lunch, they'll tow my car, they'll loan me a cup of sugar."

"Slow down," Rosalie said. "You may be overstating your case to make a point. Every silver lining has a cloud, you know."

"Speaking of silver," Verney said, lifting the cape off Rosalie's shoulders, "your crowning glory couldn't be more *beau monde*."

Rosalie smiled. "*Merci beaucoup, Vernais.*"

What am I to do? Elaine pondered, pen in hand, poetic lines tumbling in her brain. Mason's article was due in three weeks. Was she to write her poetry or his? Or both? And how long before she wrote his letter of resignation? She thumbed through notebooks she kept in the kitchen, in the car, on the bedside table. She had jotted the colorful idioms, the time-worn clichés, the clever turns of a phrase she heard from the mailman, the grocery clerk, the gas station attendant. And the girls at Salon Chic. She searched her notes from the last visit—notes of "French Impressions," and wrote:

> *You in jaunty* beret *sit*
> *At* Bistro Petit, *corner table*
> *Under Renoir's* giclee *print*
> The Luncheon of the Boating Party
> *Little Sparrow trills* La vie en rose
>
> *A* coup de grace, *this spot*
> *For intimate* tete-a-tete
> *The* café, *the song, the you*
> *Is this* déjà vu? *Don't ask*
> *I shall not risk* faux pas

Cameo

I consider pinot noir
To complement filet mignon
Garcon *charges bearing* Evian
Bon appetit, *he says. May I suggest*
Chateaubriand?

Yes, with French fries

Touche

"I want to thank you for your inspiration. You're such a wellspring of poetic expression." Elaine called Verney after reading her expanding collection of poems. "I can trace many poems to conversations in your salon. What do I owe you for the favor?"

"That's what friends are for," Verney sang. "And I'm glad you called. Saves me a nickel. You can return the favor. Desiree is coming home this weekend. She's on a three-day break. My brother Brian is driving her, and I can't handle him myself. Join us for dinner. I want you to meet Desiree."

Elaine tapped her pen on the table. "Verney, I have to keep an eye on Mason."

"You'll be next door." She waited. "I could ask one of my young clients to sit with him a couple hours."

"I want to come, but I'm uncertain." Elaine looked up the stairs and listened for Mason.

"If it's Brian you're nervous about, not to worry. He's been married three times, and he's not looking. And he doesn't know you exist. Brian's an excellent cook. Do you like lamb?"

Mason. How long had it been since she attended a dinner party? A simple dinner party of friends. No speeches, no glad handing, no posturing. No impressions to make, no reputations to destroy. Mason. Why was everything complicated with him?

"I want to meet Desiree. I'll be there."

Elaine stood at Verney's door at six. Inside she heard laughter, music. Smoke coiled from a charcoal grill in the side yard. Lamb and herbs. Rosemary. Brian appeared, tongs and platter in hand. "Hello, you must be Elaine. Right on time."

"And you must be Brian." Elaine offered her hand to shake and realized his hands were occupied. *Younger than I expected*, Elaine thought. He wore a black chef's apron with white lettering "Why does HAPPY have to be only an HOUR?"

"I'll take the chops off so they can rest for a few minutes while we have refreshments. Go on in. Verney is setting the table."

Candles flickered on either side of a bouquet of roses and reflected in the stemware. Napkins folded like origami sat on plates. Verney, in a lipstick red hostess gown, placed silverware around three settings. Elaine stopped. "Verney, it's beautiful. I didn't know this was a formal affair. Where's Desiree?"

"Oh, you know young people. She wanted to be with friends. She said she'd be back early. She wants to meet you."

"I'll bet." Elaine sniffed a rose. "It's been a busy day for me. Why did they put the laundry in the basement of a two-story house? How many times did I go up and down those stairs lugging baskets of wet clothes? I wanted to hang the linens outside on the clothesline."

"You met Brian. What do you think?" Verney refolded a napkin and winked.

"What do you mean what do I think? I think he's your brother. I think from the aroma he's a good cook. I think I'm nervous being away from Mason."

"Relax. I'll ask Brian to mix you a gin and tonic."

"I'll have to take it easy on the alcohol. I skipped lunch today so I'd have a hearty appetite."

Brian entered, bearing a platter of sizzling chops like crown jewels and presented it to Elaine. She cupped the aroma to her nose and swooned.

"Have a chair. Relax," Brian said. Elaine walked into the living room and sat on the sofa. Copies of *Good Housekeeping* and *Cosmopolitan* were fanned on the coffee table. She looked out the window, wishing she could see her house.

"Here's to Sis's new neighbor." Brian brought an iced glass to Elaine. "She says you're a poet. Cheers." They clinked glasses, then he set his glass on a table. "Don't look," he said and slipped the apron over his head.

Elaine turned her head, embarrassed, then recovered. "I'm a self-declared poet at this point. Unpublished." She sipped the drink, surprised at its mild flavor, its refreshing chill. "Nice," she said, raising her glass. "And what do you do when you aren't grilling lamb chops and mixing gin and tonics?" She noticed his eyes, chocolate brown, like Verney's. Noticed his stature, shorter than Mason's, less angular. Softer, rounded lines.

"Freelance photography. And I am published." He smiled at Elaine. "I considered writing, but why should I slave over a thousand words when I can say the same thing in one picture?" He watched her as he sipped his drink. "Now, tell me about your poetry. What do you do with it if you don't publish it?"

"It's part therapy, part escape."

"Sounds part anxiety disorder, part denial." He smiled. "Just kidding."

"Wait 'til you taste the salad dressing Brian concocted," Verney said joining them, tall drink in hand. "And the roasted vegetables. All I'm responsible for is the dessert. How can you go wrong with grasshopper pie?" She sat beside Elaine. "I'm so happy you joined us. And I'm so unhappy that Desiree ditched us."

"I think we have time for one more of these while the chops rest," Brian said. "Join me?"

Verney drained her glass. Elaine did the same.

"Thank you for a delightful dinner, Verney. And Brian. May I take a rain check on dessert?" Elaine wiped her lips and felt a warm fog encase her body. Warm, close, and misty. Candles flickered in a haze. Verney and Brian diffused into fuzzy images. Elaine braced to rise from her chair. "Oops. I think the gin and chardonnay have taken their toll. Excuse me for a few minutes."

In the bathroom, the tile floor was cool. She must have kicked her shoes off under the table. She lowered herself to her knees and spread her hands on the floor. Cool. She reached for a towel and folded it into a pillow and placed it beside the tub.

There was a knock on the door. A pause, then another knock. "Elaine, are you all right? Elaine." The door opened. "Oh, my God," Verney said. "Brian, come help me."

"I'm fine. Just tired. Please. I'm fine." Elaine lifted herself to the tub, to the sink. "I'm sorry, Verney. The wrong ending to a beautiful evening."

"Are you all right? I'll walk you home," Brian said.

"Please. Trust me. I'm all right." She steadied herself on the door, then faltered to the table to retrieve her shoes.

"Leave the dishes, Sis. I'll do them in the morning."

"You don't have to walk me home. I live next door."

"Nonsense."

"Honest, Brian. I'm OK." The voice she heard was not convincing. "I'm concerned about Mason, but I'm OK." Elaine braced against the back of the chair. "Guess I ought to get out more, or not at all," she laughed.

"Thanks for dinner, Sis," Brian said. He kissed Verney on the forehead. "I'll be right back."

"Honest, this isn't necessary," Elaine said on the sidewalk. Brian held her arm against his. "But it was so good to relax and laugh again. I hope Mason slept through the evening." She glanced at her living room window, hoping not to see him. "Verney is such a good neighbor, such a great friend."

She held his arm. "Brian. That's a beautiful name." She hummed the theme from "Brian's Song." "Isn't this where Henri Mancini mysteriously appears out of nowhere?"

"I love the music but I hated the movie. Too sappy for me." Brian slipped his arm over her shoulder. "I hope you get a chance to meet Desiree."

"Oh yes, Desiree. Tell me about her."

"Think second generation Verney." They were at Elaine's door. "I'll wait here while you check Mason. Just in case."

Elaine held the door knob, teetered toward the kitchen table, and braced against the wall. She gripped the banister and climbed the stairs. In the bathroom, she gargled with Listerine and doused her face with cold water.

"He's asleep," she said when she returned a few minutes later and saw Brian in the kitchen. "Thank you for being a gentleman."

"And they said chivalry was dead. Would you like me to sit with you for awhile? I'm a great listener."

Her arm flailed toward the staircase. "Mason is up there."

"How long has it been since he came downstairs at midnight?"

"I'd better call it a day."

"I can see why poetry is your therapy and escape. You have reason to be frustrated. You're attractive, you're talented, you're an interesting person. And you're a full-time caretaker for an invalid husband. You deserve better."

She stared at a cupboard, focusing on a drawer pull. "It's hot in here," she said, fanning herself. "Let's sit on the back porch."

Elaine sat at the table the next morning holding her head in her hands. Her tongue was thick and tasted silvery. She walked to the back porch looking for evidence of the night before and smelled burned scented candles, eucalyptus. She straightened the pillows on the couch, lifting one to her face, wondering if his scent remained. She raised the rattan shades, aligned magazines on the credenza, and returned to the kitchen. In the doorway, she stood where she stood last night and squeezed her arms in her hands. *You're attractive. You're talented. You're an interesting person.* She sat and fingered "The French Connection" poem tucked in the napkin holder.

The bedroom door opened at the top of the stairs. Mason stood in his linen suit, shirt collar open, a Panama straw in his hand. "Good morning," he said, descending. "What a wonderful day for a walk. Will you join me?"

Elaine slid her poem under the centerpiece. "Mason," she said. "You startled me. My, but you look handsome this morning. Let's have coffee first." She rose to pour a cup, hiding her flushed face in a hand towel.

"Have you done something to your hair?" he asked. "You've had it cut. I like it."

"I'm at a loss for words. Thank you. I have a new friend at the town salon. I'm her *experimentee*. I'm so happy you noticed it." Her words sounded rushed.

"How could I not?" He accepted the coffee and sat at the table. "Thank you. Did you sleep well?"

"The usual." And changing the subject, "I've been mulling your article for *The Poet* which is due soon. Any ideas?"

"*The Poet*? Oh, yes. I'm entertaining a concept or two. Perhaps it's time for lighter fare." He pulled the paper from under the centerpiece. "What's this?"

Elaine walked to the cupboard while he scanned the poem. She kept her eyes away from him, opened and closed the silverware drawer, her hands trembling, her heart pounding.

"Where did you find this? I don't remember writing it."

"How does it read, now that it's fresh in your memory?"

"It's clever, but it's not poetry. Expressive, but not literary. Metrical, but not lyrical. It doesn't speak to a higher purpose. It's just a poem. But there's a kernel of whimsical innocence here that deserves development. Someday maybe."

"Let's discuss it later," Elaine said, feeling the kitchen close in on her. "This beautiful day is beckoning. I'll show you the neighborhood."

On the sidewalk, Mason draped his arm over her shoulder. "Are you happy here? Do you miss the convenience of the city? The culture? Your friends?"

Sunlight filtered through ash trees on the boulevard. The Amtrak blew a whistle far on the other end of town. Bicyclists, an older man and woman, approached them on the street and waved. "Nice day for a walk," the man said as they rode by.

Elaine smiled and turned to Mason. "The transplant has taken."

"It was beautiful." Elaine sat across from Betty that evening on her back porch. "Like our early days together."

"Who are you talking about, Brian or Mason?"

"You talked to Verney, didn't you? That was foolish of me. Do I regret it? Yes and no." She laughed. "It'll probably make me a better poet." She looked at the pillow she and Brian had shared.

"You can dismiss it that easily?"

"I won't dismiss it." She stared at Betty. "He boosted my confidence. I found myself scratching my memory for every word he said, every gesture. It was good, but it was foolish indiscretion. When Mason and I walked this morning, it was as if nothing had happened. That was good, too."

"Like maybe too good to last?"

"Perhaps. We walked by your house and I mentioned your name. He didn't make the connection with your visit."

"Good thing. What's next?" Betty assumed her counselor pose, sitting erect with her hands folded on her lap.

"I'll keep writing. My poetry and his. Pardon my waxing poetic, but poetry emboldens me, it empowers me. Finally, I feel pregnant. Pregnant with poetry. It's the blood in my veins. It's also managing my sanity." She stopped. "Look," Two sparrows landed in the ivy outside the screen, tousling, chirping. "Must be love."

"If you'd appreciate an unsophisticated audience, I'd like to read your work."

"I'd like that. I'd like to know that you hear what I'm saying. I'm writing a poem a day, sometimes two or three. I can look at a morning sky, or see shirts hanging on a clothesline, even reflect on adolescent misbehavior in middle age, and feel a poem. I know there's art and craft involved, and I've re-read many of Mason's articles to understand how a poem works. Ask me about onomatopoeia."

"Ask me about osteoporosis."

"I submitted a poem to a local writers' group for their anthology," Elaine said. "And someday, when I mail Mason's article for the poetry magazine, I'll mail a poem of mine. I've changed my *nom de plume* to Morgan, my maiden name, Elaina Morgan. Sounds poetic, doesn't it?"

"You've thought this out, haven't you?"

"I don't want Mason to know. Not yet. I also rented a post office box to provide an address different from Mason's. The editors will reason I'm a local student of his."

The low summer sun glittered through the ivy and danced on Elaine's face.

"And Brian?"

"Please. I'm trying to forget him."

"Keep writing."

Elaine wrote and rewrote. Her manner of speech changed. "I now see life through a poetic lens," she'd say. The chenille ribs of her robe were caterpillars. The staccato beat of a woodpecker was jazz tempo. The smell of bed sheets hanging outside was summer at Grandma's farm. "I feel a poem coming on," she'd say, and pull her car to the curb, or drape a dishtowel over the oven door, or rise at four in the morning gliding out of bed without disturbing Mason. She wrote hours each day. "This is my best work to date," she'd say of every poem. She wrote, and she hurried to the post office each morning awaiting word about her poem submission.

When it arrived, she read and reread the letter of acceptance from the local writers' group. She called Betty at Good Shepherd. "Would you care to be the first to congratulate the newest published poet on your block?"

"Congratulations. But shouldn't that privilege be extended to the poet's spouse?"

"No."

"OK. What next?"

"I'm sending *my* poem to *The Poet*. Today."

In time, she composed a collection of poems, fueled by praise of Mason's work—her work, by *The Poet* readers. For the magazine's annual competition, she selected poems that reflected her new hometown and titled the chapbook *Browns Prairie*.

When an editor called to discuss publication, she assumed the call was for Mason. "No," the editor said. "I'd like to talk to Elaina Morgan."

With Mason requiring constant attention, Elaine left the house only to rush to the post office each morning. She returned one day to find him roaming the upstairs hall.

"Mason, can I help you?" she called.

"Help me find the damn bathroom."

He remained in his pajamas, ate one or two meals daily in his chair by the window watching the nest in the apple tree, the fledgling robins having tottered and flown away. Elaine called Betty about caring for him while she was in New York. "I'm scared to leave him, but I'm going." Elaine held the receiver and listened through a long silence.

"He needs twenty-four hour supervision," Betty said. "We have a vacancy at Good Shepherd. Would you be willing to admit him?"

"Let me think about it. In the meantime, can you recommend a home health care nurse? Call me if you know someone. I'll be home tonight packing."

"New York," Mason said. "You're going to New York. Aha. The editors accepted my proposal." He stood, the blanket dropping from his lap. "I suggested an anthology, you know." He rubbed his hands and looked around the room. "I'll select from years of articles and add new material."

"Mason," Elaine interrupted.

"It's about time they act," Mason continued. "That magazine would fold without my contribution. I'll keep the title, "The Last Word."

"Mason." She reached for his arm, her heart pounding.

"I'm overdue for another book publication. How long has it been? Five years?"

"Mason, listen to me. *The Poet* wants to publish a book of *my* poetry." She waited in silence. Seconds that seemed like minutes, hours, while Mason stared at her.

"That's ridiculous. *Your* poetry? What poetry?"

"I submitted a collection for their annual competition, and they offered to publish."

"What are you talking about?" His voice was monstrous.

Elaine left the room and returned with a notebook. "My poetry," she cried. She held the book before him, clinging to it like a drowning child.

Mason reached for the book. "*Browns Prairie*? That's the title?" He opened the book to the table of contents. "And what's this? "Ruby Red Cadillac?" "Avalon Revisited?" "Grass Widow

Row?" I won't have it. I won't have it, do you understand? I will not have my name sullied with your simplistic, sentimental gibberish." He threw the notebook at the wastebasket. "I struggled a lifetime to establish my position at the university. I will not allow you to exploit my name, my reputation for your puerile expression." He kicked the wastebasket. "I won't have it. Do you understand?"

Elaine was quiet. She waited again, waited until she felt control of her voice. She swallowed, then reached for him.

"Mason. Listen to me. I respect your name. I respect your reputation. I submitted under my maiden name. The editor doesn't know. She never will. She likes my poetry. She calls it fresh and accessible."

Mason trembled, then staggered to the window. He steadied himself against the frame and teetered, as if standing on the window ledge of a tall building.

"What have I done?" Elaine whispered.

When Mason slept, Elaine called Betty and asked her to come. "I told Mason about my poetry, my award, and my publication contract. I told him I didn't use his name, that I used a new pen name."

"How did he respond?"

"He was angry, angrier than I've ever seen him. He threw my book on the floor. My book of poems. My child." She cradled the book to her breast. "You had a daughter. I didn't. Mason didn't want children. This is my belated child, my miracle."

"I understand."

Elaine shook her head. "No, you don't."

Betty placed her hands on Elaine's shoulders. "Elaine. You have to do something about Mason. Today."

"Yes," Elaine said, then paused. "But why don't I feel remorse? Why am I optimistic?"

Mason arrived at Good Shepherd while a group played canasta in the Gathering Room. A lady in pink called to Nurse Betty, "Who's the new guy, my next door neighbor?"

"He's the husband of the poet Elaina Morgan."

SISTERS

Harry, you asked about your father. Sister should have told you. I promised her that if you asked, I'd tell his story as best I could. When you called here at Good Shepherd, I began thinking about what I'd say, but I don't trust my memory. So much of his story is hurtful, I buried it years ago. Worse, I don't trust that I could tell you face to face. I'll write these notes and, if I don't have the courage to talk, I'll mail this to you.

Interesting that your daughter Mimi, my only grand-niece, brought this to the forefront. I remember her as a precocious child when she visited here. Not surprising that at her age, she wants to know about her grandfather. I'm the only one alive to tell her. Tell me she's mature enough to understand tragedy.

Where to start? Maybe at the farm where we grew up, Sister and I.

So. That year, we moved to what would become the home place off Pickle Factory Road. A small farm by today's standards—80 acres, a dozen cows, chickens, and a team of Percheron horses,

Sisters

Dolly and King. "You know you're getting close to our place when you smell dill pickles," Mother would say in her smiley voice when giving directions to first-time company.

Mother was a housewife. She cooked and scrubbed and did laundry, whatever it took to keep Pa fed and comfortable and in clean overalls. In her spare time, she fussed in the perennial garden. I remember hollyhocks. Later, when the infection set in her system, the garden went to weeds.

Pa scraped enough money out of milk checks to keep the family body and soul together. Mother took in alterations and mending for spare money for us girls. Sister would be a high school senior in the fall; I had finished eighth grade. She was tall and thin, with blond, naturally curly hair, a teenage clone of Mother. I was short, *chunky* my Uncle Frank said, with mousey brown hair like Pa's.

Living close to the pickle factory had its benefits. Pa had dedicated a small patch, maybe a half-acre, to cucumbers, a project for Sister and me. I remember the patch in spring, when last year's vines were dry and dead, like gray skeletons.

In early summer, when the patch was weedless, the light green tendrils coiled and clung to each other. By late summer, prickly leaves stained our hands black from picking. I remember the hideaway that our private patch provided. We lugged bushel baskets of cucumbers under box elders and calculated the proceeds, fantasizing far from Mother's chastising voice about the things we would buy.

"If you could buy anything in the world, what would it be?" I asked Sister.

"A typewriter. And a new washing machine for Mother."

For me, it would have been a new Schwinn bicycle. But the money we earned selling cucumbers financed a trip to town before Labor Day for school supplies and clothes.

Summer vacations were a lifetime of endless days and endless nights. We worked around the house, around the farm. When Pa pitched hay on the wagon, Sister drove the team and I stomped the hay down, stumbling back and forth. We gathered eggs, picked radishes and early lettuce, swept the porch.

It's the memory of free time that I cherish. Fishing for sunnies off the dock with a cane pole and cork for a bobber. Picking chokecherries for Mother's jelly, singing our way home with purple tongues and puckered lips. At night, catching lightning bugs in a jar. Starlight, moonlight. On rainy days in our bedroom, poring over catalogs, Wish Books, that contained pinking-sheared swatches of fabric glued to the pages. Pink floral organdy for a little girl's dress. Hunter green wool for a teenage girl's coat. Navy blue and white pinstripe gabardine for the traveling woman's wardrobe.

We counted the days until the county fair with 4-H exhibits, talent contests, and my favorite, the Ferris wheel. Every month of summer vacation had a hundred weeks. Every week had a hundred days. Every day had a hundred hours. You could live an entire life in one summer.

Pa drove a rusted Chevy pickup truck with a cracked windshield and without a muffler. Weekdays, he'd haul calves to the livestock auction, and Sundays, we girls would crawl into the truck box for the ride to Emanuel Lutheran, sitting low against the cab to avoid detection. Mother complained, unusual for her. "We need a decent car to drive to church," she said one Sunday morning. Pa went to an auction soon after and bought an old hearse, 1938 Packard with wide whitewall tires and velvet curtains on the rear windows with gold braid tiebacks. Sister and I loved the comfort and space and privacy. Gawky neighbors may have pointed and laughed, but we didn't see them. No more windblown hair or straw clinging to our clothing. Mother was mortified when she saw the hearse and said she wouldn't be caught dead riding in it.

I mentioned our draft horse team, Dolly and King. Pa spoke to them as if they were human, a quiet tone of authority and respect. Their size and strength made me skittish, and I darted in and out when helping Pa harness the team. It was when I was hitching King to an evener that he spooked. Pa said I startled him. King bolted forward and smashed my leg against a gate post. Pa didn't suspect a broken bone, couldn't tolerate the delay a trip to town would incur. The pain bowled me over, and I fought to stay conscious.

"We'd better get her to a hospital, get an x-ray," Mother said, kneeling over me and stroking my hair.

"We'll do that tomorrow once the corn's cultivated." Pa looked off to the west. "Can't you see those rain clouds?"

The bone in my foot had broken when King lunged forward. I remember the ache that night, then a dull fog of pain the next day. I complained less, and Pa interpreted that to mean that my condition was non-emergency. By the time I saw a doctor, my foot had set and had to be re-broken. The doctor said I would never walk without crutches. When they removed the cast, I dragged my foot, curled at a right angle. Uncle Frank, the man who called me *chunky*, said I had a club foot. Fifty years later, I still have it.

Pa kept to himself, spent most of his time in the barn or the fields. He may have wanted a son instead of another daughter. He never raised a hand against Sister or me, or Mother. I never saw him mistreat an animal, least of all his horses. But under his calm exterior, I felt, even as a child, the threat of violence—that he had a dark side which would explode if anyone crossed his threshold. It didn't help that I knew my grandmother, his mother, had made a few trips to the insane asylum for nervous breakdowns.

Pa spoke with respect to women, tolerated kids, got along with the Scandinavian neighbors. I can't put a finger on my feelings, but I do remember a threat he made. A neighbor boy had skipped school, wrecked the family car, and was caught shoplifting. "If he was my kid, I'd drown him," Pa said.

For reasons I didn't understand, and still don't, he hated all Catholics. Wouldn't trade at their stores. Ridiculed the parishioners for getting drunk on Friday, confessing their sins on Saturday, and attending mass on Sunday. Objected to any Catholic running for public office. "The next thing you know, we'll be paying taxes to the Pope."

After he delivered his harangue, Mother dismissed it with a wave of her hand. "He has a reason to feel that way," she said with no conviction, as if she also didn't understand. "Mr. Rogers, who was president of the bank and chairman of the Catholic church board of trustees, called in a loan that Pa had made on our first farm. The loan was not due, but Mr. Rogers showed Pa the fine print, showed him his signature that proved he knew the terms and agreed to them. Pa lost the argument and the farm."

I overheard Pa relate the same story to Uncle Frank years later. "If I ever see that son-of-a-bitch on a deserted country road, I'll shoot him."

Sister and I shared the upstairs of our farm house, a long room with ceilings sloping to a half-wall, wallpapered in a design of roses and ivy. The floor was a linoleum pattern of green and white tiles. Mother had sewn coverlets, roses and ivy again, for the beds which snugged against opposite walls.

"You'll never guess who I thought about today," Sister would say as I lay half-asleep. Or, "Look how the moon shines on the floor." Or, "Shall we pray together that your foot heals?" Always, she tried to lure me into conversation. I would grunt a *yep* or a *nope*. She'd say, "Which is it?"

Victory gardens were popular then, and Mother announced her plan to expand the vegetable garden where the calf pen had been, now overgrown with six-foot ragweed and thistles. She stepped on a rusty nail in the process, washed her foot, and applied a poultice before bed to draw out the poison. It wasn't enough. Her foot ached, but the pain was tolerable. Pa was cultivating corn at the time, sun up to sun down. Mother didn't drive and wouldn't impose on the neighbors for a trip to the doctor. By the time Pa noticed her impaired speech and labored breathing, her luck had run out. Pa said blood poisoning. The doctor said tetanus.

Pa half-carried Mother to the hearse, her arm slung around his neck. She turned to us as if to say "Don't worry. I'll be home soon." But no voice.

That is my last living memory of her, stumbling and embarrassed, a black patent leather purse dangling from her arm.

After the funeral, days and weeks blurred and blended into months and seasons. Pa had assigned the household chores to Sister—cooking, cleaning, washing and ironing, everything but the new garden. He was more generous with Sister than he had been with Mother, increasing the allowance for groceries, even complimenting her on her raisin pie. She added recipes from her Home Ec class to our suppers, one an orange Jell-O salad with shredded carrots. I remember Pa's comment: "Why'd you put vegetables in the dessert?"

When Sister was to sing with the high school choir at the Decoration Day ceremony, Pa approved her buying a dress from the Spiegel catalog. I remember her walking down the stairs in that dress—pale blue with white stripes, a narrow red belt cinched at her tiny waist that accentuated her breasts and hips. Sister had become a woman. She stood in front of the closet door mirror, chin tilted up, chest out. She raised on tiptoes, smoothing her skirt. She looked as if she would dance. Or fly. I stared at her, then looked down at my bib overalls. For the first time in my life, I hated myself. I hated my crutches. I hated her. She could look forward to a normal life—marriage, kids. I would forever be an object of pity, of humiliation, of ridicule.

As spring warmed into summer, Pa lost interest in farming. He did chores morning and night. He cut and raked and hauled hay. He cultivated corn. But the resolve, the passion had vanished. I wouldn't call it sorrow or melancholy. More like indifference and an occasional burst of anger, cussing the horses if they didn't lunge forward on the first giddyup.

He pulled the rowboat out of the machine shed, caulked leaky gunwales, and replaced the oar locks. After milking at night, he'd load the boat in the pickup and drive to Round Lake. Back before the ten o'clock news, in good humor, he'd flash a stringer of blue gills. I remember him smelling like fish and citronella.

He surprised us one day when he announced he was considering a fishing trip to Canada, after the Fourth of July, between hay cuttings. First he'd get current on farm work. He'd replace tires on the truck. And he'd ask Uncle Frank to join him. My two reactions, after the announcement: happy he didn't ask me along, and who'd milk the cows? Pa must have read my mind. "I'll get the neighbor's hired man to do chores."

The Fourth was two weeks away and Pa attacked his daily routine with a new vigor. Evenings he tuned up the Evinrude outboard and changed oil and replaced tires on the truck. He dug angleworms in the cow yard and stored them in cans covered with used coffee grounds. Had it been anyone else, I would say he was excited, sometimes giddy. With the first two prerequisites of the trip satisfied, he didn't talk about inviting Uncle Frank. We didn't ask.

Pa didn't ignore us; he just let us be. I was no good at chores, lugging crutches around. Sister was preoccupied in the house, singing along with Pearl and Ade on WCCO and planning her baked dessert for the Young Lutherans' Fourth of July picnic.

Sisters

I should tell you more about our neighborhood, maybe our entire township and county, maybe our entire half of the state. Every family was headed by first generation Americans. Ancestors emigrated from Norway and Sweden in our case, or Germany. The Scandinavians were Lutheran; the Germans, Catholic. The few others, the oddballs, Irish, Finns, Poles, banded together not out of common interest but out of necessity. In late summer, three threshing crews, bonded by nationality, traveled to their respective farms. In late fall, three silo filling crews. In winter, three wood cutting crews. Between those landmark occasions, the Germans assembled to butcher a pig, the Scandinavians to build a granary.

Pa became casual about his church attendance after Mother's funeral, but Sister had learned to drive the hearse, and we went to church alone.

After Mother's death, Sister's promotion to lady of the house felt natural, even obvious. Of course we missed Mother, and at night, lying in bed, Sister talked about her—expressions she used, meals she prepared, outfits she wore—talking as if she wanted me to seal her memory inside. "Remember when she'd say 'I do declare,' and 'Bless his heart?' Remember her Easter outfit? That dusty rose crepe dress with the pink cloche hat? Remember how Pa loved the horseradish sauce she served with roast beef?"

In the morning, Sister would flit about the kitchen preparing pancakes for Pa and me. She'd stand by the screen door watching for Pa, her arms crossed behind her. "What is so rare as a day in July?" she'd say and giggle at her cleverness.

Rare indeed. That early summer, we endured endless stretches of heat and humidity. We spent days with an oscillating fan providing the only air movement. Nights we tossed and thrashed in our beds, searching for a cool spot on the pillow, waking wet with sweat, clawing for air. Early morning was the coolest.

I remember standing on crutches, handing clothes pins to Sister as she hung wet laundry on the line. When we took them down in the afternoon, the fresh clean aroma of sheets and pillow slips flapped in my face.

The morning of the Young Lutherans' Fourth of July picnic, Sister posed at the top of the stairs in her Spiegel dress, twirled on the landing, and floated down the stairs. I was used to the dress now, seeing it hanging in the closet, seeing Sister press it against her, dancing around our bedroom. But I still hated it for the loftiness, the adulthood it lent her.
"Where'd you get the lipstick?" I asked.
She feigned surprise. "Bye-bye, Sister," she said, and lifted the car keys from a nail behind the door.
When she returned late that night, I pretended to sleep. I had decided, out of spite, not to have any interest in the picnic—who came, what happened, what the other girls wore. Sister undressed in the dark, placed the dress under her blanket, and didn't say a word. In the faint light, I saw her hug her pillow. Then a soft whimper, a cry.
"What's the matter?" I asked. Nothing.
The next morning, Sister avoided my gaze, wasn't chatty about the picnic as I expected. After Pa left for field work, she spent minutes, hours in the bathroom. She would wash a few dishes, then run to the bathroom in tears. She ran upstairs, ran down with the dress bundled under her arm, and rinsed it in the kitchen sink. I thought I saw grass stains.
The magic of summer had disappeared. Sister withdrew, was short with me. "Leave me alone," she'd yell, and then run upstairs crying. Meals were silent affairs, probably to Pa's satisfaction. There were no games, no singing. I was lonely.
One morning, when Pa was in the barn milking cows, she called Aunt Leona. "Can you come over? Now?"
Aunt Leona was in the driveway by the time we finished lunch. She and Sister sat on the front porch, Sister sobbing, not speaking, only shaking her head, yes or no. I hobbled past them,

walked into the yard, then circled the house, crouching beside the porch. I heard Aunt Leona say, "Just because you're late on one period doesn't mean you're pregnant."

At supper, Pa ate what Aunt Leona had prepared, unaware of her visit. "Check the heifer in the pen every hour tomorrow," Pa said. "Come and get me when she starts calving. It's her first, and likely to be a problem."

Sister pushed her chair back and pulled an apron over her face. She ran upstairs, crying.

"What got into her?" Pa asked.

"She's pregnant." I hadn't spoken that word before, hadn't realized its power.

"Pregnant?" Pa scraped his chair backwards and banged his knees on the table. "Girl, get down here this minute."

I hustled out of the house and crouched on the porch, within hearing distance but out of sight.

Whether out of fright or obedience, Sister confessed all. Ed Schultz.

"Schultz? A German? A Catholic?" He banged the table. "What's he doing at a Lutheran picnic? Schultz. That dirty little son-of-a-bitch. Schultz. I can't believe what I'm hearing."

Sister sobbed in her apron. Pa ranted for what seemed like hours. "You'll have to get married," he said. "And soon."

I sat on the porch swing, out of sight but within earshot. A wedding, I thought. How exciting.

I avoided Pa for the next few days, but heard him stomping around the kitchen, throwing his boots in the corner, yelling at the radio. He asked me to leave the house after supper one night. I did, but I overheard him ask Sister about her period.

"Have you had one yet?"

"No."

"Well, let me know right away if you do."

He must have hoped for a false alarm. He collected himself, hustling to stay ahead of fieldwork, saving time at night to sort fishing tackle, change line in his reel, re-tie the landing net. With the disruption and turmoil, he hadn't forgotten the fishing trip. Sister drove to the Schultz home to drop the news about the late period on Ed. And Pa's insistence on a wedding.

She told me later they talked to his mother. "Now let's be civilized about this," his mother had said. "It's not the first time this has happened." Best for the families to get acquainted, she suggested, and Sister agreed. Mrs. Schultz invited our family to supper Sunday evening.

The meal was pleasant enough, and Pa was courteous, although he never looked at Ed. I remember Ed—tall, dark, wavy hair, a brush of mustache over his lip. Sister sat next to him, likely holding hands beneath the table. Both picked at their food. Neither said a word during the meal.

"Ed," Pa barked, breaking the silence after dessert. Ed lifted his head, looked as if he were facing Armageddon. Sister froze. Pa's voice softened. "We should get to know each other. Spend some time together. I'm driving to Canada in a week or two for some good fishing. Want to join me?"

"I think that's a wonderful idea," Mrs. Schultz said.

Pa planned a seven day trip: a day and a half to drive up, three days fishing, a day and a half to drive home, with one day for mechanical breakdowns or bad weather. After chores on Monday morning, Ed's dad drove him to our farm and talked to Pa about the trip, both checking the tie-down of the boat on the pickup truck and kicking the new tires. Sister had packed sandwiches and brewed a thermos of coffee.

"Aren't you worried about bears up there?" Mr. Schultz asked.

"Not to worry," Pa said. "I have my 12-gauge, and slugs."

Sisters

Sister and Ed were in the kitchen; I sat on the porch swing. Whether she sensed a premonition, or whether she felt prematurely maternal, she held his arm. "Be careful," she whispered. "Promise me you'll be careful."

None of us was a stranger to tragedy. Certainly not our family, with my horse accident, a crippled invalid for life. Mother's death, which might have been avoided with a simple inoculation. Now Sister's pregnancy. We weren't strangers to tragedy, nor were we inured to it. I'm still not. It's painful, Harry, to dredge these memories up.

Pa was late returning from the fishing trip. One day. Then two. Sister called Mrs. Schultz. No word. On the third day, Pa returned, alone. Sister ran from the house when the truck pulled into the driveway. She looked in the cab. "Where's Ed?"

Pa was silent. He stepped out of the cab, stretched his arms, and wiped his brow with a red handkerchief. "I lost him," he said. "He fell out of the boat. Stupid kid. Stood up to land a big Northern. I spent the rest of the trip looking for him. Even had the Mounties out there."

Sister stood in shock, her hand covering her mouth.

"They'll drag the lake, but I doubt if they'll find him." Pa seemed content with that and began loosening the ropes that secured the boat to the pickup. I couldn't fathom what had happened. I could imagine a fisherman standing when he felt a strike. I could see whitecaps and feel the boat rock. I could hear Pa shout, "Sit down, dammit." But I could not grasp Ed falling and disappearing beneath the boat.

"I stopped by his folks' place," Pa added. "They're driving up to Canada tomorrow."

"I'm going with them," Sister blurted.

"You're staying home."

Again, the house took on a morgue-like quality, but different this time. An accidental death lends intrigue. A young accidental death lends melodrama, at least to me. We heard no reports of a search by the Royal Canadian Mounted Police, never heard of a body being discovered, lost contact with Ed's parents. Since Ed and I attended different schools and were members of different churches, I didn't know much about him. Sister wasn't talking. I heard the Schultz place was up for sale, that they were moving if only to get away from us. I would have.

Sister collected herself by day, cried until I slept at night. When she thought she was alone, she'd pull her dress tight over her tummy and pat it. Whisper words I couldn't hear. She cooked, she cleaned, she washed, she ironed, all in sad silence. No singing or dancing.

On Mondays, she washed bed linens. At supper one Monday night, there was no aroma of roast beef, no table set, no six o'clock news on the radio. Pa walked in from the barn. Sister stood at the cupboard, her arms locked around her chest. Pa looked at the bare table. "What's going on?"

"I found these under your mattress," Sister cried. She held a billfold, a watch. "Ed's," she said. "Why were you hiding them?"

Pa flushed. He rushed at her and grabbed the billfold and watch. "You never saw it. Understand? You never saw it."

"And why didn't you give them to his parents?" Sister was hysterical.

"Listen." Pa grabbed her shoulders. "You never saw it. Understand? You never saw it."

Sister left the next day to live with Aunt Leona and Uncle Frank. Who could blame her? She called me long distance once a week, during the day, but never came to visit. She said she had chanced to meet Ed's mother in the grocery store. Yes, they were moving, as soon as they sold the farm, Mrs. Schultz had said.

Sisters

Any report from the Royal Canadian Mounted Police? Sister asked. The Mounties knew nothing about the accident until we told them, was the reply. Yes, they found the body. Hadn't you heard? Didn't your father tell you? The Mounted Police suspected foul play. But we can't rule out suicide, they said. A young man, no training, no job, with a wife and baby to support. Maybe more than he could bear. Would we sign a complaint? they asked. All the complaints in the world wouldn't bring my boy back. My boy, she said, and broke into tears. And why did the Mounties suspect foul play? Sister asked. Because they found a hole in his . . . Mrs. Schultz fell against a produce rack, righted herself, and rushed out of the store. Sister received a letter from her months later, asking about the baby. Mrs. Schultz included a check with a note that more would follow when circumstances allowed.

After you were born, Harry, Sister married Clint, the Schultz's hired man. I remember Clint—tall, thick shouldered, jovial, a man who could and would stand up to Pa if that was required. I don't know how Sister explained why your last name differed from hers. Clint was a loving father, or stepfather, and an outsider would have considered yours an average family.

I remember the day Pa died. He was listening to Ronald Reagan inveigh against socialized medicine. At the end, when the President said, "Well, make my day," Pa shouted, "I'll make your day." He sprang to his feet, collapsed, and died. I stayed on the farm until it sold, then bought a house with five acres on the highway leading into town and opened a vegetable stand. Along came Stubb, an itinerant carpenter. He needed a house; I needed someone to dig potatoes and pick sweet corn. Not exactly your perfect match, but it worked. He had simple tastes, treated me well, and thank God, didn't want children. Sister and Clint were bridesmaid and best man.

My wedding picture sits on the television set. I'm leaning on Sister, your mother, in my virginal white dress, crutches conveniently out of view. Sister looks askance, an oversized corsage weighing on her shoulder. Stubb and Clint wear boutonnieres, looking bored. Or incredulous, I can't tell. Only the preacher smiles.

I wonder how life would have changed if I had met Stubb when we were younger. Would we have fallen in love? Probably not. He would likely have spurned me, a cripple. I, with crusty resentment, would have expected rejection. I can't imagine it any other way. I have loved many people, but have never been *in love*. I loved Stubb, I guess. But he was just *there*. A functional necessity, like the refrigerator. When our husbands died, Sister and I moved closer and stayed in touch.

In her final days, Sister asked me if I would tell you, Harry, about your father, about the accident.

"No, I won't," I said.

She looked at me in a pre-death glaze. "Please?"

"Did you believe the suicide possibility?" I asked.

"Of course not."

"Did you confront Pa?"

"No."

"And you never told Harry?"

"He never asked. But if he had, I would have told him. If he asks you, tell him, please."

"I'll think about it," I said. Someday, I thought then, as a memorial to Sister, I'll record our story. As a memorial for her, and as information for you, her only son.

Harry, you said you'd visit me here at Good Shepherd on the Fourth of July, and I'm dredging through my memory to write your story. Funny that some of the memories surfaced because of dill pickles. I keep a jar in my refrigerator, and today the smell, the look, the taste transported me back to the farm. The briny odor of the factory in summer; the premium that this size cucumber brought at the factory; the squeak of biting into Mother's pickles in the basement crock.

When you called, Harry, you said you had a challenge for me. Your daughter Mimi is enrolled in a summer genealogy camp. Mimi, our family's only link to the future. Where she got her brazen confidence, I don't know. She's asking questions that you can't answer. Questions about your real father. I've seen your birth certificate, and it says *Illegitimate*. Nothing like unvarnished truth. Your knowing the truth won't better the story. Maybe it'll make it worse.

You said your wife is on duty on the Fourth of July, so you'll visit me alone. Please consider bringing Mimi. She reminds me of your mother at that age. Blond hair, tall and thin, but with a different demeanor. Your mother was happy, generous, and, I hate the word, nice. Mimi is direct, all business, mature for her age. She'll do well. Bring her, and then I'll tell both of you. All the sordid details. Who's to care? Everybody's dead. If I can't tell you, I'll give you this letter.

At least, I *think* I'll give you this letter. Upon reading it, I'm uncertain if I should tell you the *real* story. What's to be gained? You want to know how your father died? He died in a boating accident. Isn't that enough? Must I disparage Pa's memory, his reputation with what I suspect, what I believe? Maybe I should just bury the memories. It won't be much longer.

Oh, God, help me.

I love you, Harry,
Your Aunt Stella

Satyr

Last night's storm began with growls of thunder and flickers of lightning off to the west, amplifying into rumbles and flashes as it neared. Once overhead, thunder roared and lightning fired the sky. Alice huddled in her rocker beside the window, a cat sleeping in her lap. Trees shifted from black silhouettes to waving branches to whipping leaves. The storm hovered, then receded off to the east the way it had arrived, rumbles and flashes, growls and flickers. Its last remnant was a fading roll, like a freight train heading for the next county.

"The rain will be good for the garden back at the farm," Alice said as she carried the cat to the bed, then remembered there was no garden, no lawn, no grazed corral. Weeds. Only weeds.

Muggy air followed the storm and infiltrated her apartment at Good Shepherd, stifling the room with discomforting humidity. Alice had turned the air conditioner off; the rattle kept her awake. That, and the odor in the room. "Like air from a hot inner tube," she told the cat. "But it complements the chemical-tasting water."

Satyr

In the first morning light of August, she stepped outside, breathed fresh air, and walked.

A half-mile from Good Shepherd, the asphalt street gave way to gravel. Houses crowded on 50-foot lots transformed into hobby farms with outbuildings and barking dogs that jumped against chain link fences.

She bumped along the gravel road with her walking stick, enjoying the ozone of morning. A figure ahead, a man reading a letter, stood by the mailbox at the end of a driveway. As she neared him, the sounds of his farm intrigued her—cackling guinea hens, a braying donkey, bleating sheep.

"Good morning," she said, startling him. "Beautiful morning for a walk."

He nodded.

"Excuse me, sir," she said. "I hear your sheep. I'm wondering if you have goats."

He chuckled a nervous laugh and folded the letter. "Yes, I do. Are you from around here?"

"Good Shepherd. I had a small herd before I moved. I miss them."

"You're welcome to see my goats. I was about to feed them."

Alice followed him up the driveway. "Do you milk them? Sell them?"

"Just a hobby. I'm advertising the kids for sale. All my nannies had twins."

Alice related her story of her move from the farm to Good Shepherd, how she yearned for her animals, how she missed the daily routine of chores.

"You're welcome to visit as long as they're here," he said. "I may not be home. I work ten to three at the General Store." At the pen, he tossed a bucket of grain in the feeder trough. "By the way, there's a shortcut to Good Shepherd that will save you a few minutes." He pointed to a road that skirted a hay field and edged along a woodland. "It's an old logging trail. Overgrown, but still passable."

The goats nibbled at the grain, small gentle bites. Alice watched, their familiar odor and bleating returning her to her farm. After scratching the nannies' necks and petting the kids, she pulled herself away and sniffed her hands.

He walked to the barn and stood in the doorway. "Treats are in a cabinet on the left, if you're here and I'm not," he said. "By the way, my name is Merritt."

"I'm Alice and I'd better go," she said, "but I'll be back."

"You can't miss the field road. Just keep the woods on your left."

She returned to Good Shepherd unnoticed by staff, exhausted by the walk and exhilarated by the animals. Lulu the orange tabby sniffed her pant legs, her hands. Alice sat in the rocker until breakfast was served, planning a return to Mr. Merritt's farm tomorrow.

In the morning, the path beyond the mowed lawn lay draped with arched fronds of fern, beaten from rain and bent with morning dew. Not fifty feet from the building, Alice's boots were soaked, her feet sloshing inside. She'd have explaining to do when she returned.

Ahead, a patch of turquoise sky pushed through the mist. A sliver of morning sunlight sparked rain droplets into tiny rainbows. Trees showered her when the wind breathed, and in the mist, she saw phantom goats waiting for her.

She sloshed on until she found the field road that separated the woods from the hay field. Sprays of vapor drifted from a lowland bog. Spider webs threaded the path, clinging to her face. A mourning dove called; another answered. They mate for life, Alice thought. Glad it works for birds. She stopped and listened for the braying donkey, the bleating goats.

She carried a sack of grapes saved from yesterday's snack bar at Good Shepherd. Alice guessed the distance to Mr. Merritt's farm at about a mile. She would walk to the farm, feed the nannies and pet the kids, and return before morning crafts at ten. No one would know she was gone. No one except Lulu. Her cat would be watching at the window.

Back at Good Shepherd, Alice procrastinated about calling her daughter Tanya. Always good to hear her voice; always bad to hear her message. Alice still stung from her son-in-law Kurt's criticism: "Your mother talks too much. She tells everybody everything."

When Kurt lost his job at the potato factory, they lost their house. "Can we move in with you, Ma? Until Kurt finds another job?" Tanya had asked months ago.

Alice had a spare bedroom. Her doctor had advised her to hire someone to do chores. "You're not as young as you used to be." His words mocked her vision of herself. She remembers his nonnegotiable voice. "With your epileptic seizures, I can't recommend a driver's license."

The day her daughter and son-in-law moved in, Tanya spent most of it on the telephone or in front of the television. Kurt snarled around the house, grousing about the bank, the potato factory, the county welfare system. *Just like home*, Alice thought, and knew they were there for the long term.

She neither saw nor heard an indication that Kurt sought employment after his one rejection where he declared himself overqualified for the job. During the day, he pulled the shades to watch television, smoked odd-smelling cigarettes, and ate his meals on the sofa. "Get off the phone. I'm expecting a call," Kurt would yell. "And get me a beer."

Alice walked outside, fed the goats, checked the mailbox, weeded the garden, anything to avoid the mess inside. When she retreated to her bedroom, she hatched a plan to split five acres and the buildings from the farm, deed it to Tanya, and lease the cropland to the neighbor. That way she could afford to move to Good Shepherd. "One stipulation," Alice said when she notified Tanya of her plan. "You tend the goat herd and keep my room available for home visits."

When Alice called for a ride home from Good Shepherd, Tanya broke the news. "Kurt sold the goats. He said they were a pain in the ass. They weren't making you any money. And on hot days, all we'd smell is goat shit."

"Sold them? To who?"

"He hauled them to the auction barn. We got the check, but we needed groceries. We'll pay you back when he finds a job."

Alice held the phone away from her ear and rocked in her chair faster until the cat jumped.

"By the way, your grandson moved into your bedroom. He thinks his girlfriend is pregnant, and they're trying to figure out what to do."

"She's living there too?"

"Of course, Ma. I didn't raise him to welsh on his obligations."

At the farm, Alice surveyed the yard, expecting regret and finding it. No anxious bleats welcomed her home. No nannies or kids stood on their hind legs bracing against the woven wire fence. And the garden . . . Weeds were knee high. The lawn mower, out of gas or broken, stood abandoned in the half-mowed yard. A second beater pickup was parked in the drive, hood up, tools laying where they fell.

In her house, her former home, Alice fanned the blue air and coughed. Her son-in-law, her grandson, and his girlfriend sat in front of the television, feet on the coffee table around a pie tin of cigarette butts.

"Aren't you going to say hello to your grandma?" Tanya asked her son.

"Hi, Grandma."

"Coffee?" Tanya asked. "I'll make some."

"I think I'll take a walk outside."

Alice stepped over discarded auto parts, around an overflowing garbage can buzzing with bees, and headed for the barn. It might be their idea of a joke, she thought, to see how she reacted to selling the goats. They might be waiting for her, hiding from her, ready to greet her when she opened the door.

Once inside, nothing. Shafts of sunlight streamed down on the bedded floor of an empty pen. A musky aroma clung to the warm air. Quiet, vacant, except for horse flies buzzing against the windows and a pair of barn swallows balancing on a wire guarding their nest.

Back in the kitchen, Alice talked over the drone of television. "I'd better pass on the coffee. I forgot to tell the front desk I wouldn't be there for lunch. They get pretty sticky about that."

In her Good Shepherd apartment, Alice rocked with Lulu on her lap facing the window. She hadn't brought much furniture, preferring to leave most of it to Tanya. "Our stuff is trashed," Tanya had said. "It's not worth moving." Alice kept the bedroom set, reclining rocker, a kitchen table, and two side chairs. A television sat on a packing crate. Her books and records and tapes were unpacked in boxes, and a guitar leaned in the corner. Why would she need a sofa? She hadn't planned to entertain.

Blue jays pecked at the bird feeder, taunting the cat. Lulu tensed, poised to pounce. Stroking the cat calmed Alice. She refused to believe the goats were gone. Worse than gone—sold, and at an auction to an unknown bidder with a few bucks. No way of knowing how he treated animals.

She had kept the goats to the last, giving her chickens to a neighbor, the stray dogs she befriended to the Humane Society at a cost that choked her. When Alice arrived at Good Shepherd, the administrator pointed to the cat cage among her belongings.

"We generally discourage pets," she said.

"What do you call those?" Alice pointed to the parakeets and tropical fish. "Residents?"

Hazel, her neighbor across the building, stopped by for her usual Saturday morning visit to feed Lulu scraps of fish from the Friday night fish fry. "Sorry about the taste," Hazel said to the cat. "All the food here is country fresh. They just don't say what country."

"Sit awhile," Alice said. "Had any visitors lately?"

Hazel looked around the kitchen for the coffee pot. "My son. How about you?"

"I have a daughter that doesn't visit. I can't take her whining. Can't take her yelling and irresponsible behavior." Lulu jumped on her lap when Alice sat in the rocker. "Can't live with her just like I couldn't live with her dad."

"Men," Hazel said. "If we could teach our dogs to start the car, we wouldn't need them."

"We had our good times, I guess," Alice said, stroking the cat. "But damned if I can remember them." She laughed. "I remember the day I knew it was over. I was washing clothes, his clothes. You know how you sort through pockets before you toss overalls in the washer?" She rocked faster. "Well, in the watch pocket, I found a handful of lottery tickets. Ten bucks apiece. A couple hundred dollars worth. That explained the phone call I got from the feed store that the bill hadn't been paid. He said he forgot to pay it. That explained the hate mail I got from the phone company and the REA. I kicked his ass out that night. The goats were better company than he was. And a hell of a lot more predictable."

"Goats?" Hazel asked.

"My one bad habit. Raised them all my life. A lot more gratifying than raising my daughter. Turns out she inherited her father's genes for gambling. Spent hours, days, nights at the casino. Borrowed money from me for car payments, for the mortgage. I've supported enough Indians to claim them as dependents. Someday I'll believe what everyone tells me—she's beyond redemption. But so am I. I'm old. I'll save my energy for something else."

"There's plenty out there that need redemption," said Hazel. "My daughter-in-law for one. Talk about irresponsible . . ."

"Be sure to visit the county fair," the radio announcer repeated morning after morning. "Rides, exhibits, grandstand shows, the midway, dozens of food stands. Coming to town Friday, Saturday, and Sunday."

Alice loved the fair, had attended it for years, had exhibited goats as a girl in 4-H. The warm summer air suggested fair time. Gardens were in full bloom and full production. Homemakers would be canning jams and jellies. Kids would be grooming a steer, preening a Long Island duck, primping a Fuzzy Lop rabbit. Of course, there would be goats. She called the county fair office for the date of goat judging.

"Tanya," Alice called on the telephone. "Would you drive me to the fair Saturday afternoon?"

"I would, Ma, but the gas tank's empty."

"If there's enough gas to get to town, I'll fill it. There's a demolition derby, if Kurt wants to come." She stopped herself before she added, "And a beer garden."

"I'll mention it to him, but I doubt if he'll come. He doesn't do well in the heat. Or crowds."

August weather is capricious. When Alice left Good Shepherd for the fair, the sun blazed. Wind through the truck's open windows refreshed her. Goldenrods and Purple Gentians blurred as she passed. Swallows peeled off telephone wires like tiny aircraft in formation. Mowed alfalfa perfumed the roadside with intoxicating aroma. "Ah," Alice said, "I feel life again."

"If it's okay with you, I'll do some shopping while you do your fair going," Tanya said when they reached the fairgrounds. "Can you spot me a twenty?"

Alice rolled her eyes and dug in her purse.

"Thanks, Ma. How about I be back in a couple hours? I'll meet you here at the gate at four. Okay?"

The midway lay straight ahead. Barkers yelled, the merry-go-round calliope whistled, loudspeakers blared declaring this the greatest little show on earth. Alice walked through the midway, tripped on power cords that crisscrossed the ground, and caught herself. Frisky kids yelled and waved from the Tilt-a-Whirl.

Food stands lined the route to the exhibit buildings. The aroma of fried onions from a hamburger stand mingled with caramel corn and cotton candy. Alice walked past the ring-toss tent, past the penny arcade, past a carny. "Guess your weight, ma'am? Guess your age?" Past a picnic shelter toward the 4-H building.

Inside, she felt the breeze from a huge floor fan. It sucked scents of animals and fresh wood chips from the other end of the building and blew them toward the open door where she stood. Turkeys, geese, ducks, and chickens crowded in wire pens. Pigeons and rabbits slept in cages. Then, the familiar musky odor of goats.

In the judging ring in the center of the building, 4-Hers with numbered cards around their necks stood with goats haltered and leashed. The announcer called "Number 4," and a pigtailed girl in a Heidi dress led her Boer goat, spotted and floppy-eared, like a long-legged Cocker Spaniel. Alice recognized the lineup—dairy Toggenburgs, Nubians, Alpines. No *mixed heritage*, as Alice referred to her herd. The Boer stood at attention as the judge prodded and peered, asked questions, and took notes.

The announcer made cutesy small talk as the judge worked his way around the circle of contestants. "Now there's a cute pair," he said as a young woman in a pinafore led twin kids. "I'm talking about the goats, of course."

Alice leaned on the railing, nodding her head or shaking it at the judge's comments, and groaning at the announcer's banter. She walked through exhibits of turkeys, geese, ducks, chickens. Better keep an eye on the time, she thought. Distracted and disoriented, she exited the building on the opposite end from which she entered.

Fickle August weather had taken a turn while she was in the barn. Clouds covered the sun. Wind swept dust off the road. Food wrappers twirled and sailed like kites. Alice lowered her head and shielded her eyes from the wind, the dust. She looked through her fingers and saw no midway, no merry-go-round, no picnic tables.

"Tanya," she called, and the wind swallowed her words. Cars blocked her path. Buses and trailers she hadn't noticed before. She walked left, then right. A patter of rain fell. More cars and motor homes. Semi-truck cabs and trailers. She didn't remember them.

She walked to the shelter of a trailer where a small animated object caught her attention. It was leashed to the rear door of a school bus with gaudily painted images against a pale blue background. She walked toward the bus. An animal, but not a puppy. She stared at it, waiting for her vision to focus. She wiped rain from her glasses. The animal looked at her and bleated. "A goat," she said. "A pygmy goat." As she neared it, the goat trembled and wagged its tail. She knelt beside it, cupping its chin in one hand, stroking its back with the other.

"You're going to get wet out there." Alice looked up to see a man standing on the rear step of the bus.

"Do you mind?" she asked. "I've had goats all my life."

"I came out to bring Lucy in from the rain," he said. "You can bring her in if you wish."

He swept a curtain aside with his arm, exposing the interior of the bus, dark with a single light above an easel. Alice released the latch on the goat's leash and lifted it.

"Let me help you up," he said. He was a big man, past middle age but younger than Alice. He wore a Greek fisherman cap, a Burl Ives goatee, an undershirt that inflated over his belt. As she lifted her hand to him, lightning flashed and thunder roared. Rain pelted like bullets, stinging her arms and face. "Hurry."

She stumbled up the stairs, one arm cradling the kid, the other protecting her head, his hand on her elbow.

"Welcome to my studio, my humble abode." He pinched his beard. "Call me Santiago the artiste." He turned on an overhead light.

"Unusual name," she said stroking the goat.

He smiled, gold caps shining on his front teeth. "A gypsy gave it to me."

Alice handed him the goat and wiped her glasses while her eyes adjusted to the dimness. Artwork hung from every inch of the interior. Sketches, portraits, caricatures, some framed, some thumb-tacked. The subjects were people—young and old, men and women.

"I'm a caricaturist by profession," he said. "These . . ." he pointed to pictures on the wall, "are mostly dissatisfied customers. They wanted the portrait, but didn't like the result."

"You did all of these? The caricatures? The portraits?"

"You can't make a living selling portraits." He laughed. "You can't make a living selling caricatures either. But Lucy and I, we survive, don't we, girl?" He patted her head.

"Sit down," he said handing her the goat, "and wait until the rain slows. Could I get you an iced tea? I have some brewed in the fridge."

She nodded and scratched the goat's belly. Rain drummed the roof.

"Mind if I sketch you?" he asked, handing the glass. "You cradling Lucy?"

Alice sipped her tea and petted the goat.

He held a sketch pad and drew with quick strokes of charcoal.

Alice scanned the artwork wall display again. "I notice many of your subjects are framed in rainbows. Any significance?"

"Absolutely none. Sort of a trademark."

"The portraits are good. Have you approached any galleries about carrying your work?"

"Artists are a dime a dozen. I'm ashamed to say I have an MFA in visual arts. What I need is a kick in the pants."

Alice lifted her foot.

Rain hammered the bus. Wind floated the privacy curtain up and out the door. Thunder drowned the sound of music.

Music. Alice hadn't noticed it until the thunder faded. "What music is that?"

"Black Sabbath. 'Iron Man.' It's their signature song."

"Never heard of them." She stroked the little goat. "How old is Lucy?"

"I don't know. Probably a year. I've had her for a couple months, and I'm looking for another one." He glanced at Alice, glanced too long, she thought. "I checked the local want ads for animals for sale. There's a farmer south of town that has goats. You're from this area. Maybe you know him, Alex Merritt."

"I know him. He lives near me at Good Shepherd."

"This is my lucky day. I have time to drive out there before I go to work. Will you direct me?"

"What time is it? I told my daughter I'd meet her at four. And Mr. Merritt works at a grocery store in town. He probably isn't home."

"We have plenty of time. Here, I'll put Lucy in her pen." Santiago lifted the kid from Alice and buried his face in her fur.

They drove out the parking area behind the exhibit buildings, out the front gate, windshield wipers sweeping in broad arcs. "Left on Main Street," Alice said. "About a mile. I have to be back at four, you know."

Santiago nodded and glanced out the side view mirrors. Rain fell in torrents, fell faster than the wipers could accommodate. Approaching cars beamed diluted headlights. He turned the CD player volume up, drowning out the drumming rain. Alice gripped the door handle. She looked at him, saw his profile against rain racing across the window. His neck was tattooed. A hole was punched in his earlobe, and from it . . . She struggled to focus. From it dangled a five-pointed star earring.

"Oh, pay attention, Alice," she said. "Turn left at the Conoco. Watch for a mailbox on the right. 'Merritt.'"

The bus turned into the driveway, past the house, to the sheds and pens. Santiago honked the horn. He looked at his watch. "If he's not home, he should be soon. We'll wait. Take your spot on the chair holding Lucy. I'll kill time by sketching."

Alice lifted the goat from the pen and sat.

"You've had goats all your life. But not now?" Santiago sketched, glanced up, sketched. He reached for a tray of colored pastels.

"None now. I had a big herd for years, planned to keep a few plus my original pair Harry and Bess. My son-in-law sold them."

"Why goats?"

"It's a long story and painful to tell. And I doubt if you want to hear it."

"Try me. It'll give you something to do while I sketch."

SATYR

"Well, my dad was drafted in World War II and killed at Iwo Jima, two months before I was born. Mama and my brother and I lived on a small farm, a hundred miles from nowhere. She had a '37 Chevy and a widow's pension. The car worked until it needed tires, or a radiator. After that, it sat on blocks. We had a garden, chickens, goats. Times were tough. The drought started the year I was born. The summer I was five, the well went dry, and the creek slowed to a trickle. We couldn't afford to drill a new well, so my brother hiked upstream to haul water every day. Mama said we'd melt snow in the winter."

Alice took a deep breath and fondled Lucy.

"Continue," Santiago said, glancing up to sketch.

"That year, the garden dried up in July and the grasshoppers took over. We couldn't afford to feed the chickens, so we butchered them. We had three goats, a billy and two nannies. One day when I woke from my nap, we had only one nanny. Mama said the other went to Heaven, but I knew different because we had meat for supper. We milked the nanny, and that was my nourishment. In August, we butchered the billy. That left one nanny. She delivered a kid, my playmate. I named her Rainy."

Alice sipped her iced tea and fingered Lucy's dainty cloven hooves.

"Go on," Santiago said.

"Well, the drought worsened. The potatoes burned up. There was no food to store for winter. We boiled cow parsnips for vegetables. My brother shot a squirrel or an occasional pigeon with his BB gun. We were hanging on by a string. I wasn't aware of how bad things were. I had Rainy."

She gazed at Lucy sleeping in her lap and ran her fingers through its fur until she found its tiny pulse. "Do you want to hear more?"

"Continue," Santiago repeated, looking and sketching.

"Then the buzzards started circling. I'm talking turkey vultures. We had a dead box elder tree in the yard where they'd alight and glower at us. I remember Mama screaming, 'Get out of here.' She'd throw rocks at them, yelling and working up a sweat. Then she'd carry Rainy to the goat pen and me to the house. I'd plead with her to bring Rainy into the house or leave me in the goat pen. Nothing doing.

"Mid-August and still no rain. The nanny goat dried up, so there was no milk. I don't remember being hungry, but I must have been. I do remember fruit cocktail, cans of it. And dates. Where they came from, I don't know. To this day, I don't eat either of them.

"We must have been at the end of our rope. One day, a game warden came by. Said he'd seen buzzards circling and thought they had spotted a dying fawn. He drove up the driveway in a cloud of dust. Mama and my brother met him at the porch. I bet he knew he had a catastrophe staring at him. 'Everything okay?' he asked. Before Mama could answer, he said he'd take us to town. Get us food. Medical attention. A safe place to live." She stopped and looked at the wall, the windshield, the other wall, then lifted Lucy to her face.

"Continue," he said, "and hold still."

"Mama said we'd be okay if he'd just shoot those god damned buzzards. I remember him saying 'I can't do that, ma'am.' He persisted. Said he'd take us to town. Asked us what we wanted to bring along.

"'Oh, we're not going anywhere,' Mama said. 'The government check will be here in a couple days. We'll be fine.' My brother yanked her skirt. I sat by the front step playing with Rainy. Mama asked if we could have some time to think about this. She wondered who would look after the place if we were to leave. Who would feed the goats? Who would tend . . . ? She pointed to the garden, all brittle leaves and bony stems and brown vines. The buzzards circled the house and lit in the box elder tree.

"'Come on, Mama,' my brother said. 'We don't have much to pack.'

"Mama looked at me and asked the game warden if we could bring the goats. Or at least the kid. The game warden said he was sorry, but they didn't allow animals or pets where we were going. He walked to his truck and stuffed a lunchbox and tools behind the seat. He said we could all fit in front. He'd put our belongings in the back. But we'd better get going, because it was a long drive into town, and we'd have arrangements to make once we got there."

Alice stopped and sipped her tea. "You know, I should get back." She scanned the walls for a clock. "My daughter will be waiting."

"She won't be looking for you in this weather."

Alice stared through the windshield at a wall of rain. "Feels odd talking about a drought during a downpour."

"Continue."

She cuddled the goat to her breast. "I was five. I had no idea what was happening. Mama told me to put Rainy in the pen, said she guessed we were leaving. My brother ran in the house, pulled a suitcase out of the closet, and grabbed a couple of boxes from the wood room. I followed him. Mama packed groceries in boxes, picture albums, blankets, and towels in a bushel basket, and our clothes in the suitcase. She asked if I had put Rainy in the pen. I was confused. Why were we packing? Where were we going? Mother hollered, 'Put Rainy in the pen and say goodbye. We'll come back once we're settled.'

"I walked outside carrying Rainy. Buzzards stretched their long, ugly necks and flew to a cottonwood tree by the goat pen. They flapped their wings, waiting. The nanny goat called her baby as if to say, 'Come away.' Rainy stood by the fence.

"'Hurry,' Mama called. When I saw the warden lifting boxes into the truck, I knew we were leaving. 'Mama,' I said. 'Rainy.'

"'She'll be all right 'til we get back.' She seemed to be crying. Somehow, at five years old, I knew there'd be no coming back. Mama walked to get me. I held onto the woven wire pen. She lifted me, pried my fingers from the wire, and carried me to the truck. I was strong enough to struggle, frightened enough to scream. Then a buzzard swooped from the tree and landed on the goat shed.

"The truck was loaded. The warden sat behind the wheel, my brother in the middle, and me on Mama's lap at the window. I screamed for Rainy. I remember her faint *maa maa*."

Alice stopped. Santiago peered at her over his glasses. Rain pounded on the roof. "You asked why I raised goats," she said. "That's why. To vindicate myself. To seek their forgiveness."

Santiago sketched. Alice waited. She looked through the windshield again, hoping to see Mr. Merritt's car in the driveway. "What time is it? I should be getting back."

"We have plenty of time, and it's raining harder. Per chance, are you a Capricorn?"

"I don't know. I was born on New Years Day."

"You're a Capricorn."

"I don't cotton much to that crap."

"Crap?" He stopped sketching. And then, "Did you ever go back to your home place? To Rainy's pen?"

"No. Mother found it hard to talk about the farm, let alone visit it."

"Your brother. What happened to him?"

"We were separated at Social Services. I never saw him again." She looked out the windshield. "I really must be going."

"We'll wait." He stood placing the sketch behind him and rested his hand on her shoulder. "I want to show you something."

She cringed, shivering at his touch.

He walked to the sound system and pushed buttons. Sharp and metallic music played, drowning the hammer of rain.

"This is my home, and a man's home is his castle," he shouted over the music. "And every castle has a sanctuary." He opened a closet door. "This is my sanctuary. This is my altar."

A narrow closet space was draped in black. Black velvet, Alice guessed. Atop a table, a white marble slab shone. Santiago reached in a drawer and placed candle holders on either side of the marble. He pulled a lighter from his pocket and lit the candles. The candle holders were figures, half man, half goat.

Alice hugged Lucy and stared. Her head pounded from the music. She looked at Santiago, then looked at the door.

He reached for Lucy and held her close to his face. He stroked her pointed beard, then his own. "Ever notice how much a goat resembles our image of the devil?" He traced her tiny face. "The horns, the beard. The eyes. Satanic yellow eyes." He held the goat close to his face again, his nose touching her snout. "Lucy. My little Lucifer," he whispered.

Alice poised to rise and ran her fingers through her hair. She gasped, felt a scream building.

He placed the goat on the marble slab, then handed it back to Alice. She held her breath.

The rain drummed a staccato beat to the music. Alice snuggled Lucy as if she were holding a rescued child. "I'd better be going," she said. "My daughter will be looking for me. Take me back."

"You're in no position to make demands, woman." He sat and retrieved the sketch pad. "Now let me finish this. Would you like more iced tea?"

"No." She stroked the goat, finding a new unexpected strength. "What will happen to Lucy?"

Santiago tilted his head, glanced at Alice, and sketched. "What do you suspect?"

"I can't bear to think about what I suspect." She pressed the goat to her chest. "I can't let anything happen to her."

"You assume you have a lot of power."

"I won't let anything happen to her. I'll take her with me." She stood and looked at the door.

"Sit down," he said, without looking up. "You're not going anywhere."

Alice sat. The warm fur of the goat comforted her, empowered her. "I'm not afraid of you," she said. "I'm not afraid of anything. If you don't let me take Lucy, I'll stay here. It's no worse than Good Shepherd. And a helluva lot better than with my daughter and son-in-law. I could have a pet goat again."

"You're not staying here, and you're not taking Lucy."

"Watch me."

"Don't make me laugh."

"You could use some domestic help. When's the last time you cleaned this place? And when's the last time you washed that shirt?" She whiffed the smell of burning wax and turned toward the altar. "You better blow those candles out. They're dripping on your altar cloth."

He rose, pinched the candle flames, and placed the candlesticks in the drawer. He closed the closet door. "Satisfied?"

Alice glanced at the goat and nodded.

"Now, do you want to see your portrait?" He waited, holding the sketch pad to his chest, then swinging it in front of her. A large five-pointed star. Horns in the top points, ears in the middle, a goatee in the bottom. She stared and focused. The face. It was hers. Her chin, her nose, her mouth. Her drawn cheeks, her hair pulled back. Not her eyes. Yellow eyes with slotted pupils. Goat eyes. Devil eyes. "Would you like it?" he teased, swinging it toward her, then snatching it back. "You can't have it. It's one of my best works. I'll keep it."

Alice hugged Lucy. "He doesn't scare me," she said to the goat. "You and I are going to get along just fine."

Santiago rose from his chair, slid the portrait in a stack, and walked to the driver's seat. "Looks like your friend isn't going to show up. Put Lucy down and show me where the goats are." He walked to the rear door.

Alice placed Lucy in the pen and followed him outside, then stared at the bus. A multi-pastel colored arc framed the rear door. Smiley faces and gaudy flowers and peace signs adorned the light blue side walls. "I was riding in that outrageous contraption?" Alice said. Ballooned graffiti lettering on the side announced: End of the Rainbow.

The goats scrambled when Alice and Santiago appeared, rushing against the far fence and into the shed. "They're afraid of you," she said. "Mr. Merritt keeps treats in a cabinet inside the door. They'll come for them."

When Santiago walked into the barn, Alice ran behind the bus, out of sight, toward the logging trail. *If I can make it to the trees*, she thought, *he'll never find me*. She hurried past the garden, past the fence, toward the trail, toward the trees.

"Get back here, you crazy woman," she heard him call.

She ran farther into the woods, the rain-laden leaves swishing her face and soaking her hair and clothes. She stooped low and watched the end of the trail.

"I see your footsteps in the grass, but I'm not coming for you. Lucy will be disappointed if you don't return."

Alice stayed in a crouched position. *He'll leave in time*, she thought. *Then I can take the trail home*. She watched Santiago walk toward the bus and enter.

Good, she thought. *Tanya will wait awhile, then call Good Shepherd to report my absence. By then, I'll be home.*

Santiago appeared at the end of the trail holding Lucy. "This innocent kid shouldn't have to pay for your idiocy, now should she?"

The kid bleated as if being squeezed.

Alice clamped her eyes shut and covered her ears.

The kid bleated again, louder, louder.

She watched him carry the kid to the bus. He released the latch on the collar, and dangled the leash from the door handle.

"Rainy," she cried, and walked out of the woods.

Back in the bus, Santiago turned the ignition on. The wipers arced and scraped after a few cycles. "Let's go," he said, "and keep your mouth shut."

When they approached the fairground, Alice said, "Watch for a blue pickup."

It was waiting at the gate. "Keep going. I don't want my daughter to see me getting out of this hippie bus."

August weather is whimsical. It shifted again, this time to a cool breeze from the west. Rain settled the dust. Air smelled fresh and un-breathed. A pale sun peered through lingering clouds and a splatter of raindrops. Alice stood on the rear step of the bus holding Lucy. The leash dangled from the knob.

Alice had never believed in rainbows. She wouldn't expect one now.

Hug

Dr. Harold Provence lingers at the kitchen table with a second cup of coffee and scans the morning paper. It's 7:30; the radio will forecast the weather soon. Or it already has. Dr. Provence concedes he hasn't tasted the coffee, can't remember the headlines he's read, and didn't hear the report he waited for. At his age nearing retirement, distraction is commonplace, he rationalizes. Maybe it's not age. Maybe the distraction is this house. Maybe it's the *we* memories that are reduced to *I*.

Why not pack up and leave? He knows why. Because it's easier to reconcile a painful past than confront an unknown future.

Today is Wednesday, the day he makes rounds at Good Shepherd to reassure the residents that their aches and pains come with the territory. He checks his list of appointments for the morning—Hazel Benson, prescription refill; Adam Douglas, sore joints, arthritis; Alice Johnson, seizure medication; Pearl Witte, nothing specific; Stanley Klein, admissions exam.

Hug

Wednesday is the day the cleaning lady visits. He walks through the house. He hangs shirts in the bedroom and puts socks in the hamper; scrubs the toilet bowl and replaces towels in the bath; stacks unread mail and fluffs couch pillows in the living room. His wedding picture tilts where it hangs at the stair landing. He straightens it. Back in the kitchen, he loads his cup in the dishwasher. Irene would not allow the cleaning lady to see an unkempt house.

But Irene isn't here. A year ago, September 17, she was rear-ended on a quick trip to town, a trip that could have been avoided had he been thoughtful on the drive home from the clinic. Once home, he had volunteered to return; he should have insisted. For a month after the accident, Irene lay comatose before he could consider the inevitable. The accident and his decision weighed on him. Nights he played and re-played the *what if* scenarios until futility exhausted him, leaving him to sleep in agonizing fits.

The phone rings. His daughter calls from her home in Virginia. Her voice, so similar to her mother's, calms him. "Just checking in, Dad. How's your day?"

He savors her words, the grace of her voice. He accepts her invitation to fly out for the weekend of his grandson's first varsity football game, and makes a note to clear his calendar. He invents small talk—the weather, the garden, the neighbors, to keep her on the phone.

"I have to go, Dad. My day to serve lunch at the shelter."

He replaces the receiver, too soon, feeling cheated. He lifts it again and hears a dial tone, not the echo of her voice he hoped for, not one final word.

The highway north to Good Shepherd hugs the river, now in sparkling full view, now hidden by dense woodlands of jack pines and yellowed aspen. The timber stands give way to a tamed landscape, a backcountry of farm homesteads with broken barns and clapboard houses reminiscent of his boyhood. A vacated schoolhouse turned township hall abuts a fenced cemetery. Car windows down, the hum of crisp fall air calms him, like his daughter's voice.

Dr. Provence finishes his first three appointments at Good Shepherd before coffee break and, as is custom, has coffee with director Mrs. Fitzgerald and nurse Betty Brockett. They discuss Stanley Klein.

"Been here less than a month," Mrs. Fitzgerald reports. "Tends to be reclusive, as most new residents are. May have trouble making friends with our few male residents. Even more trouble with the females."

"Widowed? Married? Divorced?"

"None of the above. Lifelong bachelor. Still owns the family farm south of town. You passed it on the way in."

Dr. Provence lifts his cup and peers over the rim. "Why is he here?"

"Cardiovascular disease," Betty says. "His sister found him unconscious in the barn on a chance visit. He was hospitalized and released on the condition that he check into an assisted living facility."

"Ask for his medical file before my next visit." He checks his watch. "I'd better see Miss Pearl Witte."

Dr. Provence allows extra time for Pearl. He accuses her of imagining symptoms to justify appointments, the way he imagined sins as a boy to justify confession. But her conversations have a positive side. She is an accurate barometer of communal health at Good Shepherd.

In Pearl's apartment, Montovani music blends with an aroma of warm vanilla. Shades are drawn, a candle flickers. "Come in, Dr. Provence," she says in a lilt.

"How are we doing today?"

"Same old aches and pains. Cookies? Coffee? But of course not. We just finished coffee break." She sits at the kitchen table and slides her sweater sleeve up for the blood pressure cuff. She puts a finger over her mouth, as if to still herself. When he finishes, she fidgets with her sleeve, her hankie, her bracelet. "There might be something you could help me with, Doctor. I'd like your thoughts on my having a tummy tuck."

"Miss Witte, I can say without any thought that I wouldn't recommend it. Not at your age, and not in your condition, which is . . ." he stammers, "which is remarkable. For your age."

Pearl smoothes a crease on the tablecloth.

Dr. Provence continues, "Often that surgery is cosmetic rather than health related." He tucks the blood pressure cuff in his bag. "Might there be a reason for your request? A new romance perhaps?"

"You're so perceptive, Dr. Provence. I've been trying to attract my neighbor's attention since he arrived. We're the same age. I thought I'd turn his head if I came on like Marilyn Monroe." She laughs.

"You might do better coming on like Julia Child. Invite him for dinner. Or start with coffee and cookies. The way to a man's heart is through his stomach, you know."

"Oh, Dr. Provence. You're perceptive, but you're so old fashioned."

Stanley Klein is stoic, answers questions with a nod, sucks an unlit pipe. He hasn't shaved for days and wears a chambray shirt, pencils in the pocket, and stiff new overalls rolled at the cuff.

"Anything else I can help you with?" Dr. Provence asks after he checks his vitals and exhausts his litany of questions.

Stan sucks his pipe, shakes his head. "Can't think of any."

"I've asked to see your medical records. Any recent illnesses other than your heart issues? Surgeries? Any problems with prescriptions?"

Stan shakes his head, *No.*

Dr. Provence closes the folder and places it in his clipboard. The room is quiet, desolate; the furniture is modest: a wicker rocker and sofa, kitchen table with unmatched chairs, television, bare walls.

"There are a couple tests I'd like you to take. Not physical health tests. Multiple choice, true false."

"Don't do well with tests."

"We're not testing intelligence, Stan. I'd like to know how you'll fare in a group home. I understand you weren't given many options when you left the hospital. Any place you'd rather be? Other than home?"

Stan shakes his head. He gazes out the window.

Dr. Provence sees him withdraw, disappear. "You still have the farm. Who's tending it?"

"My sister. She checks on my dog Max."

Dr. Provence prompts him. "You must feel like a fish out of water. Your life in the country: independent and solitary. Your life here: noisy and crowded. More people in one building than in a square mile at the farm."

Stan sucks his pipe.

"Let's schedule the tests. I'll have them sent here. Take them at your convenience, but plan to complete them by Monday and give them to Mrs. Fitzgerald. I'll drop by Wednesday and see how you're doing."

Stan pats his shirt pocket as if looking for tobacco.

Dr. Provence leans forward, resting his elbows on the table. "You must miss your dog Max. Did you ask if you could bring him here?"

"There's a sixteen-pound weight limit. Max is five times that."

"Would you like me to ask Mrs. Fitzgerald to reconsider?"

Stan lifts his eyes, then drops them. "I don't think she'd budge."

"But would you like me to ask?"

Hug

"Guess it can't hurt."

Dr. Provence closes his briefcase and stands. "I'll see what I can do. See you next week, Stan."

The following Wednesday on the way to Good Shepherd, Dr. Provence slows as he approaches the mile of farmsteads, one of which will be Stan Klein's. He wonders why he feels compassion for him, why he's going the extra mile to understand his condition, his plight. He wonders, but it pleases him to feel compassion.

He slows at a driveway where a hand-painted sign, FRESH EGGS, is wired to a mailbox stuffed with yellowed newspapers. STANLEY KLEIN is stenciled in faded black paint. He follows a pair of tire ruts in the gravel drive that straddle a strip of weeds. Thistles bloom and droop in the yard. A plastic bag snagged on a barbed wire fence waves at him. He remembers the dog, but sees nothing.

He parks the car. The house, the barn, the sheds look vacant, feel abandoned, deserted, and in a way, familiar. Not unlike his boyhood home. The L-shaped farm house with open porch, the windmill, the path to the granary and barrel-roofed barn. The open machine shed, his dad unseen, greasing the corn picker. His dad . . .

At Good Shepherd, he reviews Stan's tests with Mrs. Fitzgerald. "We may have to bend some rules to get this guy acclimated," Dr. Provence says. "He's a loner and won't last long here unless we wean him away from the farm, unless we let him make trips out there now and then. Maybe bring his dog in for an occasional overnight."

"You know we have rules."

"I saw his place on the way in. A hundred and eighty degrees out of phase with Good Shepherd. I'm free on Wednesday afternoons. I could drive him there."

"You're the doctor."

"I slowed down when I passed your farm this morning." Dr. Provence sits at the table and opens the test folder in Stan's room. "I looked for your dog, but didn't see him. What breed is he?"

Stan nurses a cup of coffee, eyes down, standing at the sink. "Black Lab."

"Interesting. That's what we had when I lived on the farm. Easy keepers, affectionate pets, great watch dogs." He scratches a note on the score sheet. "Stan, it's going to take a while for you to make Good Shepherd your new home. With no live-in help, you won't be able to return to the farm."

"I have a sister," Stan says and sits opposite the doctor.

"Isn't she the one who suggested you move here?"

Stan pulls a pipe from his pocket and tamps his shirt for tobacco.

"There are no surprises in your test scores. You have issues; we all have issues. Yours appear to be tolerable, maybe even solvable. What is apparent is your problem with persons in authority. Often that can be traced to a bad experience with an abusive teacher or a minister, a law enforcement officer or a parent."

Stan looks down, looks out the window, taps his pipe in his palm.

"I'd like to work with you on this. What do you think?"

"I think I'd like to get back home. See how Max is doing."

Dr. Provence stands and places a hand on Stan's shoulder. "Tell you what. I'll arrange with Mrs. Fitzgerald for me to drive you to the farm next week after rounds. In the meantime, think about what I said. Problems that might be caused by people in authority. Will you do that?"

Stan nods his head.

"I'll stop by the kitchen on the way out and steal a hotdog. Give it to Max on the way home. Sound okay?"

He smiles.

Hug

Next Wednesday as Dr. Provence and Stan leave Good Shepherd, Pearl Witte runs to the door and waves to the car. "Oh, Dr. Providence," she calls.

Stan continues to the car and strikes a match against his pant leg to light his pipe.

"I have good news for you." She turns to confirm no one is listening. "You suggested I invite Mr. Baxter to dinner. Well, he accepted. Saturday night. I'll silently toast you over my first glass of wine."

"Great," he says. "By the way, I'm flattered. My name is *Provence*. Not *Providence*."

Pearl winks. "Oh yes it is."

Stan is quiet during the drive, pensive, rolls the windows up to relight his pipe, then rolls them down. Dr. Provence turns the radio off. He wonders if Stan is excited about returning to the farm. He doesn't show it. No sound now except wind rushing in the windows. Leaves along the treed highway are a jacquard blur of reds, yellows, greens, and browns.

In the driveway, a dog barks and follows the car to the house. Stan opens the door and calls him. Max bounds for Stan, plants his paws on his shoulders. "Down, boy." Stan scratches the dog, then walks to the house. He reaches under a floor mat for the key.

Windmill blades rotate and creak in the shifting breeze. A dog dish sits on the stoop, with remnants from the last feeding.

"Come on in. I'll brew a pot of coffee."

The kitchen air is stale. Breakfast dishes and a flyswatter sit on the table amid piles of papers. The kitchen is furnished as it would have been the day it was built: a wood burning stove with warming ovens above the cooking surface, two ovens with white porcelain handles, and water heaters on the side, a stove pipe stretching across the room to the chimney.

"Pull up a chair," Stan says. "It's chilly in here. I'll make a fire." He fills the Mr. Coffee and places kindling in the stove.

A sink cabinet holds a white enameled dish pan beside a gray towel hanging from a roller rack. Slip-pocket calendars and a decaled tin match holder decorate yellow enameled walls. Dr. Provence watches Stan through an oval mirror that hangs over a commode with a wash bowl.

Stan lights a fire in the woodstove, then rinses two cups in the sink. Dr. Provence walks to the window and looks across a pasture, across the highway, to a small cemetery on the horizon.

"You see that wagon in the barnyard?" Stan asks, relaxed and conversational. "A man stopped by and offered to buy it. Said he'd give me ten bucks. Hell, it's worth more than that just sitting there doing nothing."

Dr. Provence looks at the wagon buried in thistles, its broken box and rusted wheels suggesting it has outlived its usefulness. "That wagon, this farm, this kitchen remind me of my boyhood home." He sits at the table, tapping his fingers. "I was eighteen when I left. I remember the day. We stood in a kitchen like this." He turns to face Stan, priming him to talk. "I waited upstairs with the door closed and my suitcase packed, practicing my goodbye speech on the dog. Another Black Lab."

Stan nods, watching the coffee percolate.

"I remember having second thoughts about leaving. Four of us slept upstairs, but at that time, I was alone. I was scared. I was comfortable there. I feared leaving. Do you understand what I'm saying?"

Stan nods his head. "Leaving home isn't easy. Wasn't when I went to my grandparents, and wasn't when I went to Good Shepherd."

"I remember my dog's ears rose when he heard a car," Dr. Provence continues. "He jumped to the door and barked. I saw a car turn off the gravel and up the drive. I remember that car, a big black Buick, coming slow, negotiating the washouts in the drive

Hug

and scattering a flock of chickens. The driver, my uncle Paul, parked near a path to the front door which we never used. He wore a white shirt and black pants and wiped a handkerchief across his neck. My mother called, 'Uncle Paul is here.' I heard her greet him and invite him in. She called Dad to join us for coffee, then called me from the stairwell to come down and meet my uncle.

"My legs went weak. I staggered, then steadied myself against the bed and lifted the suitcase. I wondered if I was doing the right thing. What if this didn't work? Where would I go? I took a deep breath and walked downstairs."

Stan lifts a stove lid and adds lumber scraps to the fire, then pours coffee.

"I was a small boy for eighteen, ready to start college." Dr. Provence inhales black coffee fumes. "I wore my best clothes—white shirt, thrift shop oversized pants bunched at the waist. I carried a suitcase strapped shut with an old belt. Mother introduced me to Uncle Paul.

"I remember the kitchen smelled of fly spray. The countertop was stacked with fruit jars, dirty dishes, a coffee can. Like that . . ." Dr. Provence points to the cupboard. Stan turns to the cupboard and nods.

"A cabinet door was missing, I remember, and the silverware drawer tilted off its slide. Flies crawled everywhere, on the window screens and countertops and table. Mother held the coffee pot with a nervous smile, not able to pour because of her trembling. I was embarrassed. I knew she was anxious to finish this goodbye business.

"I walked up to Uncle Paul and offered my hand. He was older than mom and dad, red sweaty face, bulging belly. His white shirt was sweat-stained and wrinkled. I remember his words. 'Harold,' he said. 'The man of the hour.'"

Dr. Provence sips his coffee. Flies crawl on the table, and Stan grabs the flyswatter.

"My dad opened the backdoor and let it slam behind him. He didn't offer a welcome, just something casual like 'I see you made it,' and walked to the sink to wash his hands. His overalls were greasy and his shirt sleeves patched. He hadn't shaved since Sunday mass. To inform us how he felt, he said he supposed we were in a hurry, that we had a lot of miles to put on yet today." Dr. Provence sips his coffee and looks at Stan petting Max.

"Mother knew how Dad felt about his brother. Paul was the successful one, the house in town, the fancy car, the good job. Dad said that did him a lot of good. All the comforts of life, and no kids to leave it to."

Dr. Provence stops, watches Stan's reaction to his *no kids* comment.

"Where was your uncle taking you?" Stan asks, as if the words conjured a memory.

"He and Aunt Minnie were childless. For reasons I didn't know, they took an interest in me. Thought from my school grades and my interest in science, I deserved a better opportunity. They offered to send me to college, finance my education. I wonder why Dad didn't object." He pauses, as if still wondering.

"Mother poured coffee for Dad. She asked me if I wanted a cup. 'Growing boys shouldn't drink coffee,' Uncle Paul said with a laugh and asked if they had any questions.

"Dad asked what it was going to cost them.

"Nothing. Uncle Paul said I had a scholarship from his company, and he and Aunt Minnie would handle the balance. He chuckled and said, 'Of course, when he's rich and famous, we hope he repays the favor.' I scratched the dog's neck and looked at Mother.

"Uncle Paul continued with his information, holding the floor like a Sunday preacher. Classes begin on Monday. I'd get a Thanksgiving weekend break and then continue until the Friday before

Hug

Christmas. Then a two-week break. He said I'd be free to stay at school or travel home. He and Aunt Minnie would be in California for the winter, so if I traveled, I'd need bus fare. I saw my mother's strained glare.

"Dad finished his coffee and said he had to finish fixing the hay baler before chores, which he'd have to do with one less hand. He stared at me. Mother asked if we'd like a sandwich to eat on the road. Or a jar of ice water. Paul said that Minnie would have dinner waiting for us when we arrived.

"Then he asked if I wanted to give my mother and dad a goodbye hug. I froze. I didn't remember ever hugging my mother, hadn't touched her for weeks, months. And if then, it was an accidental brush. And Dad. I had never hugged him, hadn't touched him, hadn't brushed against him that I could remember.

"I looked at Mother, broken and aged. I walked to her out of obedience or pity, I don't know which. I touched her shoulders and hugged her."

He stops. "Do you see Stan, our young backgrounds are not that different?"

Stan nods his head and turns toward the window. He scratches Max's neck. "We were poor at the same time." He relights his pipe. "Looks like you did better than me though. A doctor. A big car. A family."

"Did you ever think of marriage, Stan? Or having a family?"

"Yup. Once in my late thirties. She was in a hurry. Tried to get me into bed our first time together. I figured she wanted to get pregnant. Get married. I didn't want kids. Didn't want them to go through what I suffered."

"You have a sister who lives close. Any other sisters or brothers?"

"Nope. Just us two now. Mother and Dad both dead. They're buried in that cemetery up the road. I was fifteen when Dad died. The farm was more than Mother and two kids could handle. I moved in with Grandpa and Grandma, and my mother and sister lived with an aunt until Mother died. She said she wouldn't sell the farm. Said someday it would be mine."

Stan tenses when he talks about moving, then relaxes when he walks to the stove. Max chews on a piece of firewood by the door. Dr. Provence looks at his watch. "I should be going soon. How about we finish our coffee in the car and pick up where we left off next week?"

"Stan's comfortable talking at the farm. I don't think I'd get that from him here," Dr. Provence reports to Mrs. Fitzgerald and Betty the following Wednesday. "He's agreed to return there with me after rounds today."

"What's the reason for your optimism?" Betty asks.

"He and I had similar youths. His house, his farm struck a chord with me. My plan is to share my story with him and hope he sees common ground. The difference between us is that no one interceded for him, no one intercepted his arc."

He looks out the window into a glorious fall day. "How could I not be optimistic?"

The sumac in the garden is turning red, the birch yellow. Finches crowd the feeder, their gold plumage fading to winter. Sky though the canopy of trees shines a brilliant September blue.

"I wouldn't have guessed your commonality," Mrs. Fitzgerald says.

"It's true. Interesting, isn't it, how when we're young, one person we regard with respect pays a compliment that propels us forward. Another person we regard with authority degrades us, and we live a lesser life. The person who nudged me was Uncle Paul. I hope to find who Stan's demon was."

Mrs. Fitzgerald shuffles papers. "I don't understand," she says. "It's been years since I've heard of a doctor making house calls." She looks at the clock. "I have a noon board meeting. Betty, you're in charge."

Hug

"You've observed Stan more than I," Dr. Provence says to Betty. "Care to walk to the park after lunch and share your diagnosis?"

"It's a great day for a walk," she says, "but I don't diagnose."

Betty Brockett had been Dr. Provence's nurse when he moved to Browns Prairie and began his residency at Jordan Memorial. She and his wife Irene had shopped together, attended yoga class together, joined the same book club. "You spend more time with her than I do," he had said.

During rounds, Betty had learned Dr. Provence's mannerisms, his irritants, his sources of joy. "You know me better than my wife does," he joked more than once.

Leaves blanket the sidewalk, and more leaves tumble with each breath of wind. They walk in silence, the sublime autumn air and golden aura of foliage impossible to describe and a sacrilege to verbalize.

He breaks the silence. "My time with Stan is more than his issues. They're mine too."

"I got that impression."

"When I told my story to Stan, I realized I still have issues with Dad. I stopped my story when I reached the crucible."

"Which was . . . ?"

"When I was asked to hug him." He kicks his foot, scattering leaves crunching on the sidewalk.

"Irene was aware of my issues with Dad. She encouraged me to work things out before he died. I promised her, and me, I would. I didn't."

"Your dad's been dead for years. What's the lesson learned?"

"I want to spend more time with my family. Anne called and invited me to my grandson's first varsity football game. I'm going."

"Good."

"I'm cutting back on my hours at the clinic. Taking appointments on Tuesday and Thursday only. No new patients. I'll spend Wednesdays at Good Shepherd."

"Good again."

"I want to know my grandchildren. Want them to know me. Want to share my values. Polish my legacy."

"Any impediments to your plan?'

"Yes. The house. I'm considering selling it. I don't need four bedrooms. I'm not able to make the decision today. Too many memories." He slides his hands in his pockets, head down.

Betty places a hand on his shoulder. "You're not selling the memories. You're selling the house."

After the walk, Dr. Provence and Stan drive to the farm. "We were talking about my leaving home last week," Dr. Provence says in the kitchen. "You were talking about your dad dying and moving in with your grandparents."

Stan has plugged in the percolator and sits. He looks uncertain, uncomfortable in the deafening silence. Max rubs against his leg, holding a wood stick. The phone rings, startling them both.

"Hal-low," Stan says. He is quiet for a time. "No, I don't think so." He hangs the phone in the wall cradle. "That was my sister. She drove by and saw your car in the driveway."

He sits, quiet again. The windmill creaks. Flies buzz against the window screen. "She asked me to go to church on Sunday. Almost every week, she asks me." He checks the coffee and pours two cups.

"I haven't been in that church for fifty years. Didn't even go to my mother's funeral." He stirs powdered creamer in his cup. "I probably never will go back." Max chews on the wood stick, now under the table. The rotating windmill blades chop the afternoon sunlight through the window. The kitchen smells of wood smoke. An eye-shaped mantle clock on the refrigerator is quiet, stopped at nine-thirty.

Hug

"You must have had a horrible experience to keep you away from your mother's funeral," Dr. Provence says.

"I haven't been to that church since I was fifteen." His voice breaks. "It wasn't easy for me in Catholic school. I always had trouble learning. It didn't help that my older sister was an A student. The teachers expected me to be the same. I was fifteen and still in eighth grade." He looked at the floor, out the window, anywhere but at Dr. Provence.

"The kids teased me at recess. *Dummkopf*, they called me. My grandma told me what that meant. She said I must forgive them. She quoted the bible. 'Forgive them, for they know not what they do.' At prayers that night, when we came to 'forgive us our trespasses, as we forgive those . . .' she tapped me on the shoulder. She was a great forgiver. She forgave Grandpa for boozing away all their money and for dying poor."

Dr. Provence leans forward, wanting to touch his shoulder. "So you lived through your dad's death, then your grandpa's."

Stan nodded. "Sister Justine was my eighth grade teacher. She was sick most of the year, and damned if she didn't die before the last day of school. I had problems with reading and spelling. And I couldn't remember my catechism. Sister sent notes home with me. Grandma was a devout church goer, and she'd have me practice after night chores." He paused, as if trying yet to remember.

"Go on."

"Sister would call on me to recite the commandments. I couldn't remember them. She'd tell me to name the Apostles. I could remember Peter and Paul. Then she'd say 'Stanley Klein, you will stay in the class room during recess until you memorize the commandments.'

"When the class left, she locked the door. Then she'd drag me to the cloak room carrying her ruler. She'd say 'Hold out your hands.' It hurt, but she was weak. She'd wheeze and hold her stomach. I thought she'd die."

Stan hesitates and exhales. His voice trembles, his hand quivers. He relights his pipe, lifts his cup from the table, and sets it down.

"She'd ask me the same question a week later. Same answer. Same punishment. One day, she seemed sicker than usual. She asked me to name the sacraments. I could only remember baptism, penance, and holy communion. I knew that a wedding was a sacrament, but I couldn't remember the name. And that was only four. At recess time, she told me to see the principal.

"Mr. Becker knew I was coming," Stan continues. "He met me at the rectory door and pulled me inside. 'So, Stanley Klein,' he said, 'you aren't learning your catechism.' I didn't know whether to say yes or no. He asked me why.

"We were in his office. It was dark and smelled like dust and wine. The drapes were closed. He had a small lamp on his desk and an empty glass and papers strewn around. He screamed at me. 'Answer me, Stanley Klein.'

"I told him I had a problem remembering. I tried, but I couldn't. I read things over and over, but I couldn't remember them the next day. He asked me if I was saying Sister Justine was not a good teacher. I shook my head no. Then he said if Sister Justine is a good teacher, you must be a bad student.

"I started to feel scared. I saw his face get red and his shoulders shake. He walked to the desk and took his ruler and walked behind me, blocking the door. He screamed again. 'Hold out your hands.' He struck me hard. 'Turn your hands over.' It hurt terrible. I closed my eyes. I couldn't defend myself.

"He kept beating me. On my shoulders, my arms. Then on my neck. I could smell his sweat, like musty alcohol. I folded my head into my chest.

"He called me a little son-of-a-bitch. Said he'd teach me to respect my teachers. Teach me to learn my catechism. He called

Hug

my whole family a bunch of freeloaders and said my mother never did pay for my dad's funeral mass."

He paused and looked at his coffee, looked at his pipe, looked at Max.

"You're doing great, Stan," Dr. Provence says. "And then . . ."

"I tried to get away. I ran around the desk and stumbled over a wastepaper basket. He fell on top of me, breathing in my face. My knee was right in front of his balls. I didn't even think. I gave him the knee with all my might. He screamed like a stuck pig. Then he curled up and rolled off me, and I ran out the door."

Stan stops and lights his pipe. He inhales and releases the smoke in a long, slow stream that clouds the room like incense.

"Grandma asked me about the marks on my neck," Stan continues. "I told her we were playing football at recess. She didn't see my hands. The next morning, I told her I was sick. And I was. I didn't go the school the next day or the next week or the next month. And I haven't been to church since eighth grade."

Stan looks at his hands. His face tightens. Max looks at Stan, offers him the wood stick. The wind has stopped and the windmill is silent.

"Stanley Klein," Dr. Provence begins. He reaches for Stan's hands, touches them, holds them. Farmer's hands. Working hands, large and calloused. He conjures welts, bruises, blood. "Close your eyes."

Stan bristles when touching a man, tenses, pulls back, then relaxes. He bows his head.

"Stanley Klein. This is the voice of Mr. Becker. For years, my spirit has been tormenting me. I have wanted to ask your forgiveness. I can't rest. I have been dead for years, but I need your forgiveness before I can be free from this earth. I haunt the school, the church, the rectory. I waited for you to return after I died. I waited for you at your mother's funeral."

Stan bows his head, his hands limp. Dr. Provence massages them, turns them, presses them. "Forgive me, Stanley Klein," he continues. "Please forgive me."

He releases Stan's hands and waits. He taps him on the shoulder.

"And I bless you in the name of our fathers, our mothers, and our brothers and sisters." Stan raises a finger to his forehead, his heart, and either shoulder. "Amen."

Stan nibbles his lower lip. He relaxes his jaw and lowers his eyes. He folds his hands as if praying. His shoulders slope, and he blows a breath. He looks at Dr. Provence. Quiet.

The sun is low. It silhouettes Stan's body seated at the table. It floods the kitchen and reflects off the mirror. Stan pushes his chair back and walks to the west window. He stands staring, trancelike, his hands in his pockets. He looks over the pasture where his cattle fed, over the fields where he cultivated corn, over the vacant barn where pigeons circle and alight in the haymow.

Flies buzz the window. Stan lifts the sash, and the curtain waves. The windmill creaks again. "You didn't finish your story, Doctor," Stan says.

Dr. Provence raises his head. "My story?"

"You were leaving home, and you were in the kitchen with your uncle and your mother and dad."

Dr. Provence stumbles to recover. "Ah, yes. I looked at Dad standing in the doorway. Jealous, embarrassed, angry. His was the poverty I would rise above. But I had Dad in my genes, his strengths and weaknesses, his values. A sudden urge, something supernatural led me to him. I lifted my arms and held him."

Dr. Provence rises and walks across the room to Stan. He gives him a clumsy, then a relaxed hug. He releases him, places his hands on Stan's shoulders. He backs away, checks his watch, a gift from his wife Irene. He smiles and sets the correct time on the mantel clock.

Sweet Spot

"Dearly beloved, we gather here today to witness the marriage of two of our friends, two of our neighbors, two of our family. We hear of young love. We read of young love. We sing of young love. It's almost as if love is a privilege of the young. Today, we gather to refute that notion. Or perhaps to validate it. Perhaps love is a privilege of the young, the young at heart."

"Bull crap." Hazel shifted from one cheek to another on her metal chair. She nudged her son Cliff who sat beside her. "I wish they'd get on with it."

"Friends, neighbors, and family, by bearing witness to this blessed union, we do more than observe this holy rite," Pastor Luke pontificated. "By our presence, we join the bride and groom, Pearl and Arnold, as they repeat their sacred vows. By our presence, we offer . . . nay, we pledge our support, our encouragement, our affection." Pastor Luke nodded his head at the residents of Good Shepherd and their friends and families in attendance, soliciting approbation.

Hazel leaned her walker forward, tipping it with a clang into the chair ahead. The small crowd turned from the flowered trellis that framed the wedding party. Hazel returned their glare and shifted to the other cheek. "For this, I gave up *Wheel of Fortune*?" she muttered.

In the stark and honest light of October, they sat in rows before the wedding party. The sun was low and warm, adding radiance to the bride and a healthy glow to the groom. In the opposite sky, a pale sliver of moon appeared.

Beyond the trellis, the river flowed, its jeweled surface sparkling. The bride's frilled pink dress mimicked the deckle-edged rose-to-red clouds that filtered the setting sun. A faint aroma of burning leaves drifted with the breeze. Honking geese flew upriver in a lopsided V, interrupting the ceremony.

Pearl smiled at the congregated. "I ordered doves."

"Pearl, do you take Arnold to be your lawful wedded husband?"

"I do."

"And Arnold . . ."

A shotgun blasted. Another. Then another. A duck boat drifted into view, two hunters paddling toward the reeds.

Hazel poked Cliff. "I never expected this to be a shotgun wedding."

"Christ," Hazel yelled when they returned to Good Shepherd. "What the hell is this?"

The Gathering Room was a cloud of pink balloons floating over white table linens with napkins, candles, and floral centerpieces in pink and rose and lilac. A rectangular table for the wedding party completed a circle of five round tables, six place settings each. Mrs. Fitzgerald and nurse's aide Mary stood in the doorway of the director's office. Mary approached to help Hazel; she waved her away and clanked her walker to a table. Cliff positioned a chair for her. Other residents and their guests arrived, stopping inside the door and gesturing at the sight of the extravagant décor.

"Where's Andy?" Hazel asked, picking at a dish of pink and white mints.

"He's with his mother. I see him about once a month."

"What does he do in the city?"

"She has a condo downtown. He goes to the library. Eats out. Maybe sees a movie." Cliff looked at his watch. "He should be back at the condo by now."

"I hope he knows about the perverts down there."

A young woman holding Adeline by the arm approached their table. "May we join you?" She smiled at Hazel.

"Sorry. It's saved," Hazel said.

Adeline tilted her head, and toyed with her necklace. She managed a nervous tee-hee. "Oh," she said to the young woman who held her arm, "I have to go to my apartment for a minute anyway."

"Saved? Who for?" Cliff asked when they walked away.

"Not Adeline. She's goofy."

"Eloise will join us when she finishes her shift at the Muni." Cliff looked at his watch again.

"Seat her by me. I want to talk to her." Hazel tapped her cup in the saucer, signaling for coffee. "Cheyenne phoned me from out in the oil fields."

"She did? What did she want?"

"Wants to keep in touch. I told her about you and Eloise."

Two men approached the table. "These seats saved?" one asked.

"Yup," Hazel grunted.

"Mother," Cliff said, when they walked away. He pointed his fork at her. "You don't own this place. This is not your party. I'm inviting the next people that walk in to join us. Understand?"

Hazel tapped her cup in the saucer again. Harder. A catering assistant arrived with a tray of wine glasses. "I'll be your server tonight. Care for a glass of wine? We have red, white, and pink."

"I'll have a beer," Hazel said.

"Sorry. Just wine."

Hazel waved her away.

"I'll have the red," Cliff said.

Hazel shifted her weight in the chair and looked at the clock. "I wish they'd get on with the meal. The World Series starts in a half hour."

"Mother, before Eloise gets here, I want to talk to you. I've decided to ask her to move in with me."

Hazel toyed with her napkin and aligned the silverware.

Cliff folded his hands as if praying and stared ahead. "The issue for Eloise will be her teenage daughter. But we'll be in the same school district. She won't have to make new friends."

Hazel stirred imaginary coffee and looked around the room.

Cliff continued. "She has this large house, and it's just the two of them living there. It has to be expensive heating it, now with winter coming on."

Hazel shifted in her chair and waved her coffee cup toward the catering crew in the kitchen.

"And my house is too big for me, and I'm not about to move."

Hazel stared at him with a sharp glint in her gray eyes. "Cheyenne must be talking to Eloise too, because she told me this would come up. And she said you'd have a dozen practical reasons for making it happen. Listen." She pointed a spindly finger at her son. "You don't ask someone to move in with you because it costs too much to heat two houses, or because the kids don't have to change schools, or because the house is too big. You ask them because . . . because you *love* them." Hazel glanced away and cleared her throat, as if choking on the word. "At least that's what Cheyenne thinks."

"I didn't want to embarrass you," he said. "Didn't want you to hear people say I was living in sin with some small town beer saleslady."

"I'm way past embarrassment. I like Eloise. I've already decided to give her my wedding china. I want to get rid of it anyway. Costs too much money to store."

"Now *you* listen." Cliff shook his fork at her. "You don't give away your wedding china because you want to save storage costs. You give it away because you care for someone."

"Right. Now get me some coffee. Or a beer from my fridge."

"I'll get on that, Mother," Cliff said. "I want to say hello to a few friends on the way." He passed by Grace and Mary Ellen's table. "Is this the Johnny Cash celebrity table I heard about?"

"That would be us," Grace said. "We're waiting for Johnny."

They sat with one chair leaned against the table, three chairs open. The Gathering Room bustled with residents and their wedding guests finding seats and making introductions. Candles flickered and pink balloons bounced against the ceiling whenever the door opened.

"He's auditioning for a role in *Oklahoma!*," Mary Ellen said. "It's the spring musical for Northern Lights Opera. I can't see him as Curly. Poor Jud, maybe, but not Curly."

"Wish him luck," Cliff said and maneuvered to the hall.

"His fans are expecting him here today," Grace said. "They want Johnny Cash back for the Christmas party."

"He'll probably do that. He gave up the Country Western Tribute Band. But I still see remnants of Johnny Cash around the house." Mary Ellen scanned the room, now filling with older residents and younger guests—family members, friends, neighbors, caregivers. "He enrolled in the Business Management sequence at community college. Night classes after work at Wal-Mart. I'm sure he'll tell you about it."

"Good for him. I can see him in a three-piece suit. Corner office. Company car."

"Easy, Mother. He has to make it through Accounting 101 first." She scanned the room again, then faced her mother. In the dim light, Grace's cheeks were downy soft, her eyes fixed in a smiley squint, her hair in tight gray curls fresh from the beauty salon. "I had planned to wait until Johnny came to tell you this, but . . . you are going to become . . . a grandmother."

Grace dropped her purse. "I am?"

"Yup. Once we decided it was time, I was pregnant within fifteen minutes."

"The circle of life," Grace said. She reached to hug Mary Ellen. "When's the due date? Boy or girl? Any morning sickness?"

"Easy, Mother," Mary Ellen laughed.

"This party is not for Pearl and Arnold. This party is for us. Waiter," she raised an empty glass. "Champagne."

"It's exciting and it's a challenge. Do you remember when you were first pregnant with me?"

"No. I was taking care of three other kids. Why?"

"I sometimes wonder if I can care for two kids. Johnny and the baby."

"You want my opinion? I think you're too close to the problem. Johnny has come a long way in the short time you've been married." Grace assumed a maternal pose and held her daughter's wrist. She hesitated. "I think I feel two pulses."

Mary Ellen pulled away. "Mother."

Grace continued. "Don't forget Johnny's family background. That religious zealot mother of his, teaching him all pleasure was sin. His overprotective father, making decisions for him until he left home. You must have studied arrested adolescent behavior somewhere along the line. In my opinion, that's what you're seeing."

Mary Ellen stared at pink roses and carnations in the centerpiece and massaged her tummy, feeling for life.

"In my opinion," Grace added, "in time, Johnny will be an exemplary husband and the quintessential father."

"Mother, I want to believe that so bad."

Johnny appeared behind Mary Ellen, placed his hands on her shoulders, and kissed her cheek. "How are *we* doing?" he whispered.

Grace rose to hug Johnny. "Mary Ellen told me the news. Congratulations."

"Oh, what a beautiful morning. Oh, what a beautiful day," Johnny sang, his arms out, his head back, in a sweeping gesture.

"Does that mean you got the role?" Grace asked.

"I probably could have had it. I looked at the rehearsal schedule and realized there weren't enough hours in the day to be a good employee, and student, and husband, and father. And Curly."

"I'm so excited for you two. No, you three." Grace said. "I'm so excited for myself. Why do I feel the urge to knit?"

Grace felt a tap on her shoulder. "Pardon me, is this a private party? And are these seats taken?"

"Yes and no," Grace said. "Hello, Adeline. Have a seat. You must be Adeline's daughter-in-law, Jeanine. So good to see you again. This is my daughter and son-in-law, Mary Ellen and Johnny. And they're going to have a baby. And I'm going to be a grandmother." She raised her hands to her cheeks and gasped. "Oh my God, I am so excited."

"Sit. Sit," Mary Ellen said. "Hello, Jeanine," and to Grace, "Jeanine and I work together at the hospital, you know. What a beautiful dress, Adeline. You'll have to pardon the new grandmother. She's reeling from the news."

"A baby." Adeline pointed to Mary Ellen. "You're going to have a baby?" "And you're going to be a grandmother?" She tittered and looked across the room, toying with an earring. "Oh, dear."

"All kinds of wonderful news today," Mary Ellen said.

"Everything except the shotgun blasts," Grace added. "Now when do we eat? Let me guess the menu. Pink salmon, Pink Lady apple sauce, pink champagne."

Adeline sat, an intent gaze directed at Jeanine. The Gathering Room quieted for a moment, one table's silence spreading to another, and another. Guests scanned the room, the candles and centerpieces, the billowing balloons, the vacant bridal party table. Someone near a window shouted, "I think the bride and groom are here."

Adeline continued, as if not hearing. "Shotgun blasts. I remember duck hunting at the farm. I was so nervous about Victor and the shotgun."

"Mother, that's the first time we've talked about that."

"And the smell of burning leaves today. I remember that from the farm too."

"Mother, that's wonderful. Wonderful," Jeanine said, leaning toward Adeline. "Anything else?"

"The moon. Did you see the moon?"

"Yes, yes. It was rising as the sun was setting."

"And candles, blossoms." Adeline touched the petal of a pink rose. Candle flames floated in pools of melted wax. "My May Day altar."

Jeanine squeezed her hand.

"Coming through," came a voice from behind Grace. Thelma and Adam snaked through the tables, Thelma carrying sheet music. "If they pack any more tables in here, I'm calling the fire marshal." Adam maneuvered to the piano. "Excuse us."

They sat at the piano; Adam arranged the music. He signaled to Mrs. Fitzgerald. The door opened. The Gathering Room resounded with "Here Comes the Bride." Guests stood and applauded.

Pearl led the procession, stopping to kiss her friends and greet their guests, then pressing one hand to her chest and waving the other at the balloons, the candles, the flowers. Pearl and Arnold proceeded to the wedding party table and stood with the bridesmaid and best man. They motioned for the guests to sit. "Thank you. Thank you so much for coming," Pearl said. "Please, have a glass of wine. Dinner is on the way."

Someone clinked a glass with a knife. Others joined. "Sounds like a five-alarm fire," Arnold said, and turned to kiss his wife. The crowd applauded. Waitresses marched from the kitchen carrying plates of food.

"What's this?" Hazel asked the server.

"Chicken in a creamy vegetable sauce over puff pastry, with florets of broccoli."

"Looks like a biscuit to me. And we're out of mints."

Three guests arrived, surveyed the room, and headed for Hazel and Cliff's table. "Looks like we don't have much choice," Stella said. "Hello, Hazel." She rested on her crutches and smoothed her party dress.

Cliff stood. "I'm Hazel's son, Cliff." He reached for Stella's hand, then Harry's.

"This is my nephew Harry and his daughter Mimi," Stella said. "Sorry we're late. I've been to these wedding receptions before and I never get enough to eat. We stopped at the A&W for a hamburger."

"A glass of wine with your dinner?" a server asked, holding three dinner plates.

"Why not?" Stella said. "And a 7-UP for my grandniece. I'm going to use the ladies' room. Cliff is a numbers guy too, Harry. Maybe together you can balance the national budget." She snugged crutches under her arms and lumbered away.

Hazel turned to the girl sitting beside her. "Having fun?"

"No."

Surprised at her candor, Hazel said, "Neither am I. What's your name?"

"Mimi."

"How old are you?"

"Thirteen." Mimi folded her napkin into triangles.

Hazel leaned toward the girl. "Same age as Andy. Do you know him?"

"Andy who?" Mimi unfolded the napkin and placed it on her lap.

"Do you go to school here in Browns Prairie?"

"No."

"What's your favorite subject?"

"Science."

"Science? Why science?"

Mimi raised her eyes to Hazel's. "You ask a lot of questions."

"That's an old lady's prerogative. But turnabout's fair play. Ask me some."

"Okay. Is this your only son?"

Hazel fussed with her silverware. "No. I have other sons and daughters."

"Do they love you?"

"I don't know. I suppose they do."

"I don't like broccoli," Mimi said. She pushed the vegetables to the side of her plate. "If they love you, why aren't they here?"

"Well, they're busy with their families, I suppose. And one of them is dead. He died in the Army."

"Shot?"

"Yes, I suppose he was shot."

"I don't like green peppers either." Mimi steered small squares of green into a pile. "Shooting a person is hard to understand, isn't it?"

"Sometimes we don't have much choice."

"How old was he?"

Hazel hesitated. "He was only seven days from being twenty."

"That's young. Was he married?"

"No."

"Did he have a girlfriend?"

"Yes. He was engaged to be married. To a nice . . ." Hazel dropped her fork and pushed her plate away. "You ask a lot of questions too."

"How did you feel when you found out he died? What did you do?"

"I don't know. I don't remember. Now that's enough."

"Did you want to hate someone? Did you want to get revenge but didn't know how?"

"He died an honorable death. He was defending his country."

"Defending his country? From what?"

Hazel shrugged and clenched her jaw. She turned to the window. Outside, in the garden courtyard, a spotlighted flag hung limp and lifeless. The flag. Like the one folded in a wooden box on her table.

"He was defending us from the enemy, of course. Now stop it. What are you, some kind of freak?"

"Didn't you think *what a waste?* Didn't you wonder what he would have become? Don't you wish he was here now? Here beside you?"

"Stop it, I said."

Mimi planted her elbows on the table, rested her chin in her hands, and stared at Hazel. "What was his name?"

"I haven't spoken his name in fifty years."

"My counselor says we have to name our demons before we can conquer them."

"Stop it. I won't have you calling my Danny a demon."

"Danny. Danny Boy. *Oh Danny boy, oh Danny boy, I love you so.* We sang that in Chorus."

Hazel choked and wiped her face with a pink napkin. "I don't want to talk about my dead son." She pushed away from the table. "I'm going to my apartment, Cliff. Let me be alone." She rose, swung her walker around, and headed through the crowd of chattering wedding guests, avoiding a latecomer.

"Sorry. I was delayed," Rayanna said. She slipped into a chair. "I'm Rayanna, Woody's mother," she pointed to the best man at the wedding party table, "and a lifelong friend of the groom."

"I'm Mrs. Fitzgerald, director here at Good Shepherd. This is Alice, and this is Mary, our aide."

"What a beautiful day for a wedding." Rayanna glanced at the head table and waved to her son. "Look at the bride. Glowing." She waved to Arnold and blew him a kiss. "Did the bride remember her lines? Both words?"

"We heard her rehearse days before the wedding. *I do. I do.* I DO. I do?"

"She'll be good for Arnold. Alice, good to meet you."

"Thank you," Alice said. "You knew Arnold? He's a great guy."

"He is. He and my late husband logged together. If we weren't such good friends, that would be me sitting next to him. But you know how friendship trumps romance."

Rayanna looked around. The room had darkened, and Mrs. Fitzgerald rose to walk to her office. Soon the chandeliers dimmed to a low party level of light through the pink balloons. Candles flickered. Guests had pushed their empty plates with crumbled pink napkins forward. "Nice place," Rayanna said. "How about you, Mary? Is it tough working among all these *golden oldies*?" She made quotation marks with her fingers.

"Alice is one of my favorites," Mary gushed. "She has a cat named Lulu. The only pet in the building, other than the fish and birds."

"Those fish and birds were my argument for getting Lulu in here. I came close to owning a pet goat this summer," Alice said.

"That's where we'd draw the line," Mrs. Fitzgerald said, returning. "Rayanna, you're the best man's mother?"

"Yes. I'm surprised to say we don't see much of each other. He loves me and I love him. His wife? Not so much."

"In-laws can be an issue," Alice said. "Take my daughter and son-in-law, for example."

"The big issue is how much Woody resembles his dead father. Nothing Oedipal, you understand, but I . . . "

"We studied that in Psychology," Mary blurted, smiling, then flushed when the attention turned to her. "Oedipus and Electra and the complexes named for them. There are such things? Here in my small world?"

"There are," Rayanna said. "And delusions of grandeur and Faustian bargains."

Alice snapped, "I could tell you about Faustian bargains." She sipped her wine. "Who is that lady with hair that rivals Pearl's?" she asked Mrs. Fitzgerald.

Mrs. Fitzgerald glanced over her shoulder. "That's Verney, proprietress of Salon Chic up town. She does Pearl's hair." She waved to Verney.

Verney raised a cupped hand to her mouth. "What do you think of the hair?" Verney pointed to Pearl. At the bridal party table, Pearl chatted with Arnold, then Bonnie, then reached in front of Arnold to chat with Woody, all the while holding a forkful of chicken a la king.

"Nice," Elaine said, "if you're talking to me. Where'd she buy it?"

"*Au contraire.* That's all hers. Keep her away from candles, though. Poof. Fireball," Verney said. "And what do you think of the best man? I think we ought to audition him for membership in the club."

"Is he married?" Nurse Betty asked.

"Guess it depends on what day of the week you're talking about."

"Forget it. What's the latest gossip around town?"

"Well, you heard about Rosalie getting rear-ended? They took her to the hospital. Nothing serious, I guess."

"I hope she was wearing clean underwear," Betty said.

"I hope she was *wearing* underwear. Now give me the lowdown on your trip to New York, Elaine. Did you bring me a souvenir?"

Elaine looked at Mason, slumped in his chair, reading a small book or sleeping, she couldn't tell. She snipped a rose from the centerpiece with her fingernails and placed it in his lapel.

"I was a star until I arrived at the publisher's offices. Picked up at the airport, dropped off at a swanky hotel. Chocolates on the pillow. Daily rate about as much as our monthly mortgage payment. We met and talked about the poetry colllection. They knew they had a rube in their presence. What did I have in mind for foreign language translations or soft cover editions? Even Braille, for God's sakes. I just threw up my hands and said you're in this business, not me.

"I looked the editor straight in the eye." She stared at Betty. "Be advised though. You ain't seen nothing yet. There's a lot more poetry where this came from. Treat me right, and you'll get it." She sat straight in her chair and pounded her fist on the table.

"What did they say?"

"Well, my editor was sweet and said we'd work it out. The gal from Legal packed up her briefcase and sneered."

"So there's more poetry coming?" Betty asked.

"One poem a day. On a good day, two or three." She stopped when she heard chairs sliding forward and saw Thelma and Adam walking toward them.

"Excuse us," Thelma said. They negotiated a path to the piano again. Thelma opened sheet music and placed it on the stand.

"What now?" Verney asked.

Mrs. Fitzgerald walked to her office and dimmed the lights in the Gathering Room. Candles on the tables glistened like fireflies.

Adam raised his hands and dropped them on the keyboard, playing the "Grand March from Aida."

The door of the kitchen opened and caterers rolled out the wedding cake on a draped cart. Multi-tiered layers of white frosting festooned with pink roses. Two more caterers marched with silver candelabras of pink candles.

Adam ploughed into the music, his fingers like long-legged spiders spanning the octaves. Pearl attempted a look of surprise. Arnold smiled. The attendants set the candelabras on the table and stood. They waited. Adam played. Measure after measure. Guests shifted their gaze from the bride and groom to the musician. Adam's head nodded, his shoulders swayed.

Thelma looked at the crowd, then at the bridal table. Arnold gave a *cut it* gesture. Thelma tapped Adam's shoulder. No response. Measure after triumphant measure. Finally the coda. Hard, strong strokes, then arms flailing high. *Finis*. Adam threw his head back and grinned.

Guests applauded. The bride and groom rose to cut the cake. Aide Mary crouched toward their table carrying a camera. "Smile," she said as the two held the knife.

"I think I'm going to cry," Verney said. "But not until I have a piece of cake."

A waitress set a carafe of coffee on Verney's table and said, "Cake in just a minute." She followed Thelma and Adam to their table with a second carafe.

"Adam, you were great," Dr. Provence said. "I didn't know that old upright had life in it. It does."

Thelma and Adam sat. "Thanks." Adam lifted his head and stared at the balloons.

"We practiced a couple duets which we can play later," Thelma said. "Maybe premier one of Adam's original compositions."

Adam scowled. "Not today. Maybe not ever. Stan," he said. "Did I scare the dog with my crescendos?"

Stan reached to the floor and scratched Max's head. "Nope."

"He flinched each time you hit that out-of-tune key," Dr. Provence said.

Thelma chuckled. "He and I both."

A waitress lifted the carafe and shook it. "Cake in just a minute."

"How goes the checkers match, Stan and Wayne?" Dr. Provence asked.

Wayne sat erect in his chair, stoic and indifferent, a dried flower in his lapel from his daughter's funeral. He looked at Stan. Stan looked at Max.

"Nothing more exciting than a good game of checkers, right?" Dr. Provence joked.

"I guess he's beating me," Stan said. "We don't keep score."

"Oh, yes we do," Wayne corrected. "I'm winning, twelve to four."

"Keep your voices down," Thelma said, shushing the two men. "Pearl will hear us and schedule a checkers tournament."

"Hopefully she'll be preoccupied for a while," Adam said.

Thelma laughed. "Think of the sleep she'll get, now that she's married. Wayne," she continued. "I miss your daughter's visits. Annette. She was like one of the family and one of the staff."

"Thanks," Wayne mumbled. He slouched in his chair and glanced at his watch.

"She always had a kind word. And a sample pack of Ibuprofen, when I couldn't get them from this guy." She poked Dr. Provence.

"My sympathies to you, Wayne," Dr. Provence said. "I don't think I could survive my daughter's death. And Annette died in the line of duty, as they say. She should get special recognition in the Home Health Care Hall of Fame, if there is such a thing."

"There isn't," Wayne said.

"Neither rain, nor snow, nor sleet. That ought to be the motto of the medical profession, not the post office."

"What difference does it make?"

Adam turned to Wayne and cocked his head. "The difference it makes is that she died so that others could live. She's a martyr and she's a hero." Adam's voice rose to a wail.

"Nothing heroic about helping that son-of-a-bitch."

"You must think you have a lot of power. Power over your children, that is. Guess what. You don't. She was an adult. She would decide who to help. Not you."

The two men were separated by Stan, who scratched Max's head. Dr. Provence eyed them both, prepared to intervene.

"I know something about powerlessness," Adam said. "I'll tell you about it someday." The server arrived, balancing five plates of wedding cake.

"But not today," Thelma said. "Today is a day of celebration. Let's eat our cake." She inspected her piece and dug a pink floret of roses out of the frosting.

Thelma surveyed the room. The party was winding down. The room was quiet now, with an occasional clink of fork against plate, a snippet of hushed conversation, Pearl's melodious laugh. She noticed Woody rolling his chair behind the bride and groom toward Bonnie.

"Hey, bridesmaid. What are you doing after the show?" Woody whispered. "Arnold gave me the key to his apartment for the night. I thought maybe a few of us might continue where we leave off."

"Thanks for the offer, but I have a chemistry test coming up," Bonnie said. "You might have trouble finding party animals in this crowd."

"Anyone not currently enrolled in Medicare is invited."

"That would be you, me, Mary the aide, and that little girl over there."

"Guess you're right. You and I have the privilege of proposing a toast. Want to go first?"

"Go ahead."

Woody stood and raised his glass. "Ladies and gentlemen." The guests quieted. "It's a tradition for the best man to offer a toast to the bride and groom. My acquaintance with the bride is brief, but I like what I see. My familiarity with the groom goes way back. Arnold was a friend of my father, my mother," he pointed to Rayanna, "and me. So here's a toast to friendship." He lifted his glass and rested his hand on Arnold's shoulder.

"What is friendship? Maybe it's love. Maybe it's attraction. Maybe it's feeling that I want to be with you when I'm up, when I'm down, when I'm in need, when I have something to share. Maybe it's excitement when I see you in the doorway, or hear your voice on the telephone, or feel the grip of your handshake. Maybe it's comfort in knowing that I can trust you with my innermost thoughts and feelings. That you'll not judge me, but accept me as I am, unconditionally. This is how I feel about you, my friend.

"So Arnold and Pearl, here's to friendship, old and new. Cheers."

Arnold stood and hugged Woody while the guests applauded. Then he clinked a knife on his wine glass. The crowd hushed. "Now, a word from my bride."

As Pearl stood, Mrs. Fitzgerald slipped into her office and dimmed the Gathering Room lights. Night had fallen, and streetlamps glowed through the windows. Flames in the candelabras flickered like tiny torches. Pearl stood between the candles and smiled. "If I was allowed only *a* word, it would be *thanks*. So good to be with friends and neighbors and family. I can't tell you how much this means to me." She stopped and smiled at Arnold. "What did I do to deserve this?" She glanced at Bonnie. "Don't answer that. Honest, I've waited all my life for this moment. Before I forget, we have a special guest to introduce." She walked toward Dr. Provence's table. "Stan, would you introduce Max, please."

Stan lifted the dog's front end and waved a black paw, then patted his shirt pocket for a pipe. The crowd applauded.

"One more item of business," Pearl continued. She reached for the bouquet beside her plate and jiggled it toward Thelma.

"No, no," Thelma yelled.

"Just kidding, my friend." She handed the bouquet to Bonnie and kissed her cheek. More applause.

"Funny, isn't it, we come to Good Shepherd to spend the end of our lives. And suddenly, it's the beginning. So many wonderful friends. So many memories in the making. How sweet it is."

At their table, Betty sipped water, and Verney whispered to her, "I wonder who pumped sunshine up her ass." Betty spewed water across the table, dousing the candle and spraying Mason. He shook his head as if waking from a bad dream. He grabbed the pink napkin from a giggling Elaine and whimpered, "Close the window."

"I'm sorry. I'm sorry," Betty mouthed.

"So, thank you for coming," Pearl said. "Thank you for being our friends. Thank you for being our family." She sat. The crowd applauded.

"May I propose a toast?" Bonnie stood and raised her glass. "I hope you like angels, Arnold."

"One angel is enough." He laughed and pulled Pearl to him.

"Last year at this time, Pearl, Aunt Pearl, was just another branch on a lackluster family tree," Bonnie began. "What a joy it's been to get to know her. I promise I won't tell your secrets, Pearl, if you don't tell mine."

Pearl shook her head, *No.*

"What a joy it's been to be part of this auspicious day. If anybody deserves to live happily ever after, it's this lady. Arnold, I hope you like pink. Because I can't see Pearl changing."

"I hope she doesn't," he said.

"So, here's to the happy couple. Arnold, early in your marriage, you may find it hard to get the last word in a discussion. In time, you'll learn to get the last two words. Just make sure they're 'Yes, dear.' Cheers."

The guests applauded. Knives clinked against glasses. Arnold reached to kiss the bride. Bonnie snuggled between them, kissing them both. "How sweet it is," she said.

Pearl placed her hand on Arnold's shoulder. "Arnold, my handsome husband," she said to the crowd. "Will you say a few words to bring this delightful day to a happy ending?"

"I'll try." He stood tall, scanned the room, and raised his glass. "How sweet it is, indeed. Here's to happy endings." He sipped the wine. "I guess we're all suckers for a happy ending. We want health. We want companions. We want our needs met. And we have those, at least for today." He placed his hand on Pearl's shoulder, then looked across the room to a figure leaning on a walker in the shadowed hallway. He continued. "But tonight, when this sweet day is over, we'll go to sleep with the same problems we woke up with this morning. There are no endings, let alone happy ones."

Hazel dabbed her cheek and nodded, *Yes, yes*.

"If we're lucky," Arnold continued, "life goes on. And on. And on."

Acknowledgments
Editors Deb Schlueter and Sharon Harris
Layout and cover designer Tarah L. Wolff
Readers Members of Jackpine Writer's Bloc
Marge Barrett, Flo Golod and Bonnie West

Made in the USA
San Bernardino, CA
19 January 2014